Walter Scott

Tales of a Grandfather - History of Scotland

Vol. II

SALZWASSER VERLAG

Walter Scott

Tales of a Grandfather - History of Scotland

Vol. II

Reprint of the original, first published in 1861.

1st Edition 2022 | ISBN: 978-3-37506-753-3

Verlag (Publisher): Salzwasser Verlag GmbH, Zeilweg 44, 60439 Frankfurt, Deutschland
Vertretungsberechtigt (Authorized to represent): E. Roepke, Zeilweg 44, 60439 Frankfurt, Deutschland
Druck (Print): Books on Demand GmbH, In de Tarpen 42, 22848 Norderstedt, Deutschland

TALES OF A GRANDFATHER.

HISTORY OF SCOTLAND.

BY

SIR WALTER SCOTT, BART.

WITH NOTES.

IN SIX VOLUMES.

II.

BOSTON:
TICKNOR AND FIELDS.
M DCCC LXI.

CONTENTS OF VOL. II.

FIRST SERIES.

(CONTINUED.)

CHAPTER XXXIII.

SECOND SERIES.

CHAPTER XXXIV.

CHAPTER XXXV.

CHAPTER XXXVI.

CHAPTER XXXVII.

CHAPTER XXXVIII.

TALES OF A GRANDFATHER.

FIRST SERIES.

(CONTINUED.)

TALES OF A GRANDFATHER.

CHAPTER XXIV.

IMPROVEMENT ON SCOTTISH LAWS — DISPUTES BETWEEN ENGLAND AND SCOTLAND — INVASION OF ENGLAND — BATTLE OF FLODDEN, AND DEATH OF JAMES IV.

[1502—1513.]

DURING the season of tranquillity which followed the marriage of James and Margaret, we find that the King, with his Parliament, enacted many good laws for the improvement of the country. The Highlands and Islands were particularly attended to, because, as one of the acts of Parliament expressed it, they had become almost savage for want of justices and sheriffs. Magistrates were therefore appointed, and laws made for the government of those wild and unruly people.

Another most important act of Parliament permitted the King, and his nobles and barons, to let their land, not only for military service, but for a payment in money or in grain; a regulation which tended to introduce quiet, peaceful farmers into lands occupied, but left uncultivated, by tenants of a military character. Regulations also took place for attendance on Parliament, and the representation of the different orders of society in that assembly.

The possessors of lands were likewise called on to plant wood, and make enclosures, fish-ponds, and other improvements.

All these regulations show that the King entertained a sincere wish to benefit his subjects, and entertained liberal views of the mode of accomplishing that object. But the unfortunate country of Scotland was destined never to remain any long time in a state of peace or improvement; and, accordingly, towards the end of James's reign, events occurred which brought on a defeat still more calamitous than any which the kingdom had yet received.

While Henry VII., the father-in-law of James, continued to live, his wisdom made him very attentive to preserve the peace which had been established betwixt the two countries. His character, was, indeed, far from being that of a generous prince, but he was a sagacious politician, and granted, from an enlightened view of his own interest, what perhaps he would otherwise have been illiberal enough to refuse. On this principle, he made some allowance for the irritable pride of his son-in-law and his subjects, who were as proud as they were poor, and made it his study to remove all the petty causes of quarrel which arose from time to time. But when this wise and cautious monarch died, he was succeeded by his son, Henry VIII., a prince of a bold, haughty, and furious disposition, impatient of control or contradiction, and rather desirous of war than willing to make any concessions for the sake of peace. James IV. and he resembled each other perhaps too nearly in temper to admit of their continuing intimate friends.

The military disposition of Henry chiefly directed him to an enterprise against France; and the King of France, on his part, desired much to renew the old alliance with

Scotland, in order that the apprehension of an invasion from the Scottish frontiers might induce Henry to abandon his scheme of attacking France. He knew that the splendor in which King James lived had exhausted the treasures which his father had left behind him, and he concluded that the readiest way to make him his friend was to supply him with sums of money, which he could not otherwise have raised. Gold was also freely distributed amongst the counsellors and favorites of the Scottish King. This liberality showed to great advantage, when compared with the very opposite conduct of the King of England, who delayed even to pay a legacy, which had been left by Henry, his father, to his sister, the Queen of Scotland.

Other circumstances of a different kind tended to create disagreements between England and Scotland. James had been extremely desirous to increase the strength of his kingdom by sea, and its commerce; and Scotland, presenting a great extent of sea-coast, and numerous harbors, had at this time a considerable trade. The royal navy, besides one vessel called the Great Michael, supposed to be the largest in the world, and which, as an old author says, "cumbered all Scotland to get her fitted out for sea," consisted, it is said, of sixteen ships of war. The King paid particular attention to naval affairs, and seemed never more happy than when inspecting and exercising his little navy.

It chanced that one John Barton, a Scottish mariner, had been captured by the Portuguese, as far back as the year 1476. As the King of Portugal refused to make any amends, James granted the family of Barton letters of reprisals, that is, a warrant empowering them to take all Portuguese vessels which should come in their way, until their loss was made up. There were three brothers, all daring men, but especially the eldest, whose name was Andrew Barton. He had two strong ships, the larger called the Lion, the lesser the Jenny Pirwen, with which it would appear he cruised in the British Channel, stopping not only Portuguese vessels, but also English ships bound for Portugal. Complaints being made to King Henry, he fitted out two vessels, which were filled with chosen men, and placed under the command of Lord Thomas Howard and Sir Edward Howard, both sons to the Earl of Surrey. They found Barton and his vessels cruising in the Downs, being guided to the place by the captain of a merchant vessel, whom Barton had plundered on the preceding day.

July, 1511.

On approaching the enemy, the noble brothers showed no ensign of war, but put up a willow wand on their masts, as being the emblem of a trading-vessel. But when the Scotsman attempted to make them bring to, the English threw out their flags and pennons, and fired a broadside of their ordnance. Barton then knew that he was engaged with the King of England's ships of war. Far from being dismayed at this, he engaged boldly, and, distinguished by his rich dress and bright armor, appeared on deck with a whistle of gold about his neck, suspended by a chain of the same precious metal, and encouraged his men to fight valiantly.

The fight was very obstinate. If we may believe a ballad of the time, Barton's ship was furnished with a peculiar contrivance, suspending large weights, or beams, from his yard-arms, to be dropped down upon the enemy when they should come alongside. To make use of this contrivance, it was necessary that a person should ascend the mainmast, or in naval language, go aloft. As the English apprehended much mischief from the consequences of this manœuvre, Howard had stationed a Yorkshire gentleman, named Hustler, the best archer in the ship, with strict injunctions to shoot every one who should attempt to go aloft to let fall the beams of Barton's vessel. Two men were successively killed in the attempt, and Andrew Barton himself, confiding in the strong armor which he wore, began to ascend the mast. Lord Thomas Howard called out to the archer to shoot true, on peril of his life. "Were I to die for it," said Hustler, "I have but two arrows left." The first which he shot bounded from Barton's armor without hurting him; but as the Scottish mariner raised his arm to climb higher, the archer took aim where the armor afforded him no protection, and wounded him mortally through the arm-pit.

Barton descended from the mast. "Fight on," he said, "my brave hearts; I am a little wounded, but not slain. I will but rest awhile, and then rise and fight again, meantime, stand fast by Saint Andrew's Cross," meaning the Scottish flag, or ensign. He encouraged his men with his whistle, while the breath of life remained. At length the whistle was heard no longer, and the Howards, boarding the Scottish vessel, found that her daring captain was dead. They carried the Lion into the Thames, and it is remarkable that Barton's ship became the second man-of-war in the English navy. When the Kings wanted to equip a fleet, they hired or pressed into their service merchant vessels, and put soldiers on board of them. The ship called the Great Henry was the first built especially for war, by the King, as his own property, — this captured vessel was the second.

James IV. was highly incensed at this insult, as he termed it, on the flag of Scotland, and sent a herald to demand satisfaction. The King of England justified his conduct on the ground of Barton's being a pirate, — a charge which James could not justly deny; but he remained not the less heated and incensed against his brother-in-law. Another misfortune aggravated his resentment, though the subject of misunderstanding was of ancient date.

While Henry VII. was yet alive, Sir Robert Ker of Fairniehirst, chief of one branch of the clan of Ker, an officer of James's household, and a favorite of that monarch, held the office of warden on the Middle Marches of Scotland. In exercising this office with rather unusual strictness, he had given offence to some of the more turbulent English Borderers, who resolved to assassinate him. Three of these, namely Heron, called the Bastard, because a natural brother of Heron of Ford, with Starhed and Lilburn, surrounded the Scottish warden, at a meeting upon a day of truce, and killed him with their lances.

Henry VII., with the pacific policy which marked his proceedings towards Scotland, agreed to surrender the guilty persons. Lilburn was given up to King James, and died in captivity; Starhed escaped for a time, by flying into the interior parts of England; the Bastard Heron caused it to be rumored that he was dead of the plague, and made himself be transported in a coffin, so that he passed unsuspected through the party sent to arrest him, and skulked on the Borders, waiting for a quarrel between the kingdoms, which might make it safe for him to show himself. Henry VII., anxious to satisfy James, arrested his legitimate brother, and Heron of Ford was delivered up instead of the Bastard. But when Henry VIII. and James were about to disagree, both the Bastard Heron and Starhed began to show themselves more publicly.

Starhed was soon disposed of, for Sir Andrew, commonly called Dand Ker, the son of the murdered Sir Robert, sent two of his dependents, called Tait, to accomplish his vengeance upon the English Borderer. They surprised and put him to death accordingly, and brought his head to their patron, who exposed it publicly at the cross of Edinburgh, exulting in the revenge he had taken. But the Bastard Heron continued to rove about the Border, and James IV. made the public appearance of this criminal a subject of complaint against Henry VIII., who perhaps was not justly responsible for it.

While James was thus on bad terms with his brother-in-law, France left no measures unattempted which could attach Scotland to her side. Great sums of money were sent to secure the good-will of those courtiers in whom James most confided. The Queen of France, a young and beautiful princess, flattered James's taste for romantic gallantry, by calling herself his mistress and lady-love, and conjuring him to march three miles upon English ground for her sake. She sent him, at the same time, a ring from her own finger; and her intercession was so powerful, that James thought he could not in honor dispense with her request. This fantastical spirit of chivalry was his own ruin, and very nearly that of the kingdom also.

At length, in June or July, 1513, Henry VIII. sailed to France with a gallant army, where he formed the siege of Terouenne. James IV. now took a decided step. He sent over his principal herald to the camp of King Henry before Terouenne, summoning him in haughty terms to abstain from aggressions against James's ally, the King of France, and upbraiding him, at the same time, with the death of Barton, the impunity of the Bastard Heron, the detention of the legacy of Henry VII. to his daughter, the Scottish Queen, and all the subjects of quarrel which had occurred since the death of that monarch. Henry VIII. answered this letter, which he justly considered as a declaration of war, with equal bitterness, treating the King of Scots as a perjured man, because he was about to break the peace which he had solemnly sworn to observe. His summons he rejected with scorn. "The King of Scotland was not," he said, "of sufficient importance to determine the quarrel between England and France." The Scottish herald returned with this message, but not in time to find his master alive.

James had not awaited the return of his embassy to commence hostilities. Lord Home, his Lord High-Chamberlain, had made an incursion into England with an army of about three or four thousand men. They collected great booty; but marching carelessly and without order, fell into an ambush of the English Borderers, concealed among the tall broom, by which Millfield Plain, near Wooler, was then covered. The Scots sustained a total defeat, and lost near a third of their numbers in slain and wounded. This was a bad commencement of the war.

Meanwhile James, contrary to the advice of his wisest counsellors, determined to invade England with a royal army. The Parliament were unwilling to go into the King's measures. The tranquillity of the country, ever since the peace with England, was recollected, and as the impolitic claim of the supremacy seemed to be abandoned, little remained to stir up the old animosity between the kingdoms. The King, however, was personally so much liked, that he obtained the consent of the Parliament to this fatal and unjust war; and orders were given to assemble all the array of the kingdom of Scotland upon the Borough-moor of Edinburgh, a wide common, in the midst of which the royal standard was displayed from a large stone, or fragment of rock, called the Hare-stone.

Various measures were even in this extremity resorted to for preventing the war. One or two of them seem to have been founded upon a knowledge, that the King's temper was tinged with a superstitious melancholy, partly arising from constitutional habits, partly from the remorse which he always entertained for his accession to his father's death. It was to these feelings that the following scene was doubtless addressed: —

As the King was at his devotions in the church of Linlithgow, a figure, dressed in an azure-colored robe, girt with a girdle, or sash of linen, having sandals on his feet, with long, yellow hair, and a grave, commanding countenance, suddenly appeared before him. This singular-looking person paid little or no respect to the royal presence, but pressing up to the desk at which the King was seated, leaned down on it with his arms, and addressed him with little reverence. He declared, that "his mother laid her commands on James to forbear the journey which he proposed, seeing that neither he, nor any who went with him, would thrive in the undertaking." He also cautioned the King against frequenting the society of women, and using their counsel; "If thou dost," said he, "thou shalt be confounded and brought to shame."

These words spoken, the messenger escaped from among the courtiers so suddenly, that he seemed to disappear. There is no doubt that this person had been dressed up to represent Saint John, called in Scripture the adopted son of the Virgin Mary. The Roman Catholics believed in the possibility of the souls of departed saints and apostles appearing on earth, and many impostures are recorded in history of the same sort with that I have just told you.

Another story, not so well authenticated, says, that a proclamation was heard at the market-cross of Edinburgh, at the dead of night, summoning the King, by his name and titles, and many of his nobles and principal leaders, to appear before the tribunal of Pluto within the space of forty days. This also has the appearance of a stratagem, invented to deter the King from his expedition.

But neither these artifices, nor the advice and entreaty of Margaret, the Queen of Scotland, could deter James from his unhappy expedition. He was so well beloved, that he soon assembled a great army, and placing himself at their head, he entered England near the castle of Twisell, on the 22d of August, 1513. He speedily obtained possession of the Border fortresses of Norham, Wark, Etall, Ford, and others of less note, and collected a great spoil. Instead, however, of advancing with his army upon the country of England, which lay defenceless before him, the King is said to have trifled away his time in an intercourse of gallantry with Lady Heron of Ford, a beautiful woman, who contrived to divert him from the prosecution of his expedition until the approach of an English army.

While James lay thus idle on the frontier, the Earl of Surrey, that same noble and gallant knight who had formerly escorted Queen Margaret to Scotland, now advanced at the head of an army of twenty-six thousand men. The Earl was joined by his son Thomas, the Lord High Admiral, with a large body of soldiers who had been disembarked at Newcastle. As the warlike inhabitants of the northern counties gathered fast to Surrey's standard, so on the other hand, the Scots began to return home in great numbers; because, though, according to the feudal laws, each man had brought with him provisions for forty days, these being now nearly expended, a scarcity began to be felt in James's host. Others went home to place their booty in safety.

Surrey, feeling himself the stronger party, became desirous to provoke the Scottish King to fight. He therefore sent James a message, defying him to battle; and the Lord Thomas Howard, at the same time, added a message, that as King James had often complained of the death of Andrew Barton, he, Lord Thomas, by whom that deed was done, was now ready to maintain it with his sword in the front of the fight. James returned for answer, that to meet the English in battle was so much his wish, that had the message of the Earl found him at Edinburgh, he would have laid aside all other business to have met him on a pitched field.

But the Scottish nobles entertained a very different opinion from their King. They held a council, at which Lord Patrick Lindsay was made President, or Chancellor. This was the same person, who, in the beginning of the King's reign, had pleaded so well for his brother, to whose titles and estate he afterwards succeeded. He opened the discussion, by telling the Council a parable of a rich merchant, who would needs go to play at dice with a common hazarder, or sharper, and stake a rose-noble of gold against a crooked half-penny. "You my lords," he said, "will be as unwise as the merchant, if you risk your King, whom I compare to a precious rose-noble, against the English general, who is but an old crooked churl, lying in a chariot. Though the English lose the day, they lose nothing but this old churl and a parcel of mechanics; whereas so many of our common people have gone home, that few are left with us but the prime of our nobility." He therefore gave it as his advice, that the King should withdraw from the army, for safety of his person, and that some brave nobleman should be named by the Council, to command in the action. The Council agreed to recommend this plan to the King.

But James, who desired to gain fame by his own military skill and prowess, suddenly broke in on the Council, and told them, with much heat, that they should not put such a disgrace upon him. "I will fight with the English," he said, "though you had all sworn the contrary. You may shame yourselves by flight, but you shall not shame me; and as for Lord Patrick Lindsay, who has got the first vote, I vow, that when I return to Scotland, I will cause him to be hanged over his own gate."

In this rash and precipitate resolution to fight at all risks, the King was much supported by the French ambassador, De la Motte. This was remarked by one of our old acquaintances, the Earl of Angus, called Bell-the-Cat, who, though very old, had come out to the field with his sovereign. He charged the Frenchman with being willing to sacrifice the interests of Scotland to those of his own country, which required that the Scots and English should fight at all hazards; and Angus, like Lord Lindsay, alleged the difference between the parties, the English being many of them men but of mean rank, and the Scottish army being the flower of their nobility and gentry. Incensed at his opposition, James said to him scornfully, "Angus, if you are afraid, you may go home." The Earl, on receiving such an insult, left the camp that night; but his two sons remained, and fell in the fatal battle, with two hundred of the name of Douglas.

While King James was in this stubborn humor, the Earl of Surrey had advanced as far as Wooler, so that only four or five miles divided the armies. The English leader inquired anxiously for some guide, who was acquainted with the country, which is intersected and divided by one or two large brooks, which unite to form the river Till, and is, besides, in part mountainous. A person well mounted, and completely armed, but having the visor of his helmet lowered, to conceal his face, rode up, and then dismounting, knelt down before the Earl, and offered to be his guide, if he might obtain pardon of an offence of which he had been guilty. The Earl assured him of his forgiveness, providing he had not committed treason against the King of England, or personally wronged any lady, — crimes which Surrey declared he would not pardon. "God forbid," said the cavalier, "that I should have been guilty of such shameful sin; I did but assist in killing a Scotsman who ruled our Borders too strictly, and often did wrong to Englishmen." So saying, he raised the visor of his helmet, which hid his face, and showed the countenance of the Bastard Heron, who had been a partner in the assassination of Sir Robert Ker, as you were told before. His appearance was most welcome to the Earl of Surrey, who readily pardoned him the death of a Scotsman at that moment, especially since he knew him to be as well acquainted with every pass and path on the eastern frontier, as a life of constant incursion and depredation could make him.

The Scottish army had fixed their camp upon a hill called Flodden, which rises to close in, as it were, the extensive flat called Millfield Plain. 6th Sept. This eminence slopes steeply towards the plain, and there is an extended piece of level ground on the top, where the Scots might have drawn up their army, and awaited at great advantage the attack of the English. Surrey liked the idea of venturing an assault on that position so ill, that he resolved to try whether he could not prevail on the King to abandon it. He sent a herald to invite James to come down from the height, and join battle in the open plain of Millfield below, — reminded him of the readiness with which he had accepted his former challenge, — and hinted that it was the opinion of the English chivalry assembled for battle, that any delay of the encounter would sound to the King's dishonor.

We have seen that James was sufficiently rash and imprudent, but his impetuosity did not reach to the pitch Surrey perhaps expected. He refused to receive the messenger into his presence, and returned for answer to the message, that it was not such as it became an earl to send to a king.

Surrey, therefore, distressed for provisions, was obliged to resort to another mode of bringing the Scots to action. He moved northward, sweeping round the hill of Flodden, keeping out of the reach of the Scottish artillery, until, crossing the Till near Twisell Castle, he placed himself, with his whole army, betwixt James and his own kingdom. The King suffered him to make this flank movement without interruption, though it must have afforded repeated and advantageous opportunities for attack. But when he saw the English army interposed betwixt him and his dominions, he became alarmed lest he should be cut off from Scotland. In this apprehension he was confirmed by one Giles Musgrave, an Englishman, whose counsel he used upon the occasion, and who assured him, that if he did not descend and fight with the English army, the Earl of Surrey would enter Scotland, and lay

9th Sept.

waste the whole country. Stimulated by this apprehension, the King resolved to give signal for the fatal battle.

With this view the Scots set fire to their huts, and the other refuse and litter of their camp. The smoke spread along the side of the hill, and under its cover the army of King James descended the eminence, which is much less steep on the northern than the southern side, while the English advanced to meet them, both concealed from each other by the clouds of smoke.

The Scots descended in four strong columns, all marching parallel to each other, having a reserve of the Lothian men commanded by Earl Bothwell. The English were also divided into four bodies, with a reserve of cavalry led by Dacre.

The battle commenced at the hour of four in the afternoon. The first which encountered was the left wing of the Scots, commanded by the Earl of Huntly and Lord Home, which overpowered and threw into disorder the right wing of the English, under Sir Edmund Howard. Sir Edmund was beaten down, his standard taken, and he himself in danger of instant death, when he was relieved by the Bastard Heron, who came up at the head of a band of determined outlaws like himself, and extricated Howard. It is objected to the Lord Home by many Scottish writers, that he ought to have improved his advantage, by hastening to the support of the next division of the Scottish army. It is even pretended, that he replied to those who urged him to go to the assistance of the King, that "the man did well that day who stood and saved himself." But this seems invented, partly to criminate Home, and partly to account for the loss of the battle in some other way than by the superiority of the English. In reality, the English cavalry, under Dacre, which acted as a reserve, appear to have kept the victors in check; while Thomas Howard, the Lord High Admiral, who commanded the second division of the English, bore down, and routed the Scottish division commanded by Crawford and Montrose, who were both slain. Thus matters went on the Scottish left.

Upon the extreme right of James's army, a division of Highlanders, consisting of the clans of MacKenzie, MacLean, and others, commanded by the Earls of Lennox and Argyle, were so insufferably annoyed by the volleys of the English arrows, that they broke their ranks, and, in despite of the cries, entreaties, and signals of De la Motte, the French ambassador, who endeavored to stop them, rushed tumultuously down hill, and being attacked at once in flank and rear by Sir Edward Stanley, with the men of Cheshire and Lancashire, were routed with great slaughter.

The only Scottish division which remains to be mentioned, was commanded by James in person, and consisted of the choicest of his nobles and gentry, whose armor was so good, that the arrows made but slight impression upon them. They were all on foot, — the King himself had parted with his horse. They engaged the Earl of Surrey, who opposed to them the division which he personally commanded. The Scots attacked with the greatest fury, and, for a time, had the better. Surrey's squadrons were disordered, his standard in great danger, Bothwell and the Scottish reserve were advancing, and the English seemed in some risk of losing the battle. But Stanley, who had defeated the Highlanders, came up on one flank of the King's division; the Admiral, who had conquered Crawford and Montrose, assailed them on the other. The Scots showed the most undaunted courage. Uniting themselves with the reserve under Bothwell, they formed into a circle, with their spears extended on every side, and fought obstinately. Bows being now useless, the English advanced on all sides with their bills, a huge weapon which made ghastly wounds. But they could not force the Scots either to break or retire, although the carnage among them was dreadful. James himself died amid his warlike peers and loyal gentry. He was twice wounded with arrows, and at length despatched with a bill. Night fell without the battle being absolutely decided, for the Scottish centre kept their ground, and Home and Dacre held each other at bay. But during the night, the remainder of the Scottish army drew off in silent despair from the bloody field, on which they left their King, and their choicest nobles and gentlemen.

This great and decisive victory was gained by the Earl of Surrey on 9th September, 1513. The victors had about five thousand men slain, the Scots twice that number at least. But the loss lay not so much in the number of the slain, as in their rank and quality. The English lost very few men of distinction. The Scots left on the field the King, two bishops, two mitred abbots, twelve earls, thirteen lords, and five eldest sons of peers. The number of gentlemen slain was beyond calculation;—there is scarcely a family of name in Scottish history who did not lose a relative there.

The Scots were much disposed to dispute the fact, that James IV. had fallen on Flodden Field. Some said, he had retired from the kingdom, and made a pilgrimage to Jerusalem. Others pretended, that in the twilight, when the fight was nigh ended, four tall horsemen came into the field, having each a bunch of straw on the point of their spears, as a token for them to know each other by. They said these men mounted the King on a dun hackney, and that he was seen to cross the Tweed with them at nightfall. Nobody pretended to say what they did with him, but it was believed he was murdered in Home Castle; and I recollect, about forty years since, that there was a report, that in cleaning the draw-well of that ruinous fortress, the workmen found a skeleton wrapt in a bull's hide, and having a belt of iron round the waist. There was, however, no truth in this rumor. It was the absence of this belt of iron which the Scots founded upon to prove that the body of James could not have fallen into the hands of the English, since they either had not that token to show, or did not produce it. They contended, therefore, that the body over which the enemy triumphed, was not that of James himself, but of one of his attendants, several of whom, they said, were dressed in his armor.

But all these are idle fables, invented and believed because the vulgar love what is mysterious, and the Scots readily gave credit to what tended to deprive their enemies of so signal a trophy of victory. The reports are contrary to common sense. Lord Home was the Chamberlain of James IV., and high in his confidence. He had nothing whatever to gain by the King's death, and therefore we must acquit him of a great crime, for which there could be no adequate motive. The consequence of James's death proved, in fact, to be the Earl's ruin, as we shall see presently.

It seems true, that the King usually wore the belt of iron in token of his repentance, for his father's death, and the share he had in it. But it is not unlikely that he would lay aside such a cumbrous article of penance in a day of battle; or the English, when they despoiled his person, may have thrown it aside as of no value. The body which the English affirm to have been that of James, was found on the field by Lord Dacre, and carried by him to Berwick, and presented to Surrey. Both of these lords knew James's person too well to be mistaken. The body was also acknowledged by his two favorite attendants, Sir William Scott and Sir John Forman, who wept at beholding it.

The fate of these relics was singular and degrading. They were not committed to the tomb, for the Pope, being at that time in alliance with England against France, had laid James under a sentence of excommunication, so that no priest dared pronounce the funeral-service over them. The royal corpse was therefore embalmed, and sent to the monastery of Sheen, in Surrey. It lay there till the Reformation, when the monastery was given to the Duke of Suffolk; and after that period, the body, which was lapped up in a sheet of lead, was suffered to toss about the house like a piece of useless lumber. Stow, the historian, saw it flung into a waste room among old pieces of wood, lead, and other rubbish. Some idle workmen, "for their foolish pleasure," says the same writer, "hewed off the head; and one Lancelot Young, master-glazier to Queen Elizabeth, finding a sweet smell come from thence, owing, doubtless, to the spices used for embalming the body, carried the head home, and kept it for some time; but in the end, caused the sexton of Saint Michael's, Wood Street, to bury it in the charnel-house."

Such was the end of that King once so proud and powerful. The fatal battle of Flodden, in which he was slain, and his army destroyed, is justly considered as one of the most calamitous events in Scottish history.

CHAPTER XXV.

Consequences of the Battle of Flodden — The Queen Dowager Margaret assumes the Regency, and marries the Earl of Angus — The Duke of Albany recalled from France — Contests between his Party and that of Margaret — Rencounter between the Douglases and Hamiltons on the High Street of Edinburgh — Storming of Jedburgh — The Duke of Albany's final Departure from Scotland.

[1513 — 1524.]

The event of the defeat at Flodden threw all Scotland into a degree of mourning and despair, which is not yet forgotten in the southern counties, on whom a great part of the loss fell, as their inhabitants, soldiers from situation and disposition, composed a considerable portion of the forces which remained with the King's army, and suffered, of course, a great share in the slaughter which took place. The inhabitants of the smaller towns on the Border, as Selkirk, Hawick, Jedburgh, and others, were almost entirely cut off, and their songs and traditions preserve to this day the recollection of their sufferings and losses.

Not only a large proportion of the nobility and of the baronage, who had by right of birth the important task of distributing justice and maintaining order in their domains, but also the magistrates of the burghs, who, in general, had remained with the army, had fallen on the field; so that the country seemed to be left open to invasion and conquest, such as had taken place after the loss of the battles of Dunbar and Halidon-Hill. Yet the firm courage of the Scottish people was displayed in its noblest colors in this formidable crisis; — all were ready to combat, and more disposed, even from the excess of the calamity, to resist, than to yield to the fearful consequences which might have been expected.

Edinburgh, the metropolis, or capital city of Scotland, set a noble example of the conduct which should be adopted under a great national calamity. The provost, bailies, and magistracy of that city, had been carried by their duty to the battle, in which most of them, with the burghers and citizens who followed their standard, had fallen with the King. A certain number of persons, called *Presidents*, at the head of whom was George Towrs of Inverleith, had been left with a commission to discharge the duty of magistrates during the absence of those to whom the office actually belonged. The battle was fought, as we have said, on the 9th of September. On the 10th, being the succeeding day, the news reached Edinburgh, and George Towrs, and the other Presidents, published on that day a proclamation, which would do honor to the annals of any country in Europe. The Presidents must have known that all was lost; but they took every necessary precaution to prevent the public from yielding to a hasty and panic alarm, and to prepare with firmness the means of public defence.

"Whereas," says this remarkable proclamation, "news have arrived, which are yet uncertain, of misfortune which hath befallen the King and his army, we strictly command and charge all persons within the city to have their arms in readiness, and to be ready to assemble at the tolling of the common bell of the town, to repel any enemy who may seek to attack the city. We also discharge all women of the lower class, and vagabonds of every description, from appearing on the street to cry and make lamentations; and we command women of honest fame and character to pass to the churches, and pray for the King and his army, and for our neighbors who are with the King's host." In this way the gallant George Towrs took measures at once for preventing the spreading of terror and confusion by frantic and useless lamentation, and for defence of the city, if need should arise. The simplicity of the order showed the courage and firmness of those who issued it, under the astounding national calamity which had been sustained.

The Earl of Surrey did not, however, make any endeavor to invade Scotland, or to take any advantage of the great victory he had obtained, by attempting the conquest of that country. Experience had taught the English, that though it might be easy for them to overrun their northern neighbors, to ravage provinces, and to take castles and cities, yet that the obstinate valor of the Scots, and their love of independence, had always, in the long run, found means of expelling the invaders. With great moderation and wisdom, Henry, or his ministers, therefore, resolved rather to conciliate the friendship of the Scots, by foregoing the immediate advantages which the victory of Flodden afforded them, than to commence another invasion, which, however distressing to Scotland, was likely, as in the Bruce and Baliol wars, to terminate in the English also sustaining great loss, and ultimately being again driven out of the kingdom. The English counsellors remembered that Margaret, the widow of James, was the sister of the King of England, — that she must become

Regent of the kingdom, and would naturally be a friend to her native country. They knew that the late war had been undertaken by the King of Scotland against the wish of his people; and with noble as well as wise policy, they endeavored rather to render Scotland once more a friendly power, than, by invasion and violence, to convert her into an irreconcilable enemy. The incursions which followed the battle of Flodden extended only to the Borders; no great attempt against Scotland was made, or apparently meditated.

Margaret, the Queen Dowager, became Regent of Scotland, and guardian of the young King, James V., who, as had been too often the case on former similar occasions, ascended the throne when a child of not two years old.

But the authority of Margaret was greatly diminished, and her character injured, by a hasty and imprudent marriage which she formed with Douglas, Earl of Angus, the grandson of old Bell-the-Cat. That celebrated 6th August, 1514. person had not long survived the fatal battle of Flodden, in which both his sons had fallen. His grandson, the inheritor of his great name, was a handsome youth, brave, high-born, and with all the ambition of the old Douglases, as well as with much of their military talents. He was, however, young, rash, and inexperienced; and his elevation to be the husband of the Queen Regent excited the jealousy and emulation of all the other nobles of Scotland, who dreaded the name and the power of the Douglas.

A peace now took place betwixt France and England, and Scotland was included in the treaty; but this could hardly be termed fortunate, considering the distracted state of the country, which, freed from English ravages,

and no longer restrained by the royal authority, was left to prosecute its domestic feuds and quarrels with the usual bloody animosity. The nation, or rather the nobles, disgusted with Margaret's regency, chiefly on account of her marriage with Angus, and that young lord's love of personal power, now thought of calling back into Scotland John, Duke of Albany, son of that Robert who was banished during the reign of James III. This nobleman was the nearest male relation of the King, being the cousin-
18th May, german of his father. The Queen was by many
1515. considered as having forfeited the right of regency by her marriage, and Albany, on his arrival from France, was generally accepted in that character.

John, Duke of Albany, had been born and bred in France, where he had large estates by his mother, a daughter of the Earl of Boulgone; and he seems always to have preferred the interests of that kingdom to those of Scotland, with which he was only connected by hereditary descent. He was a weak and passionate man, taking up opinions too slightly, and driven out of his resolutions too easily. His courage may justly be suspected; and, if not quite a fool, he was certainly not the wise man whom Scotland required for a governor. He brought over with him, however, a large sum of money from France; and as his manners were pleasing, his birth high, and his pretensions great, he easily got the advantage over Queen Margaret, her husband the Earl of Angus, and other lords who favored her interest.

After much internal disturbance, Queen Margaret was obliged altogether to retire from Scotland and to seek ref-
18th Oct. uge at her brother's court, where she bore a daugh-
1515. ter, Lady Margaret Douglas, of whom you will hear more hereafter. In the mean time, her party in

Scotland was still further weakened. Lord Home was one of her warmest supporters; this was the same nobleman who commanded the left wing at the battle of Flodden, and was victorious on that day, but exposed himself to suspicion by not giving assistance to the other divisions of the Scottish army. He and his brethren were enticed to Edinburgh, and seized upon, tried, and beheaded, upon accusations which are not known. This severity, 8th Oct.
however, was so far from confirming Albany's 1516.
power, that it only excited terror and hatred; and his situation became so difficult that to his friends in secret he expressed nothing but despair, and wished that he had broken his limbs when he first left his easy and quiet situation in France, to undertake the government of so distracted and unruly a country as Scotland. In fact, he accomplished a retreat to France, and, during his absence, committed the wardenry of the Scottish fron- 8th June,
tiers to a brave French knight, the Chevalier 1517.
de la Bastie, remarkable for the beauty of his person, the gallantry of his achievements, but destined, as we shall see, to a tragical fate.

The office of warden had belonged to the Lord Home; and his friends, numerous, powerful, and inhabiting the eastern frontier, to which the office belonged, were equally desirous to avenge the death of their chief, and to be freed from the dominion of a stranger like De la Bastie, the favorite of Albany, by whose authority Lord Home had been executed. Sir David Home of Wedderburn, one of the fiercest of the name, laid an ambush for the unfortunate warden, near Langton, in Berwickshire. De la Bastie, seeing his life aimed at, was compelled to fly, in the hope of gaining the castle of Dunbar; but near the town of Dunse, his horse stuck fast in a morass. The

19th Sept., 1517. pursuers came up and put him to death. Sir David Home knitted the head, by the long locks which the deceased wore, to the mane of his horse, rode with it in triumph to Home Castle, and placed it on a spear on the highest turret. The hair is said to be yet preserved in the charter-chest of the family. By this cruel deed, Wedderburn considered himself as doing a brave and gallant action in avenging the death of his chief and kinsman, by putting to death a friend and favorite of the Regent, although it does not appear that De la Bastie had the least concern in Lord Home's execution.

The decline of Albany's power enabled Queen Margaret and her husband to return to Scotland, leaving their infant daughter in the charge of her maternal uncle, King Henry. But after their return to their own country, the Queen Dowager quarrelled, to an irreconcilable pitch, with her husband Angus, who had seized upon her revenues, and paid her little attention or respect, associating with other women, and giving her much cause for uneasiness. She at length separated from him, and endeavored to procure a divorce, which she afterwards obtained. By this domestic discord, the power of Angus was considerably diminished; but he was still one of the first men in Scotland, and might have gained the complete government of the kingdom, had not his power been counterbalanced by that of the Earl of Arran. This nobleman was the head of the great family of Hamilton; he was connected with the royal family by blood, and had such extensive possessions and lordships as enabled him, though inferior in personal qualities to the Earl of Angus, to dispute with that chief of the more modern Douglases the supreme administration. All, or almost all, the great men of Scotland were in league with one or other of these powerful earls; each of whom supported those who followed him, in right or wrong, and oppressed those who opposed him, without any form of justice, but merely at his own pleasure. In this distracted state of things, it was impossible for the meanest man in Scotland to obtain success in the best-founded suit, unless he was under the protection either of Angus or Arran; and to whichever he might attach himself, he was sure to become an object of hatred and suspicion to the other. Under pretence, also, of taking a side, and acting for the interests of their party, wicked and lawless men committed violences of every kind, burned, murdered, and plundered, and pretended that they did so in the cause of the Earl of Angus, or of his rival the Earl of Arran.

At length, on the 30th of April, 1520, these two great factions of the Douglases and the Hamiltons came both to Edinburgh to attend a Parliament, in which it was expected that the western noblemen would in general take part with Arran, while those of the east would side with Angus. One of the strongest supporters of Arran was the Archbishop of Glasgow, James Beaton, a man remarkable for talents, but unfortunately also for profligacy. He was at this time Chancellor of Scotland; and the Hamiltons met within his palace, situated at the bottom of Blackfriars-Wynd, one of those narrow lanes which run down from the High Street of Edinburgh to the Cowgate. The Hamiltons, finding themselves far the more numerous party, were deliberating upon a scheme of attacking the Douglases, and apprehending Angus. That earl heard of their intentions, and sent his uncle, Gawain Douglas, Bishop of Dunkeld (a scholar and a poet), to remonstrate with Beaton, and to remind him, that it was his business as a churchman to preserve peace; Angus offering at the same time to withdraw out of the town, if he and his friends should be permitted to do so in safety. The Chancellor had, however, already assumed armor, which he wore under his rochet, or bishop's dress. As he laid his hand on his heart, and said, "Upon my conscience, I cannot help what is about to happen," the mail which he wore was heard to rattle. "Ha, my lord!" said the Bishop of Dunkeld, "I perceive that your conscience is not sound, as appears from its clatters." And leaving him after this rebuke, he hastened back to his nephew, the Earl of Angus, to bid him defend himself like a man. "For me," he said, "I will go to my chamber and pray for you."

Angus collected his followers, and hastened, like a sagacious soldier, to occupy the High Street of the city. The inhabitants were his friends, and spears were handed out to such of the Douglases as had them not; which proved a great advantage, the Hamiltons having no weapons longer than their swords.

In the mean time, Sir Patrick Hamilton, a wise and moderate man, brother to the Earl of Arran, advised his brother strongly not to come to blows; but a natural son of the Earl, Sir James Hamilton of Draphane, notorious for his fierce and cruel nature, exclaimed that Sir Patrick only spoke this "because he was afraid to fight in his friend's quarrel."

"Thou liest, false bastard!" said Sir Patrick; "I will fight this day where thou darest not be seen."

Immediately they all rushed towards the street, where the Douglases stood drawn up to receive them.

Now the Hamiltons, though very numerous, could only come at their enemies by thronging out of the little steep lanes which open into the High Street, the entrance of which the Douglases had barricaded with carts, barrels, and suchlike lumber. As the Hamiltons endeavored to force their way, they were fiercely attacked by the Douglases with pikes and spears. A few who got out on the street were killed or routed. The Earl of Arran, and his son the bastard, were glad to mount upon a coal-horse, from which they threw the load, and escaped by flight. Sir Patrick Hamilton was killed, with many others; thus dying in a scuffle which he had done all in his power to prevent. The confusion occasioned by this skirmish was greatly increased by the sudden appearance of Sir David Home of Wedderburn, the fierce Border leader who slew De la Bastie. He came with a band of eight hundred horse to assist Angus, and finding the skirmish begun, made his way into the city by bursting open one of the gates with sledge-hammers. The Hamiltons fled out of the town in great confusion; and the consequences of this skirmish were such, that the citizens of Edinburgh called it *Clean-the-Causeway*, because the faction of Arran was, as it were, swept from the streets. This broil gave Angus a great advantage in his future disputes with Arran; but it exhibits a wild picture of the times, when such a conflict could be fought in the midst of a populous city.

A year after this battle, the Duke of Albany returned from France, again to assume the Regency. He appears to have been encouraged to take this step by the King of France, who was desirous of recovering his influence in the Scottish councils, and who justly considered Angus as a friend of England. The Regent being successful in again taking up the reins of government, Angus was in his turn obliged to retire to France, where he spent his time so well, that he returned much wiser and more experienced than he had been esteemed before his banishment.

Albany, on the contrary, showed himself neither more prudent nor more prosperous than during his first government. He threatened much, and did little. He broke the peace with England, and invaded that country with a large army; then made a dishonorable truce with Lord Dacre, who commanded on the English frontier, and finally retired without fighting, or doing anything to support the boasts which he had made. This mean and poor-spirited conduct excited the contempt of the Scottish nation, and the Duke found it necessary to retreat once more to France, that he might obtain money and forces to maintain himself in the Regency, which he seemed to occupy rather for the advantage of that country than of Scotland.

The English, in the mean while, maintained the war which Albany had rekindled, by destructive and dangerous incursions on the Scottish frontiers; and that you may know how this fearful kind of warfare was conducted, I will give you some account of the storming of Jedburgh, which happened at this time.

Jedburgh was, after the castle and town of Roxburgh had been demolished, the principal town of the county. It was strongly walled, and inhabited by a class of citizens, whom their neighborhood to the English frontier made familiar with war. The town was also situated near those mountains in which the boldest of the Scottish Border clans had their abode.

The Earl of Surrey (son of him who had vanquished the Scots at Flodden, and who was now Duke of Norfolk) advanced from Berwick to Jedburgh in September, 1523, with an army of about ten thousand men. The Border chieftains, on the Scottish frontier, could only oppose to this well-appointed army about fifteen or eighteen hundred of their followers; but they were such gallant soldiers, and so willing to engage in battle, that the brave English general, who had served in foreign countries as well as at home, declared he had never met their equal. "Could forty thousand such men be assembled," said Surrey, "it would be a dreadful enterprise to withstand them."* But the force of numbers prevailed, and the English carried the place by assault. There were six strong towers within the town, which continued their defence after the walls were surmounted. These were the residences of persons of rank, walled round, and capable of strong resistance. The Abbey also was occupied by the Scots, and most fiercely defended. The battle continued till late in the night, and the English had no way of completing the victory, but by setting fire to the town; and even in this extremity, those who manned the towers and the Abbey continued their defence. The next day Lord Dacre was despatched to attack the Castle of Fairniehirst, within about three miles of Jedburgh, the feudal fortress of Sir Andrew Ker, a border chief, formerly mentioned. It was taken, but with great loss to the besiegers. In the evening, Lord Dacre, contrary to Surrey's commands, chose to encamp with his cavalry without the limits of the camp which the latter had chosen. About eight at night, when the English leaders were at supper, and concluded all resistance over, Dacre's quarters were attacked, and his horses all cut loose. The terrified animals, upwards of fifteen hundred in number, came galloping down to Surrey's camp, where they were received with showers of

* "Surrey to Cardinal Wolsey, — and who adds, 'I assure your Grace I found the Scots, at this time, the boldest men and the hotest, that ever I sawe any nacion.' The praise from Surrey is great, as he had often been employed on severe foreign service." — PINKERTON, vol. ii. p. 220.

arrows and volleys of musketry; for the English soldiers, alarmed by the noise, thought the Scots were storming their intrenchments, and shot off their shafts at a hazard. Many of the horses ran into Jedburgh, which was still in flames, and were seized and carried off by the Scottish women, accustomed like their husbands to the management of horses. The tumult was so great, that the English imputed it to supernatural interference, and Surrey alleged that the Devil was seen visibly six times during the confusion. Such was the credulity of the times; but the whole narrative may give you some notion of the obstinate defence of the Scots, and the horrors of a Border foray.

The Scots, on their side, were victorious in several severe actions, in one of which the Bastard Heron, who had contributed so much to Surrey's success at Flodden, was slain on the field.

The young King of Scotland, though yet a boy, began to show tokens of ill-will towards the French and Albany. Some nobles asked him what should be done with the French whom the Regent had left behind. "Give them," said James, "to Davie Home's keeping." Sir David Home, you must recollect, was the chieftain who put to death Albany's friend, De la Bastie, and knitted his head by the hair to his saddlebow.

Albany, however, returned again from France with great supplies of money, artillery, arms, and other provisions for continuing the war. These were furnished by France, because it was the interest of that country at all hazards to maintain the hostility between Scotland and England. The Regent once more, with a fine army, made an attack upon Norham, a castle on the English frontier; but when he had nearly gained this fortress, he suddenly, with his usual cowardice, left off the assault, on learning that Surrey was advancing to its relief. After this second dishonorable retreat, Albany left Scotland, detested and despised alike by the nobles and the common people, who felt that all his undertakings had ended in retreat and disgrace. In the month of May, 1524, he took leave of Scotland, never to return.

CHAPTER XXVI.

THE EARL OF ANGUS'S ACCESSION TO THE GOVERNMENT — INEFFECTUAL ATTEMPTS OF BUCCLEUCH AND LENNOX TO RESCUE THE YOUNG KING FROM THE POWER OF ANGUS — ESCAPE OF JAMES — BANISHMENT OF ANGUS, AND THE REST OF THE DOUGLASES.

[1524 — 1528.]

QUEEN MARGARET, who hated her husband Angus, as I have told you, now combined with his enemy, Arran, to call James V., her son (though then only twelve years old), to the management of the public affairs; but the Earl of Angus, returning at this crisis from France, speedily obtained a superiority in the Scottish councils, and became the head of those nobles who desired to maintain a friendly alliance with England rather than to continue that league with France which had so often involved Scotland in quarrels with their powerful neighbor.

Margaret might have maintained her authority, for she was personally much beloved; but it was the fate or the folly of that Queen to form rash marriages. Like her brother, Henry of England, who tired of his wives, Margaret seems to have been addicted to tire of her husbands; but she had not the power of cutting the heads from the spouses whom she desired to be rid of. Having obtained a divorce from Angus, she married a young man of little power and inferior rank, named Henry Stewart, a younger son of Lord Evandale. She lost her influence by that ill-advised measure.* Angus, therefore, rose to the supreme authority in Scotland, obtained possession of the person of the King, transacted everything in the name of James, but by his own authority, and became, in all respects, the Regent of Scotland, though without assuming the name.

The talents of the Earl of Angus were equal to the charge he had assumed, and as he reconciled himself to his old rival the Earl of Arran, his power seemed founded on a sure basis. He was able to accomplish a treaty of peace with England, which was of great advantage to the kingdom. But, according to the fashion of the times, Angus was much too desirous to confer all the great offices, lands, and other advantages in the disposal of the crown, upon his own friends and adherents, to the exclusion of all the nobles and gentry, who had either taken part against him in the late struggle for power, or were not decidedly his partisans. The course of justice also was shamefully perverted, by the partiality of Angus for his friends, kinsmen, and adherents.

An old historian says, "that there dared no man strive at law with a Douglas, or yet with the adherent of a Douglas; for if he did, he was sure to get the worst of his lawsuit.† And," he adds, "although Angus travelled

* "Henry, her brother, now perhaps revolving his own divorce from Catherine of Aragon, could not reprobate the example, while he despised the meanness of her nuptials. Yet James, incensed at Stewart's presumption, the marriage having been private, and the royal consent not requested, sent Lord Erskine with a body of men to the Castle of Stirling, where his mother resided with her new husband, and Margaret surrendering him, he was imprisoned for a time."—PINKERTON, vol. ii. p. 275.

† Pitscottie, p. 319. "The tyranny of the house of Douglas became every day more intolerable to the nation. To bear the name was esteemed sufficient to cover the most atrocious crime, even in the streets

through the country under the pretence of punishing thieves, robbers, and murderers, there were no malefactors so great as those which rode in his own company."

The King, who was now fourteen years old, became disgusted with the sort of restraint in which Angus detained him, and desirous to free himself from his tutelage. His mother had doubtless a natural influence over him, and that likewise was exerted to the Earl's prejudice. The Earl of Lennox, a wise and intelligent nobleman, near in blood to the King, was also active in fostering his displeasure against the Douglases, and schemes began to be agitated for taking the person of the King out of the hands of Angus. But Angus was so well established in the government, that his authority could not be destroyed except by military force; and it was not easy to bring such to bear against a man so powerful, and of such a martial character.

At length it seems to have been determined to employ the agency of Sir Walter Scott of Buccleuch, a man of great courage and military talent, head of a numerous and powerful clan, and possessed of much influence on the Border. He had been once the friend of Angus, and had even scaled the walls of Edinburgh with a great body of his clan, in order to render the party of the Earl uppermost in that city. But of late he had attached himself to Lennox, by whose counsel he seems to have been guided in the enterprise which I am about to give you an account of.

Some excesses had taken place on the Border, probably by the connivance of Buccleuch, which induced Angus to

of the capital; and during the sitting of Parliament, a baron who had murdered his opponent on the threshold of the principal church was permitted to walk openly abroad, solely because he was a Douglas; and no one, by his arrestment, dared to incur the vengeance of its chief." — TYTLER, vol. v. p. 207; PINKERTON, vol. ii. p. 282.

march to Jedburgh, bringing the King in his company, lest he should have made his escape during his absence. He was joined by the clans of Home and Ker, both in league with him, and he had, besides, a considerable body of chosen attendants. Angus was returning from this expedition, and had passed the night at Melrose. The Kers and Homes had taken leave of the Earl, who, with the King and his retinue, had left Melrose, when a band of a thousand horsemen suddenly appeared on the side of an eminence called Halidon Hill, and, descending into the valley, interposed between the Earl and the bridge by which he must pass the Tweed on his return northward.

"Sir," said Angus to the King, "yonder comes Buccleuch, with the Border thieves of Teviotdale and Liddesdale, to interrupt your Grace's passage. I vow to God they shall either fight or fly. You shall halt upon this knoll with my brother George, while we drive off these banditti, and clear the road for your Grace."

The King made no answer, for in his heart he desired that Buccleuch's undertaking might be successful; but he dared not say so.

Angus, meantime, despatched a herald to charge Buccleuch to withdraw with his forces. Scott replied, "that he was come, according to the custom of the Borders, to show the King his clan and followers, and invite his Grace to dine at his house." To which he added, "that he knew the King's mind as well as Angus." The Earl advanced, and the Borderers, shouting their war-cry of Bellenden, immediately joined battle, and fought stoutly; but the Homes and Kers, who were at no great distance, returned on hearing the alarm, and coming through the little village of Darnick, set upon Buccleuch's men, and decided the fate of the day. The Border riders fled, but Buccleuch and his followers fought bravely in their retreat, and turning upon the Kers, slew several of them; in particular, Ker of Cessford, a chief of the name, who was killed by the lance of one of the Elliots, a retainer of Buccleuch. His death occasioned a deadly feud between the clans of Scott and Ker, which lasted for a century, and cost much blood. This skirmish took place on the 25th of July, 1526. About eighty Scotts were slain on the field of battle, and a sentence was pronounced against Buccleuch and many of his clan, as guilty of high treason. But after the King had shaken off the yoke of the Douglases, he went in person to Parliament to obtain the restoration of Buccleuch, who, he declared on his kingly word, had come to Melrose without any purpose of quarrel, but merely to pay his duty to his Prince, and show him the number of his followers. In evidence of which, the King said, that the said Wat was not clad in armor, but in a leathern coat (a buff-coat, I suppose), with a black bonnet on his head. The family were restored to their estates accordingly; but Sir Walter Scott was long afterwards murdered by the Kers, at Edinburgh, in revenge of the death of the Laird of Cessford.

The Earl of Lennox, being disappointed in procuring the King's release by means of Buccleuch, now resolved to attempt it in person. He received much encouragement from the Chancellor Beaton (distinguished at the skirmish called Clean-the-Causeway), from the Earl of Glencairn, and other noblemen, who saw with displeasure the Earl of Angus confining the young King like a prisoner, and that all the administration of the kingdom centered in the Douglases. Lennox assembled an army of ten or twelve thousand men, and advanced upon Edinburgh from Stirling. Angus and Arran, who were still closely leagued together, encountered Lennox with an inferior force, near the village of Newliston. The rumor that a battle was about to commence soon reached Edinburgh, when Sir George Douglas hastened to call out the citizens in arms to support his brother, the Earl of Angus. The city bells were rung, trumpets were sounded, and the King himself was obliged to mount on horseback, to give countenance to the measures of the Douglases, whom in his soul he detested. James was so sensible of his situation, that he tried, by every means in his power, to delay the march of the forces which were mustered at Edinburgh. When they reached the village of Corstorphine, they heard the thunder of the guns; which inflamed the fierce impatience of George Douglas to reach the field of battle, and also increased the delays of the young King, who was in hopes Angus might be defeated before his brother could come up. Douglas, perceiving this, addressed the King in language which James never forgot nor forgave: "Your Grace need not think to escape us," said this fierce warrior; "if our enemies had hold of you on one side, and we on the other, we would tear you to pieces ere we would let you go."

Tidings now came from the field of battle that Lennox had been defeated, and that Angus had gained the victory. The young King, dismayed at the news, now urged his attendants to gallop forward, as much as he had formerly desired them to hang back. He charged them to prevent slaughter, and save lives, especially that of Lennox. Sir Andrew Wood, one of the King's cupbearers, arrived in the field of battle time enough to save the Earl of Glencairn, who was still fighting gallantly, by assistance of some strong ground, though he had scarce thirty men left alive; and Wood contrived to convey him safe out of the field. But Lennox, about whose safety the King was so anxious, was already no more. He had been slain, in cold blood, by that bloodthirsty man, Sir James Hamilton of Draphane, who took him from the Laird of Pardivan, to whom he had surrendered himself. This deed seemed to flow from the brutal nature of the perpetrator, who took such a pleasure in shedding blood, that he slashed with his own hand the faces of many of the prisoners. Arran, the father of this ferocious man, bitterly lamented the fate of Lennox, who was his nephew. He was found mourning beside the body, over which he had spread his scarlet cloak. "The hardiest, stoutest, and wisest man that Scotland bore," he said, "lies here slain."

After these two victories, the Earl of Angus seemed to be so firmly established in power, that his followers set no bounds to their presumption, and his enemies were obliged to fly and hide themselves. Chancellor Beaton, disguised as a shepherd, fed sheep on Bogrian-knowe, until he made his peace with the Earls of Angus and Arran, by great gifts, both in money and in church lands. Angus established around the King's person a guard of a hundred men of his own choice, commanded by Douglas of Parkhead; he made his brother George, whom James detested, Master of the Royal Household; and Archibald of Kilspindie, his uncle, Lord Treasurer of the Realm. But the close restraint in which the King found himself, only increased his eager desire to be rid of all the Douglases together. Force having failed in two instances, James had recourse to stratagem.

He prevailed on his mother, Queen Margaret, to yield up to him the Castle of Stirling, which was her jointure-house, and secretly to put it into the hands of a governor whom he could trust. This was done with much caution.

Thus prepared with a place of refuge, James watched with anxiety an opportunity of flying to it; and he conducted himself with such apparent confidence towards Angus that the Douglases were lulled into security, and concluded that the King was reconciled to his state of bondage, and had despaired of making his escape.

James was then residing at Falkland, a royal palace conveniently situated for hunting and hawking, in which he seemed to take great pleasure. The Earl of Angus at this period left the court for Lothian, where he had some urgent business, — Archibald Douglas of Kilspindie went to Dundee, to visit a lady to whom he was attached, — and George Douglas had gone to St. Andrews, to extort some further advantages from Chancellor Beaton, who was now Archbishop of that See, and Primate of Scotland. There was thus none of the Douglases left about the King's person, except Parkhead, with his guard of one hundred men, in whose vigilance the others confided.

The King thought the time favorable for his escape. To lay all suspicion asleep, he pretended he was to rise next morning at an early hour, for the purpose of hunting the stag. Douglas of Parkhead, suspecting nothing, retired to bed after placing his watch. But the King was no sooner in his private chamber, than he called a trusty page, named John Hart: "Jockie," said he, "dost thou love me?"

"Better than myself," answered the domestic.

"And will you risk anything for me?"

"My life, with pleasure," said John Hart.

The King then explained his purpose, and dressing himself in the attire of a groom, he went with Hart to the stable, as if for the purpose of getting the horses ready for the next day's hunt. The guards, deceived by their appearance, gave them no interruption. At the stables three good horses were saddled and in readiness, under charge of a yeoman or groom, whom the King had intrusted with his design.

James mounted with his two servants, and galloped, during the whole night, as eager as a bird just escaped from a cage. At daylight he reached the bridge of Stirling, which was the only mode of passing the river Forth, except by boats. It was defended by gates, which the King, after passing through them, ordered to be closed, and directed the passage to be watched. He was a weary man when he reached Stirling Castle, where he was joyfully received by the governor, whom his mother had placed in that strong fortress. The drawbridges were raised, the portcullises dropped, guards set, and every measure of defence and precaution resorted to. But the King was so much afraid of again falling into the hands of the Douglases, that, tired as he was, he would not go to sleep until the keys of the castle were placed in his own keeping, and laid underneath his pillow.

July, 1528.

In the morning there was great alarm at Falkland. Sir George Douglas had returned thither, on the night of the King's departure, about eleven o'clock. On his arrival, he inquired after the King, and was answered by the porter as well as the watchmen upon guard, that he was sleeping in his chamber, as he intended to hunt early in the morning. Sir George therefore retired to rest in full security. But the next morning he learned different tidings. One Peter Carmichael, bailie of Abernethy, knocked at the door of his chamber, and asked him if he knew "what the King was doing that morning?"

"He is in his chamber, asleep," said Sir George.

"You are mistaken," answered Carmichael; "he passed the bridge of Stirling this last night."

On hearing this, Douglas started up in haste, went to the King's chamber, and knocked for admittance. When no answer was returned, he caused the door to be forced, and when he found the apartment empty, he cried, "Treason! — The King is gone, and none knows whither." Then he sent post to his brother, the Earl of Angus, and despatched messengers in every direction, to seek the King, and to assemble the Douglases.

When the truth became known, the adherents of Angus rode in a body to Stirling; but the King was so far from desiring to receive them, that he threatened, by sound of trumpet, to declare any of the name of Douglas a traitor who should approach within twelve miles of his person, or who should presume to meddle with the administration of government. Some of the Douglases inclined to resist this proclamation; but the Earl of Angus and his brother resolved to obey it, and withdrew to Linlithgow.

Soon afterwards, the King assembled around him the numerous nobility, who envied the power of Angus and Arran, or had suffered injuries at their hands; and, in open Parliament, accused them of treason, declaring, that he had never been sure of his life all the while that he was in their power. A sentence of forfeiture was, therefore, passed against the Earl of Angus, and he was driven into exile, with all his friends and kinsmen. And thus the Red Douglases, of the house of Angus, shared almost the same fate with the Black Douglases, of the elder branch of that mighty house; with this difference, that as they had never risen so high, so they did not fall so irretrievably; for the Earl of Angus lived to return and enjoy his estates in Scotland, where he again played a distinguished part. But this was not till after the death of James V., who retained during his whole life an implacable resentment against the Douglases, and never permitted one of the name to settle in Scotland while he lived.

James persevered in this resolution even under circumstances which rendered his unrelenting resentment ungenerous. Archibald Douglas of Kilspindie, the Earl of Angus's uncle, had been a personal favorite of the King before the disgrace of his family. He was so much recommended to James by his great strength, manly appearance, and skill in every kind of warlike exercise, that he was wont to call him his Graysteil, after the name of a champion in a romance then popular.* Archibald, becoming rather an old man, and tired of his exile in England, resolved to try the King's mercy. He thought that as they had been so well acquainted formerly, and as he had never offended James personally, he might find favor from their old intimacy. He, therefore, threw himself in the King's way one day as he returned from hunting in the park at Stirling. It was several years since James had seen him, but he knew him at a great distance, by his firm and stately step, and said, "Yonder is my Graysteil, Archibald of Kilspindie." But when they met, he showed no appearance of recognizing his old servant. Douglas turned, and still hoping to obtain a glance of favorable recollection, ran along by the King's side; and although James trotted his horse hard against the hill, and Douglas wore a heavy shirt of mail under his clothes, for fear of assassination, yet Graysteil was at the castle-gate as soon as the King.† James passed him, and entered the castle;

* See a reprint of "The History of Sir Eger, Sir Grahame, and Sir Gray Steil," in a volume of "Early Metrical Tales, 12mo, W. and D. Laing, Edin., 1826."

† Godscroft adds, "The King approaching, Douglas fell upon his knees and craved pardon, and promised from thenceforward to abstain

but Douglas, exhausted with exertion, sat down at the gate, and asked for a cup of wine. The hatred of the King against the name of Douglas was so well known, that no domestic about the court dared procure for the old warrior even this trifling refreshment. The King blamed, indeed, his servants for their discourtesy, and even said, that but for his oath never to employ a Douglas, he would have received Archibald of Kilspindie into his service, as he had formerly known him a man of great ability. Yet he sent his commands to his poor Graysteil to retire to France, where he died heart-broken soon afterwards. Even Henry VIII. of England, himself of an unforgiving temper, blamed the implacability of James on this occasion, and quoted an old proverb, —

> "A King's face
> Should give grace."

from all meddling in public affairs, and to lead a quiet and a private life. The King went by without giving him any answer, and trotted a good round pace up the hill." — p. 262.

CHAPTER XXVII.

CHARACTER OF JAMES V. — HIS EXPEDITION TO PUNISH THE BORDER FREEBOOTERS — HIS ADVENTURES WHEN TRAVELLING IN DISGUISE — RUSTIC HUNTING PALACE IN ATHOLE — INSTITUTION OF THE COLLEGE OF JUSTICE — GOLD MINES OF SCOTLAND — ENCOURAGEMENT OF LEARNING.

[1528 — 1540.]

FREED from the stern control of the Douglas family, James V. now began to exercise the government in person, and displayed most of the qualities of a wise and good prince. He was handsome in his person, and resembled his father in the fondness for military exercises, and the spirit of chivalrous honor which James IV. loved to display. He also inherited his father's love of justice, and his desire to establish and enforce wise and equal laws, which should protect the weak against the oppression of the great. It was easy enough to make laws, but to put them in vigorous exercise was of much greater difficulty; and in his attempt to accomplish this laudable purpose, James often incurred the ill-will of the more powerful nobles. He was a well-educated and accomplished man; and, like his ancestor, James I., was a poet and a musician. He had, however, his defects. He avoided his father's failing of profusion, having no hoarded treasures to employ on pomp and show; but he rather fell into the opposite fault, being of a temper too parsimonious; and though he loved state and display, he endeavored to gratify that taste as economically as possible, so that he has been censured as rather close and covetous. He was also, though the foibles seem inconsistent, fond of pleasure, and disposed to too much indulgence. It must be added, that when provoked, he was unrelenting even to cruelty; for which he had some apology, considering the ferocity of the subjects over whom he reigned. But, on the whole, James V. was an amiable man, and a good sovereign.

His first care was to bring the Borders of Scotland to some degree of order. These, as you were formerly told, were inhabited by tribes of men, forming each a different clan, as they were called, and obeying no orders, save those which were given by their chiefs. These chiefs were supposed to represent the first founder of the name, or family. The attachment of the clansmen to the chief was very great: indeed, they paid respect to no one else. In this the Borderers agreed with the Highlanders, as also in their love of plunder, and neglect of the general laws of the country. But the Border men wore no tartan dress, and served almost always on horseback, whereas the Highlanders acted always on foot. You will also remember that the Borderers spoke the Scottish language, and not the Gaelic tongue used by the mountaineers.

May, 1529.

The situation of these clans on the frontiers exposed them to constant war; so that they thought of nothing else but of collecting bands of their followers together, and making incursions, without much distinction, on the English, on the Lowland (or inland) Scots, or upon each other. They paid little respect either to times of truce or treaties of peace, but exercised their depredations without regard to either, and often occasioned wars betwixt England and Scotland which would not otherwise have taken place.

It is said of a considerable family on the Borders, that when they had consumed all the cattle about the castle, a pair of spurs was placed on the table in a covered dish, as a hint that they must ride out and fetch more. The chiefs and leading men told down their daughters' portions according to the plunder which they were able to collect in the course of a Michaelmas moon, when its prolonged light allowed them opportunity for their freebooting excursions. They were very brave in battle, but in time of peace they were a pest to their Scottish neighbors. As their insolence had risen to a high pitch after the field of Flodden had thrown the country into confusion, James V. resolved to take very severe measures against them.

His first step was to secure the persons of the principal chieftains by whom these disorders were privately encouraged. The Earl of Bothwell, the Lord Home, Lord Maxwell, Scott of Buccleuch, Ker of Fairniehirst, and other powerful chiefs, who might have opposed the King's purposes, were seized, and imprisoned in separate fortresses in the inland country.

James then assembled an army, in which warlike purposes were united with those of sylvan sport; (June, 1529.) for he ordered all the gentlemen in the wild districts which he intended to visit, to bring in their best dogs, as if his only purpose had been to hunt the deer in those desolate regions. This was intended to prevent the Borderers from taking the alarm, in which case they would have retreated into their mountains and fastnesses, from whence it would have been difficult to dislodge them.

These men had indeed no distinct idea of the offences

which they had committed, and consequently no apprehension of the King's displeasure against them. The laws had been so long silent in that remote and disorderly country, that the outrages which were practised by the strong against the weak, seemed to the perpetrators the natural course of society, and to present nothing that was worthy of punishment.

Thus, as the King, in the beginning of his expedition, suddenly approached the Castle of Piers Cockburn of Henderland, that baron was in the act of providing a great entertainment to welcome him, when James caused him to be suddenly seized on, and executed. Adam Scott of Tushielaw, called the King of the Border, met the same fate. But an event of greater importance, was the fate of John Armstrong of Gilnockie, near Langholm.

This freebooting chief had risen to great consequence, and the whole neighboring district of England paid him *black-mail*, that is, a sort of tribute, in consideration of which he forbore plundering them. He had a high idea of his own importance, and seems to have been unconscious of having merited any severe usage at the King's hands. On the contrary, he came to meet his sovereign at a place about ten miles from Hawick, called Carlinrigg Chapel, richly dressed, and having with him twenty-four gentlemen, his constant retinue, as well attired as himself. The King, incensed to see a freebooter so gallantly equipped, commanded him instantly to be led to execution, saying, "What wants this knave, save a crown, to be as magnificent as a king?" John Armstrong made great offers for his life, offering to maintain himself, with forty men, ready to serve the King at a moment's notice, at his own expense; engaging never to hurt or injure any Scottish subject, as indeed had never been his practice;

and undertaking, that there was not a man in England, of whatever degree, duke, earl, lord, or baron, but he would engage, within a short time, to present him to the King dead or alive. But when the King would listen to none of his offers, the robber-chief said, very proudly, "I am but a fool to ask grace at a graceless face; but had I guessed you would have used me thus, I would have kept the Border-side, in despite of the King of England and you both; for I well know that King Henry would give the weight of my best horse in gold to know that I am sentenced to die this day."

John Armstrong was led to execution, with all his men, and hanged without mercy. The people of the inland counties were glad to get rid of him; but on the Borders he was both missed and mourned, as a brave warrior and a stout man-at-arms against England.

Such were the effects of the terror struck by these general executions, that James was said to have made "the rush bush keep the cow;" that is to say, that even in this lawless part of the country, men dared no longer make free with property, and cattle might remain on their pastures unwatched. James was also enabled to draw profit from the lands which the crown possessed near the Borders, and is said to have had ten thousand sheep at one time grazing in Ettrick Forest, under the keeping of one Andrew Bell, who gave the King as good an account of the profits of the flock, as if they had been grazing in the bounds of Fife, then the most civilized part of Scotland.

On the other hand, the Borders of Scotland were greatly weakened by the destruction of so many brave men, who, notwithstanding their lawless course of life, were true defenders of their country; and there is reason to censure the extent to which James carried his severity, as being to a certain degree impolitic, and beyond doubt cruel and excessive.

In the like manner James proceeded against the Highland chiefs; and, by executions, forfeitures, and other severe measures, he brought the Northern mountaineers, as he had already done those of the South, into comparative subjection. He then set at liberty the Border chiefs, and others whom he had imprisoned, lest they should have offered any hindrance to the course of his justice.

As these fiery chieftains, after this severe chastisement, could no longer as formerly, attack each other's castles and lands, they were forced to vent their deadly animosities in duels, which were frequently fought in the King's presence, his royal permission being first obtained. Thus, Douglas of Drumlanrig and Charteris of Amisfield did battle together in presence of the King, each having accused the other of high treason. They fought on foot with huge two-handed swords. Drumlanrig was somewhat blind, or short-sighted, and being in great fury, he struck about him without seeing where he hit, and the Laird of Amisfield was not more successful, for his sword broke in the encounter; upon this, the King caused the battle to cease, and the combatants were with difficulty separated. Thus the King gratified these unruly barons, by permitting them to fight in his own presence, in order to induce them to remain at peace elsewhere.

James V., like his father James IV., had a custom of going about the country disguised as a private person, in order that he might hear complaints which might not otherwise reach his ears, and perhaps that he might enjoy amusements which he could not have partaken of in his avowed royal character. This is also said to have been a custom of James IV., his father, and several adventures are related of what befell them on such occasions. One or two of these narratives may help to enliven our story.

When James V. travelled in disguise, he used a name which was known only to some of his principal nobility and attendants. He was called the Goodman (the tenant, that is) of Ballengiech. Ballengiech is a steep pass which leads down behind the castle of Stirling. Once upon a time, when the court was feasting in Stirling, the King sent for some venison from the neighboring hills. The deer was killed, and put on horses' backs to be transported to Stirling. Unluckily they had to pass the castle-gates of Arnpryor, belonging to a chief of the Buchanans, who chanced to have a considerable number of guests with him. It was late, and the company were rather short of victuals, though they had more than enough of liquor. The chief, seeing so much fat venison passing his very door, seized on it; and to the expostulations of the keepers, who told him it belonged to King James, he answered insolently, that if James was King in Scotland, he, Buchanan, was King in Kippen; being the name of the district in which the castle of Arnpryor lay. On hearing what had happened, the King got on horseback, and rode instantly from Stirling to Buchanan's house, where he found a strong, fierce-looking Highlander, with an axe on his shoulder, standing sentinel at the door. This grim warder refused the King admittance, saying, that the Laird of Arnpryor was at dinner, and would not be disturbed. "Yet go up to the company, my good friend," said the King, "and tell him that the Goodman of Ballengiech is come to feast with the King of Kippen." The porter went grumbling into the house, and told his master that there was a fellow with a red beard at the gate, who called himself the Goodman of Ballengiech, who said he was come to dine with the King of Kippen. As soon as Buchanan heard these words, he knew that the King was come in person, and hastened down to kneel at James feet, and to ask forgiveness for his insolent behavior. But the King, who only meant to give him a fright, forgave him freely, and, going into the castle, feasted on his own venison which Buchanan had intercepted. Buchanan of Arnpryor was ever afterwards called the King of Kippen.

Upon another occasion, King James, being alone and in disguise, fell into a quarrel with some gypsies, or other vagrants, and was assaulted by four or five of them. This chanced to be very near the Bridge of Cramond; so the King got on the bridge, which, as it was high and narrow, enabled him to defend himself with his sword against the number of persons by whom he was attacked. There was a poor man thrashing corn in a barn near by, who came out on hearing the noise of the scuffle, and seeing one man defending himself against numbers, gallantly took the King's part with his flail, to such good purpose that the gypsies were obliged to fly. The husbandman then took the King into the barn, brought him a towel and water to wash the blood from his face and hands, and finally walked with him a little way towards Edinburgh, in case he should be again attacked. On the way, the King asked his companion what and who he was. The laborer answered, that his name was John Howieson, and that he was a bondsman on the farm of Braehead, near Cramond, which belonged to the King of Scotland. James then asked the poor man, if there was any wish in the world which he would particularly desire should be gratified; and honest John confessed, he should think himself the happiest man in Scotland were he but proprietor of the farm on which he wrought as a laborer. He then asked the King, in turn, who *he* was; and James replied, as usual, that he was the Goodman of Ballengiech, a poor man who had a small appointment about the palace; but he added, that if John Howieson would come to see him on the next Sunday, he would endeavor to repay his manful assistance, and at least give him the pleasure of seeing the royal apartments.

John put on his best clothes, as you may suppose, and appearing at a postern gate of the palace, inquired for the Goodman of Ballengiech. The King had given orders that he should be admitted; and John found his friend, the goodman, in the same disguise which he had formerly worn. The King, still preserving the character of an inferior officer of the household, conducted John Howieson from one apartment of the palace to another, and was amused with his wonder and his remarks. At length, James asked his visitor if he should like to see the King; to which John replied, nothing would delight him so much, if he could do so without giving offence. The Goodman of Ballengiech, of course, undertook that the King would not be angry. "But," said John, "how am I to know his Grace from the nobles who will be all about him?"—"Easily," replied his companion; "all the others will be uncovered,—the King alone will wear his hat or bonnet."

So speaking, King James introduced the countryman into a great hall, which was filled by the nobility and officers of the crown. John was a little frightened, and drew close to his attendant; but was still unable to distinguish the King. "I told you that you should know him by his wearing his hat," said the conductor. "Then," said John, after he had again looked around the room, "it must be either you or me, for all but us two are bare-headed."

The King laughed at John's fancy; and that the good yeoman might have occasion for mirth also, he made him a present of the farm of Braehead, which he had wished so much to possess, on condition that John Howieson, or his successors, should be ready to present an ewer and basin for the King to wash his hands, when his Majesty should come to Holyrood Palace, or should pass the bridge of Cramond. Accordingly, in the year 1822, when George IV. came to Scotland, the descendant of John Howieson of Braehead, who still possesses the estate which was given to his ancestor, appeared at a solemn festival, and offered his Majesty water from a silver ewer, that he might perform the service by which he held his lands.

James V. was very fond of hunting, and when he pursued that amusement in the Highlands he used to wear the peculiar dress of that country, having a long and wide Highland shirt, and a jacket of tartan velvet, with plaid hose, and everything else corresponding. The accounts for these are in the books of his chamberlain, still preserved.

On one occasion, when the King had an ambassador of the Pope along with him, with various foreigners of distinction, they were splendidly entertained by 1533.
the Earl of Athole in a huge and singular rustic palace. It was built of timber, in the midst of a great meadow, and surrounded by moats, or fosses, full of the most delicate fish. It was enclosed and defended by towers, as if it had been a regular castle, and had within it many apartments, which were decked with flowers and branches, so that in treading them one seemed to be in a

garden. Here were all kinds of game, and other provisions in abundance, with many cooks to make them ready, and plenty of the most costly spices and wines. The Italian ambassador was greatly surprised to see, amongst rocks and wildernesses which seemed to be the very extremity of the world, such good lodging and so magnificent an entertainment. But what surprised him most of all, was to see the Highlanders set fire to the wooden castle as soon as the hunting was over, and the King in the act of departing. "Such is the constant practice of our Highlanders," said James to the ambassador; "however well they may be lodged over night, they always burn their lodging before they leave it." By this the King intimated the predatory and lawless habits displayed by these mountaineers.

The reign of James V. was not alone distinguished by his personal adventures and pastimes, but is honorably remembered on account of wise laws made for the government of his people, and for restraining the crimes and violence which were frequently practised among them; especially those of assassination, burning of houses, and driving of cattle, the usual and ready means by which powerful chiefs avenged themselves of their feudal enemies.

For the decision of civil questions, James V. invented and instituted what is called the College of Justice, being the Supreme Court of Scotland in civil affairs. It consisted of fourteen judges (half clergy, half laity,) and a president, who heard and decided causes. A certain number of learned men, trained to understand the laws, were appointed to the task of pleading the causes of such as had lawsuits before these judges, who constituted what is popularly termed the Court of Session. These men were called advocates; and this was the first establishment of a body regularly educated to the law, which has ever since been regarded in Scotland as an honorable profession, and has produced many great men.

James V. used great diligence in improving his navy, and undertook what was at the time rather a perilous task, to sail in person round Scotland, May, 1540. and cause an accurate survey to be made of the various coasts, bays, and islands, harbors, and roadsteads of his kingdom, many of which had been unknown to his predecessors, even by name.

This active and patriotic prince ordered the mineral wealth of Scotland to be also inquired into. He obtained miners from Germany, who extracted both silver and gold from the mines of Leadhills, in the upper part of Clydesdale. The gold was of fine quality, and found in quantity sufficient to supply metal for a very elegant gold coin, which, bearing on one side the head of James V. wearing a bonnet, has been thence called the bonnet-piece. It is said, that upon one occasion the King invited the ambassadors of Spain, France, and other foreign countries, to hunt with him in Crawford Moor, the district in which lie the mines I have just mentioned. They dined in the castle of Crawford, a rude old fortress. The King made some apology for the dinner, which was composed of the game they had killed during the hunting and hawking of the day, but he assured his guests that the dessert would make them some amends, as he had given directions that it should consist of the finest fruits which the country afforded. The foreigners looked at each other in surprise, on hearing the King talk of fruits being produced amidst the black moors and barren mountains around them. But the dessert made its appearance in the shape of a number of covered saucers, one of which was placed before each guest, and being examined was found full of gold bonnet-pieces, which they were desired to accept as the fruit produced by the mountains of Crawford Moor. This new sort of dessert was no doubt as acceptable as the most delicate fruits of a southern climate. The mines of the country are now wrought only for lead, of which they produce still a very large quantity.

Although, as we have mentioned, James was a good economist, he did not neglect the cultivation of the fine arts. He rebuilt the palace of Linlithgow, which is on a most magnificent plan, and made additions to that of Stirling. He encouraged several excellent poets and learned men, and his usual course of life appears to have been joyous and happy. He was himself a poet of some skill, and he permitted great freedom to the rhymers of his time, in addressing verses to him, some of which conveyed severe censures of his government, and others satires on his foibles.*

James also encouraged the sciences, but was deceived by a foreigner, who pretended to have knowledge of the art of making gold. This person, however, who was either crack-brained or an impostor, destroyed his own credit by the fabrication of a pair of wings, with which he proposed to fly from the top of Stirling Castle. He actually made the attempt, but as his pinions would not work easily, he fell down the precipice, and broke his thigh-bone.

* "The two excellent comic songs, entitled 'The Gaberlunzie Man,' and 'We 'll gae nae mair a roving,' are said to have been founded upon the success of his amorous adventures when travelling in the disguise of a beggar. The latter is perhaps the best comic ballad in any language." — *Note*, Canto vi., *Lady of the Lake.*

As the kingdom of Scotland, except during a very short and indecisive war with England, remained at peace till near the end of James's reign, and as that monarch was a wise and active prince, it might have been hoped that he at least would have escaped the misfortunes which seemed to haunt the name of Stewart. But a great change, which took place at this period, led James V. into a predicament as unhappy as attended any of his ancestors.

CHAPTER XXVIII.

Abuses of the Church of Rome — Reformation in England — and in Scotland — War with England, and Death of James V.

[1536 — 1542.]

You remember, my dear child, that James V. was nephew to Henry VIII. of England, being a son of Margaret, sister of that monarch. This connection, and perhaps the policy of Henry, who was aware that it was better for both countries that they should remain at peace together, prevented for several years the renewal of the destructive wars between the two divisions of the island. The good understanding would probably have been still more complete, had it not been for the great and general change in religious matters, called in history the Reformation. I must give you some idea of the nature of this alteration, otherwise you cannot understand the consequences to which it led.

After the death of our blessed Saviour Jesus Christ, the doctrine which he preached was planted in Rome, the principal city of the great Roman empire, by the Apostle Peter, as it is said, whom the Catholics, therefore, term the first Bishop of Rome. In process of time, the Bishops of Rome, who succeeded, as they said, the Apostle in his office, claimed an authority over all others in Christendom. Good and well-meaning persons, in their reverence for the religion which they had adopted, admitted these pretensions without much scrutiny. As the Christian religion was more widely received, the emperors and kings who embraced it thought to distinguish their piety by heaping benefits on the Church, and on the bishops of Rome in particular, who at length obtained great lands and demesnes as temporal princes; while, in their character of clergymen, they assumed the title of Popes, and the full and exclusive authority over all other clergymen in the Christian world. As the people of those times were extremely ignorant, any little knowledge which remained was to be found among the clergy, who had some leisure to study; while the laity, that is, all men who were not clergymen, learned little, excepting to tilt, fight, and feast. The Popes of Rome, having established themselves as heads of the Church, went on, by degrees, introducing into the simple and beautiful system delivered to us in the Gospèl, other doctrines, many of them inconsistent with, or contradictory of, pure Christianity, and all of them tending to extend the power of the priests over the minds and consciences of other men. It was not difficult for the Popes to make these alterations. For, as they asserted that they were the visible successors of Saint Peter, they pretended that they were as infallible as the Apostle himself, and that all that they published in their ordinances, which they called Bulls, must be believed by all Christian men, as much as if the same had been enjoined in the Holy Scripture itself. We shall notice two or three of these innovations.

Some good men, in an early age of Christianity, had withdrawn from the world to worship God in desert and desolate places. They wrought for their bread, gave alms to the poor, spent their leisure in the exercise of devotion, and were justly respected. But by degrees, as well-meaning persons bestowed great sums to support associations of such holy men, bequeathed lands to the monasteries or convents in which they lived, and made them wealthy, the monks, as they were called, departed from the simplicity of their order, and neglected the virtues which they undertook to practise. Besides, by the extravagant endowments of these convents, great sums of money and large estates were employed in maintaining a useless set of men, who, under pretence of performing devotional exercises, withdrew themselves from the business of the world, and from all domestic duties. Hence, though there continued to be amongst the monks many good, pious, and learned men, idleness and luxury invaded many of the institutions, and corrupted both their doctrines and their morals.

The worship also of saints, for which Scripture gives us no warrant whatever, was introduced in those ignorant times. It is natural we should respect the memory of any remarkably good man, and that we should value anything which has belonged to him. The error lay in carrying this natural veneration to extremity, — in worshipping the relics of a saintly character, such as locks of hair, bones, articles of clothing, and other trumpery, and in believing that such things are capable of curing sickness, or of working other miracles shocking to common sense. Yet the Roman Church opened the way to this absurdity, and imputed to these relics, which were often a mere imposture, the power, which God alone possesses, of altering those laws of nature which his wisdom has appointed. The Popes also encouraged and enjoined the worship of saints, that is, the souls of holy men deceased, as a sort of subordinate deities, whose intercession may avail us before the throne of God, although the Gospel has expressly declared that our Lord Jesus Christ is our only Mediator. And, in virtue of this opinion, not only were the Virgin Mary, the apostles, and almost every other person mentioned in the Gospels, erected by the Roman Catholics into the office of intercessors with the Deity, but numerous others, some of them mere names, who never existed as men, were canonized, as it was called, that is, declared by the Pope to be saints, and had altars and churches dedicated to them. Pictures also, and statues, representing these alleged holy persons, were exhibited in churches, and received the worship which ought not, according to the second commandment, to be rendered to any idol or graven image.

Other doctrines there were, about fasting on particular days, and abstaining from particular kinds of food, all of which were gradually introduced into the Roman Catholic faith, though contrary to the Gospel.

But the most important innovation, and that by which the priests made most money, was the belief that the Church, or, in other words, the priest, had the power of pardoning such sins as were confessed to him, upon the culprit's discharging such penance as the priest imposed on him. Every person was, therefore, obliged to confess himself to a priest, if he hoped to have his sins pardoned; and the priest enjoined certain kinds of penance, more or less severe, according to the circumstances of the offence. But, in general, these penances might be excused, providing a corresponding sum of money were paid to the Church, which possessed thus a perpetual and most lucrative source of income, which was yet more increased by the belief in Purgatory.

We have no right, from Scripture, to believe in the existence of any intermediate state betwixt that of happiness, which we call Heaven, to which good men have access immediately after death, or that called Hell, being the place of eternal punishment, to which the wicked are consigned with the devil and his angels. But the Catholic priests imagined the intervention of an intermediate state, called Purgatory. They supposed that many, or indeed that most people, were not of such piety as to deserve immediate admission into a state of eternal happiness, until they should have sustained a certain portion of punishment; but yet were not so wicked as to deserve instant and eternal condemnation. For the benefit of these, they invented the intermediate situation of Purgatory, a place of punishment, to which almost every one, not doomed to Hell itself, was consigned for a greater or less period, in proportion to his sins, before admission into a state of happiness. But here lay the stress of the doctrine. The power was in the Church to obtain pardon, by prayer, for the souls who were in Purgatory, and to have the gates of that place of torture opened for their departure sooner than would otherwise have taken place. Men, therefore, whose consciences told them that they deserved a long abode in this place of punishment, left liberal sums to the Church to have prayers said for the behoof of their souls. Children, in like manner, procured masses (that is, a particular sort of devotional worship practised by Catholics) to be said for the souls of their deceased parents. Widows did the same for their departed husbands, — husbands for their wives. All these masses and prayers could only be obtained by money, and all this money went to the priests.

But the Pope and his clergy carried the matter still further, and not only sold, as they pretended, the forgiveness of Heaven to those who had committed sins, but also granted them (always for money) a liberty to break through the laws of God and the Church. These licenses were called indulgences, because those who purchased them were indulged in the privilege of committing irregularities and vices, without being supposed answerable to the Divine wrath.

To support this extraordinary fabric of superstition, the Pope assumed the most extensive powers, even to the length of depriving kings of their thrones, by his sentence of excommunication, which declared their subjects free from their oath of allegiance, and at liberty to rise up against their sovereign and put him to death. At other times, the Pope took it upon him to give the kingdoms of the excommunicated prince to some ambitious neighbor. The rule of the Church of Rome was as severe over inferior persons as over princes. If a layman read the Bible, he was accounted guilty of a great offence; for the priests well knew that a perusal of the Sacred Scriptures would open men's eyes to their extravagant pretensions. If an individual presumed to disbelieve any of the doctrines which the Church of Rome taught, or to entertain any which were inconsistent with these doctrines, he was tried as a heretic, and subjected to the horrid punishment of being burnt alive; and this penalty was inflicted without mercy for the slightest expressions approaching to what the Papists called heresy.

This extraordinary and tyrannical power over men's consciences was usurped during those ages of European history which are called dark, because men were at that period without the light of learning and information. But the discovery of the art of printing began, in the fifteenth century, to open men's minds. The Bible, which had been locked up in the hands of the clergy, then became common, and was generally read; and wise and good men in Germany and Switzerland made it their study to expose the errors and corruptions of the See of Rome. The doctrine of saint-worship was shown to be idolatrous, — that of pardons and indulgences, a foul encouragement to vice, — that of Purgatory, a cunning means of extorting money, — and the pretensions of the Pope to infallibility, a blasphemous assumption of the attributes proper to God alone. These new opinions were termed the doctrines of the Reformers, and those who embraced them became gradually more and more numerous. The Roman Catholic priests attempted to defend the tenets of their Church by argument; but as that was found difficult, they endeavored, in most countries of Europe, to enforce them by violence. But the Reformers found protection in various parts of Germany. Their numbers seemed to increase rather than diminish, and to promise a great revolution in the Christian world.

Henry VIII., the King of England, was possessed of some learning, and had a great disposition to show it in this controversy. Being, in the earlier part of his reign, sincerely attached to the Church of Rome, he wrote a book in defence of its doctrines, against Martin Luther, one of the principal Reformers. The Pope was so much gratified by this display of zeal, that he conferred on the King the appellation of Defender of the Faith, — a title which Henry's successors continue to retain, although in a very different sense from that in which it was granted.

Now Henry, you must know, was married to a very good princess, named Catherine, who was a daughter of the King of Spain, and sister to the Emperor of Germany. She had been in her youth contracted to Henry's elder brother Arthur; but that prince dying, and Henry becoming heir of the throne, his union with Catherine had taken place. They had lived long together, and Catherine had borne a daughter, Mary, who was the natural heir-apparent of the English crown. But at length Henry VIII. fell deeply in love with a beautiful young woman, named Ann Bullen, a maid of honor in the Queen's retinue, and he became extremely desirous to get rid of Queen Catherine, and marry this young lady. For this purpose he applied to the Pope, in order to obtain a divorce from the good Queen, under pretence of her having been contracted to his elder brother before he was married to her. This, he alleged, seemed to him like marrying his brother's wife, and therefore he desired that the Pope would dissolve a marriage, which, as he alleged, gave much pain to his conscience. The truth was, that his conscience would have given him very little disturbance, had he not wanted to marry another, a younger and more beautiful woman.

The Pope would have probably been willing enough to gratify Henry's desire, at least his predecessors had granted greater favors to men of less consequence; but then Catherine was the sister of Charles V., who was at once Emperor of Germany and King of Spain, and one of the wisest, as well as the most powerful, princes in Christendom. The Pope, who depended much on Charles's assistance for checking the Reformation, dared not give him the great offence, which would have been occasioned by encouraging his sister's divorce. His Holiness, therefore, evaded giving a precise answer to the King of England from day to day, week to week, and year to year. But this led to a danger which the Pope had not foreseen.

Henry VIII., a hot, fiery, and impatient prince as ever lived, finding that the Pope was trifling with him, resolved to shake off his authority entirely. For this purpose, he denied the authority of the Pope in England, and declared, that he himself was the only Head of the English Church, and that the Bishop of Rome had nothing to do with him or his dominions. Many of the bishops and clergymen of the English Church adopted the Reformed doctrines, and all disowned the supreme rule, hitherto ascribed to the Pope.

But the greatest blow to the papal authority was the dissolution of the monasteries, or religious houses, as they were called. The King seized on the convents, and the lands granted for their endowment, and, distributing the wealth of the convents among the great men of his court, broke up forever those great establishments, and placed an insurmountable obstacle in the way of the Catholic religion being restored, after the interest of so many persons had been concerned in its being excluded.

The motive of Henry VIII.'s conduct was by no means praiseworthy, but it produced the most important and salutary consequences; as England was for ever afterwards, except during the short reign of his eldest daughter, freed from all dependence upon the Pope, and from the superstitious doctrines of the Roman Catholic religion.

Now here, returning to Scottish history, you must understand that one of Henry's principal wishes was to prevail upon his nephew, the young King of Scotland, to make the same alteration of religion in his country, which had been introduced into England. Henry, if we can believe the Scottish historians, made James the most splendid offers, to induce him to follow this course. He proposed to give him the hand of his daughter Mary in marriage, and to create him Duke of York; and, with a view to the establishment of a lasting peace between the countries, he earnestly desired a personal meeting with his nephew in the north of England.

There is reason to believe that James was at one period somewhat inclined to the Reformed doctrines; at least, he encouraged a Scottish poet, called Sir David Lindsay of the Mount,* and also the celebrated scholar, George Buchanan, in composing some severe satires against the corruptions of the Roman Catholic religion; but the King was, notwithstanding, by no means disposed altogether to fall off from the Church of Rome. He dreaded the power of England, and the rough, violent, and boisterous manners of Henry, who disgusted his nephew by the imprudent violence with which he pressed him to imitate his steps. But, in particular, James found the necessity of adhering to the Roman Catholic faith, from the skill, intelligence, and learning of the clergy, which rendered them far more fit to hold offices of state, and to assist him in administering the public business, than the Scottish nobility, who were at once profoundly ignorant, and fierce, arrogant, and ambitious in the highest degree.

The Archbishop Beaton, already mentioned, and his nephew, David Beaton, who was afterwards made a cardinal, rose high in James's favor; and, no doubt, the influence which they possessed over the King's mind was

* "Lindsay," says Dr. M'Crie, "had long lashed the vices of the clergy, and exposed the absurdity and superstitions of popery in the most popular and poignant satires, being protected by James V., who retained a strong attachment to the companion of his early sports, and the poet who had often amused his leisure hours." — *Life of Knox*, vol i. p. 50.

exerted to prevent his following the example of his uncle Henry in religious affairs.

The same influence might also induce him to seek an alliance with France, rather than with England; for it was natural that the Catholic clergy, with whom James advised, should discountenance, by every means in their power, any approaches to an intimate alliance with Henry, the mortal enemy of the Papal See. James V. accordingly visited France, and obtained the hand of Magdalen, the daughter of Francis I., with a large portion. Much joy was expressed at the landing of this princess
1st Jan., 1537. at Leith,* and she was received with as great splendor and demonstration of welcome, as the poverty of the country would permit. But the young Queen was in a bad state of health, and died within forty days after her marriage.

After the death of this princess, the King, still inclin-
June, 1538. ing to the French alliance, married Mary of Guise, daughter of the Duke of Guise, thus connecting himself with a family, proud, ambitious, and attached, in the most bigoted degree, to the Catholic cause. This connection served, no doubt, to increase James's disinclination to any changes in the established Church.

But whatever were the sentiments of the sovereign, those of the subjects were gradually tending more and more towards a reformation of religion. Scotland at this time possessed several men of learning who had studied abroad, and had there learned and embraced the doctrines of the great Reformer, Calvin. They brought with them, on their return, copies of the Holy Scripture, and could

* "At landing, the Queen upon her knees kissed the ground, and thanking God for her safety, prayed for happiness to the country and its people." — PITSCOTTIE, p. 373; DRUMMOND, fol. 104.

give a full account of the controversy between the Protestants, as they are now called, and the Roman Catholic Church. Many among the Scots, both of higher and lower rank, became converts to the new faith.

The Popish ministers and counsellors of the King ventured to have recourse to violence, in order to counteract these results. Several persons were seized upon, tried before the Spiritual Courts of the Bishop of St. Andrews, and condemned to the flames. The modesty and decency with which these men behaved on their trials, and the patience with which they underwent the tortures of a cruel death, protesting at the same time their belief in the doctrines for which they had been condemned to the stake, made the strongest impression on the beholders, and increased the confidence of those who had embraced the tenets of the Reformers. Stricter and more cruel laws were made against heresy. Even the disputing the power of the Pope was punished with death; yet the Reformation seemed to gain ground in proportion to every effort to check it.

The favors which the King extended to the Catholic clergy, led the Scottish nobility to look upon them with jealousy, and increased their inclination towards the Protestant doctrines. The wealth of the abbeys and convents, also, tempted many of the nobles and gentry, who hoped to have a share of the Church-lands, in case of these institutions being dissolved, as in England. And although there were doubtless good men as well as bad among the monks, yet the indolent, and even debauched lives of many of the order, rendered them generally odious and contemptible to the common people.

The popular discontent was increased by an accident which took place in the year 1537. A matron of the highest rank, Jane Douglas, sister of the banished Earl of Angus, widow of John Lyon, Lord of Glamis, and wife of Archibald Campbell of Kepneith, was accused of having practised against the life of James, by the imaginary crime of witchcraft, and the more formidable means of poison. Her purpose was alleged to be the restoration of the Douglases to Scotland, and to their estates and influence in that country. This lady was burnt alive on the Castle-hill of Edinburgh; and the spectators, filled with pity for her youth and beauty, and surprised at the courage with which she endured the sentence, did not fail to impute her execution less to any real crime, than to the King's deep-rooted hatred against the house of Douglas. Another capital punishment, though inflicted on an object of general dislike, served to confirm the opinion entertained of James's severity, not to say cruelty, of disposition. We have mentioned Sir James Hamilton of Draphane, called the Bastard of Arran, as distinguished on account of the ferocity of his disposition, and the murders which he committed in cold blood. This man had been made Sheriff of Ayr, and had received other favors from the King's hand. Notwithstanding, he was suddenly accused of treason by a cousin and namesake of his own; and on that sole testimony condemned and executed. Upon this occasion, also, public opinion charged James with having proceeded without sufficient evidence of guilt.

In the mean time, Henry continued to press the King of Scotland, by letters and negotiations, to enter into common measures with him against the Catholic clergy. He remonstrated with his nephew upon his preferring to improve his royal revenue by means of herds and flocks, which he represented as an unprincely practice, saying, that if he wanted money, he, his kind uncle, would let him have what sums he pleased; or, that the wealth of the Catholic convents and monasteries was a fund which lay at his command whenever he liked to seize it. Lastly, the English ambassador, Sir Ralph Sadler, insisted, as directed by his instructions, upon the evil doctrines and vicious lives of the clergy, against whom he urged the King to take violent measures.

Much of this message was calculated to affront James, yet he answered temperately. He acknowledged that he preferred living on his own revenue, such as it was, to becoming dependent upon another king, even though that king was his uncle. He had no pretext or motive, he said, to seize the possessions of the clergy, because they were always ready to advance him money when he had need of it. Those among them who led vicious lives, he would not fail, he added, to correct severely; but he did not consider it as just to punish the whole body for the faults of a few. In conclusion, King James suffered a doubtful promise to be extracted from him that he would meet Henry at York, if the affairs of his kingdom would permit.

The King of Scotland was now brought to a puzzling alternative, being either obliged to comply with his uncle's wishes, break off his alliance with France, and introduce the Reformed religion into his dominions, or by adhering to France and to the Catholic faith, to run all the hazards of a war with England. The churchmen exercised their ull authority over the mind of James at this crisis. The old of France was not spared to determine his resolution; id it may be supposed that the young Queen, so nearly nnected with the Catholic house of Guise, gave her in-ence to the same party. James at length determined to appoint his uncle; and after the haughty Henry had remained six days at York, in the expectation of meeting him, he excused himself by some frivolous apology. Henry was, as might have been expected, mortally offended, and prepared for war.

A fierce and ruinous war immediately commenced. Henry sent numerous forces to ravage the Scottish Border. James obtained success in the first considerable action, to his unutterable satisfaction, and prepared for more decisive hostility. He assembled the array of his kingdom, and marched from Edinburgh as far as Fala, on his way to the Border, when tidings arrived, 1st November, 1542, that the English general had withdrawn his forces within the English frontier. On this news, the Scottish nobles, who with their vassals had joined the royal standard, intimated to their sovereign, that though they had taken up arms to save the country from invasion, yet they considered the war with England as an impolitic measure, and only undertaken to gratify the clergy; and that, therefore, the English having retired, they were determined not to advance one foot into the enemy's country. One Border chieftain alone offered with his retinue to follow the King wherever he chose to lead. This was John Scott of Thirlstane, whom James rewarded with an addition to his paternal coat-of-arms, with a bunch of spears for the crest, and the motto, "*Ready, aye Ready.*"

James, finding himself thus generally thwarted and deserted by the nobility, returned to Edinburgh, dishonored before his people, and in the deepest dejection of mind.

To retaliate the inroads of the English, and wipe out the memory of Fala Moss, the King resolved that an army of ten thousand men should invade England on the Western border; and he imprudently sent with them his peculiar favorite, Oliver Sinclair, who shared with the priests the unpopularity of the English war, and was highly obnoxious to the nobility, as one of those who engrossed the royal favor to their prejudice.

The army had just entered English ground, at a place called Solway Moss, when this Oliver Sinclair was raised upon the soldiers' shields to read to the army a commission, which, it was afterwards said, named Lord Maxwell commander of the expedition. But no one doubted at the time that Oliver Sinclair had himself been proclaimed commander-in-chief; and as he was generally disliked and despised, the army instantly fell into a state of extreme confusion. Four or five hundred English Borderers, commanded by Thomas Dacre and John Musgrave, perceived this fluctuation, and charged the numerous squadrons of the invading army. The Scots fled without even attempting to fight. Numbers of noblemen and gentlemen suffered themselves to be made prisoners, rather than face the displeasure of their disappointed sovereign.

The unfortunate James had lately been assaulted by various calamities. The death of his two sons, and the disgrace of the defection at Fala, had made a deep impression on his mind, and haunted him even in the visions of the night. He dreamed he saw the fierce Sir James Hamilton, whom he had caused to be put to death upon slight evidence. The bloody shade approached him with a sword, and said, "Cruel tyrant, thou hast unjustly murdered me, who was indeed barbarous to other men, but always faithful and true to thee; wherefore now shalt thou have thy deserved punishment." So saying, it seemed to him as if Sir James Hamilton cut off first one arm and then another, and then left him, threatening to come back soon and cut his head off. Such a dream was very likely to arise in the King's mind, perturbed as it was by misfortunes, and even perhaps internally reproaching himself for Sir James Hamilton's death. But to James the striking off his arms appeared to allude to the death of his two sons, and he became convinced that the ultimate threats of the vision presaged his own death.

The disgraceful news of the battle, or rather the rout of Solway, filled up the measure of the King's despair and desolation. He shut himself up in the palace of Falkland, and refused to listen to any consolation. A burning fever, the consequence of his grief and shame, seized on the unfortunate monarch. They brought him tidings that his wife had given birth to a daughter; but he only replied, "Is it so?" reflecting on the alliance which had placed the Stewart family on the throne; "then God's will be done. It came with a lass, and it will go with a lass." With these words, presaging the extinction of his house, he made a signal of adieu to his courtiers, spoke
14th Dec., 1542. little more, but turned his face to the wall, and died of the most melancholy of all diseases, a broken heart. He was scarcely thirty-one years old; in the very prime, therefore, of life. If he had not suffered the counsels of the Catholic priests to hurry him into a war with England, James V. might have been as fortunate a prince as his many good qualities and talents deserved.

CHAPTER XXIX.

NEGOTIATIONS FOR A MARRIAGE BETWEEN THE YOUNG QUEEN MARY AND PRINCE EDWARD OF ENGLAND — THEIR FAILURE — INVASION OF SCOTLAND — CARDINAL BEATON'S ADMINISTRATION AND DEATH — BATTLE OF PINKIE — QUEEN MARY IS SENT TO FRANCE, AND THE QUEEN DOWAGER BECOMES REGENT — PROGRESS OF THE REFORMATION — QUEEN MARY RESOLVES TO RETURN TO SCOTLAND.

[1542 — 1560.]

THE evil fortunes of Mary Stewart, who succeeded her father in the crown of Scotland, commenced at her very birth, and could scarce be considered as ceasing during the whole period of her life. Of all the unhappy princes of the line of Stewart, she was the most uniformly unfortunate. She was born 7th December, 1542, and in a few days after became, by her father's death, the infant Queen of a distracted country.

Two parties strove, as is usual in minorities, to obtain the supreme power. Mary of Guise, the Queen-Mother, with Cardinal David Beaton, were at the head of that which favored the alliance with France. Hamilton, Earl of Arran, the nearest male relation of the infant Queen, was chief of the other, and possessed more extended popularity; for the nobles dreaded the bold and ambitious character of the Cardinal, and the common people detested him, on account of his cruel persecution of the 2d Dec.,
Reformers. The Earl of Arran, however, was 1542

but a fickle and timid man, with little, it would seem, to recommend him, besides his high birth. He was, however, preferred to the office of Regent.

Henry VIII. is said to have expressed much concern for the death of his nephew, saying, there would never again reign a King in Scotland so nearly related to him, or so dear to him, and blaming, not the late James V., but his evil counsellors, for the unfortunate dispute between them. At the same time, Henry formed a plan of uniting the kingdoms of England and Scotland, by a marriage betwixt the infant Queen of Scotland and his only son, Edward VI., then a child. He took into his counsels the Earl of Glencairn and other Scottish nobles made prisoners in the rout of Solway, and offered to set them at liberty, provided, on their return to Scotland, they would undertake to forward the match which he proposed. They were released accordingly, upon giving pledges that they would return in case the treaty should not be accomplished.

Archibald, Earl of Angus, with his brother, Sir George Douglas, took the same opportunity of returning into Scotland, after fifteen years' exile. They had been indebted to Henry for support and protection during that long space of time. He had even admitted them to be members of his Privy Council, and by the countenance he afforded them, had given great offence to the late King James. When, therefore, the influence of the Douglases, naturally attached to him by gratitude, was added to that of Glencairn and the others who had been made prisoners at Solway, and to the general weight of the Protestants, favorable, of course, to an alliance with England, Henry must be considered as having a party in Scotland in every way favorable to his views.

But the impatient temper of the English monarch ruined

his own scheme. He demanded the custody of the young Queen of Scotland till she should be of age to complete the marriage to be contracted by the present league, and he insisted that some of the strongest forts in the kingdom should be put into his hands. These proposals alarmed the national jealousy of the Scots, and the characteristic love of independence and liberty which we find that people have always displayed. The nation at large became persuaded that Henry VIII., under pretence of a union by marriage, nourished, like Edward I. in similar circumstances, the purpose of subduing the country. The exiled lords who had agreed to assist Henry's views, could be of no use to him, in consequence of the extravagance of his propositions. They told Sir Ralph Sadler, the English ambassador, frankly, that the nation could not endure the surrender of the Queen's person to Henry's charge, — that their own vassals would not take arms for them in such a cause, — that the old women of Scotland, with their distaffs, nay, the very stones in the streets, would arise and fight against it.*

* Sir George Douglas protested, from the beginning, against this rash assumption of King Henry. "I assure you," said he, "it is impossible to be done at this time: for there is not so little a boy, but he will hurl stones against it, and the wives will handle their distaffs, and the commons universally will rather die in it, yea, and many noblemen, and all the clergy be fully against it." — SIR RALPH SADLER'S *State Papers and Letters*, vol. i. p. 70. Of an after conference with Sir Adam Otterburne, Provost of Edinburgh, Sir Ralph relates: "'If,' said Sir Adam, 'your lad were a las, and our las were a lad, wold you then be so ernest in this matier; and coulde you be content that our lad should mary your las, and so be king of England?' I answered, that, considering the great good that might ensue of it, I shoulde not show myself zelous to my country if I shoulde not consente unto it. 'Well,' said he, 'if you had the las and we the lad, we coulde be well content with it; but I cannot beleve that your nacyon coulde agree to have a Scotte to be kyng of England. And lykewise I assure you, said he,

Henry was with difficulty prevailed upon to defer the time for giving him the custody of Queen Mary's person, until she should be ten years old. But even this modified proposition excited the greatest jealousy; and Sir George Douglas, Henry's chief advocate, only ventured to recommend acquiescence in the King's proposal, as a means of gaining time. He told the Scottish nobles of a certain king, who was so fond of an ass, that he insisted his chief physician should teach the animal to speak, upon pain of being himself put to death. The physician consented to undertake the case, but gave the King to understand that it would be ten years before the operation of his medicines could take effect. The King permitted him to set to work accordingly. Now one of the physician's friends seeing him busy about the animal, expressed his wonder that so wise a man should undertake what was contrary to nature; to which the physician replied: "Do you not see I have gained ten years' advantage? If I had refused the King's orders, I must have been instantly put to death; but as it is, I have the advantage of a long delay, during which the King may die, the ass may die, or I may die myself. In either of the three cases, I am freed from my trouble." — "Even so," said Sir George Douglas, "if we agree to this treaty we avoid a bloody and destructive war, and have a long period before us, during which the King of England, his son Prince Edward, or the infant Queen Mary, may one of them die, so that the treaty will be broken off." Moved by such reasons, a Parliament, which consisted almost entirely of

that our nacyon being a stout nacyon, will never agree to have an Englishman to be king of Scotland. And though the hale nobilite of the realme wolde consent unto it, zet our comen people and the stenes in the strete wolde ryse and rebelle against it.'" — *Ibid.* vol. ii. p. 560.

the lords of the English party, consented to the match with England, and the Regent Arran also agreed to it.

But while one part of the Scottish nobles adopted the resolution to treat with King Henry on his own terms, the Queen-Mother and Cardinal Beaton were at the head of another and still more numerous faction, who adhered to the old religion, and to the ancient alliance with France, and were, of course, directly opposed to the English match. The fickle temper of the Regent contributed to break off the treaty which he had subscribed. Within a fortnight after he had ratified the conditions of the match with England, he reconciled himself to the Cardinal and Queen-Mother, and joined in putting a stop to the proposed marriage.

The English King, if he could have been watchful and patient, might perhaps have brought the measure, which was alike important to both countries, once more to bear. But Henry, incensed at the Regent's double dealing, determined for immediate war. He sent a fleet and army into the Frith of Forth, which landed, and finding no opposition, burnt the capital of Scotland, and its seaport, and plundered the country around. Sir Ralph Evers, and Sir Brian Latoun, were, at the same time, employed in making inroads on the Border, which were of the fiercest and most wasteful description. The account of the ravage is tremendous. In one foray they numbered 192 towers, or houses of defence, burnt or razed; 403 Scots slain, and 816 made prisoners; 10,386 cattle, 12,492 sheep, 1,296 horses, and 850 bolls of corn, driven away as spoil. Another list gives an account of the destruction of seven monasteries, or religious houses; sixteen castles, or towers; five market-towns, 243 villages, thirteen mills, and three hospitals, all pulled down or burnt.

The exploits of the English leaders might gratify Henry's resentment, but they greatly injured his interest in Scotland, for the whole kingdom became united to repel the invaders; and even those who liked the proposed match with England best, were, to use an expression of the time, disgusted with so rough a mode of wooing. The Douglases themselves, bound to Henry by so many ties, were obliged, on seeing the distress and devastation of the country, to take part in the war against him, and soon found an opportunity to do so.

It seems Henry had conferred upon his two successful leaders, Evers and Latoun, all the lands which they had conquered, or should be able to conquer upon the Border, and, in particular, the fine counties of Merse and Teviotdale. "I will write the instrument of possession upon their own bodies, with sharp pens, and in blood-red ink," said the Earl of Angus, because they destroyed the tombs of my ancestors at the Abbey of Melrose." He accordingly urged Arran, the Regent, or Governor, as he was called, to move towards the frontiers, to protect them. Arran was with difficulty prevailed on to advance southward to Melrose, with scarce so many as five hundred men in his company. The English leaders were lying at Jedburgh with five thousand men. Three thousand of these were regular soldiers, paid by the King of England; the rest were Borderers, amongst whom there were many Scottish clans who had taken the red cross, and submitted themselves to the dominion of England. With these forces Evers and Latoun made a sudden march, to surprise the Governor and his handful of men; but they failed, for the Scots retreated beyond the Tweed, to the hills near Galashiels.

The English then prepared to retire to Jedburgh, and

the Governor, acting by Angus's advice, followed them, and watched their motions. In the mean time, succors began to come in to the Scottish army. A bold young man, Norman Leslie, the Master of Rothes, was the first to come up with three hundred horse, from Fife, gallantly armed. Afterwards the Lord Buccleuch joined them with a few of his clan, who arrived at full speed, and assured them that the rest of the Scots would be presently on the field. This Border chieftain was a man of great military sagacity, and knew the ground well. He advised the Governor and Angus to draw up their men at the foot of a small eminence, and to send their horses to the rear. The English, seeing the horses of the Scots ascend the hill, concluded they were in flight, and turned hastily back to attack them, hurrying in confusion, as to an assured conquest. Thus they came in front of the Scottish army, who were closely and firmly drawn up at the very moment when they themselves were in confusion from their hasty advance. As the Scots began to charge, the Earl of Angus, seeing a heron arise out of the marsh, cried out, "O that I had my white hawk here, that we might all join battle at once!" The English, surprised and out of breath, (and having besides the wind in their face, which blew the smoke of the gunpowder, and the sun in their eyes,) were completely defeated, and compelled to take to flight. The Scottish Borderers, who had joined them during their prosperity, perceiving their own countrymen to be victorious, threw away their red crosses (the distinction which they had assumed as subjects of England), and fell upon the English, for the purpose of helping those against whom they had come to the field, and making amends for their desertion of the Scottish cause. These renegades made a pitiful slaughter, and the Scots in general, provoked, probably, by the late ravages of the English, showed themselves so cruel to the vanquished, that they seemed to deserve the severe blow which the nation soon afterwards received. Tradition says that a beautiful young maiden, called Lillyard, followed her lover from the little village of Maxton, and when she saw him fall in battle, rushed herself into the heat of the fight, and was killed, after slaying several of the English. From this female, they called the field of battle Lillyard's Edge,* to this day.

This battle was fought in 1545. A thousand English men were killed, together with their two leaders, of whom Evers was buried in the Abbey of Melrose, which he had repeatedly plundered, and finally burnt. A great many prisoners were made. One was Thomas Read, an alderman of the city of London, whom we are surprised to meet with in such a predicament. This worthy citizen had, we are informed, refused to pay his share of a benevolence, as it was called, that is, of a sum of money, which Henry demanded from the citizens of London. It seems that though the power of the King could not throw the alderman into jail until he paid the money, yet he could force him to serve as a soldier; and there is a letter to

* "The spot on which it was fought is so called from an Amazonian Scottish woman of that name, who is reported, by tradition, to have distinguished herself in the same manner as Squire Witherington.—(See *Chevy Chase.*) The old people point out her monument, now broken and defaced. The inscription is said to have been legible within this century, and to have run thus:—

"'Fair Maiden Lillyard lies under this stane,
Little was her stature but great was her fame;
Upon the English louns she laid mony thumps,
And when her legs were cutted aff, she fought upon her stumps.'"

—Note, *Eve of St. John*, SIR WALTER SCOTT'S *Poetical Works*, vol. iv. p. 199.

Lord Evers, directing that Read should be suojected to all the rigors and hardships of the service, that he might know what soldiers suffered when in the field, and be more ready another time to assist the King with money to pay them. It is to be supposed that the alderman had a large ransom to pay to the Scotsman who had the good luck to get him for a prisoner.

Henry VIII. was extremely offended at this defeat of Lillyard's Edge, or Ancram-moor, as it is frequently called, and vented his displeasure in menaces against the Earl of Angus, notwithstanding their connection by the Earl's marriage with the King's sister. Angus treated the threats of the English monarch with contempt. "Is our royal brother-in-law," he said, "angry with me for being a good Scotsman, and for revenging upon Ralph Evers the destruction of my ancestors' tombs at Melrose? They were better men than Evers, and I could in honor do no less. And will my royal brother-in-law take my life for that? Little does King Henry know the skirts of Cairntable" (a mountain near Douglas Castle); "I can keep myself there against all his English host."

The truth is, that at no period of their history had the Scottish people ever been more attached to France, and more alienated from England, than now; the proposed match between the young Queen and the English Prince of Wales being generally regarded with an abhorrence which was chiefly owing to the vindictive and furious manner in which Henry conducted the war. Of all the Scottish nobles who had originally belonged to the English party, Lennox alone continued friendly to Henry; and he being obliged to fly into England, the King caused him to marry Lady Margaret Douglas, daughter of his sister Margaret, by her second husband, the Earl of Angus, and of course the King's niece. Their son was the unhappy Henry Lord Darnley, of whom we shall have much to say hereafter.

The King of France now sent a powerful body of auxiliary troops to the assistance of the Scots, besides considerable supplies of money, which enabled them to retaliate the English ravages, so that the Borders on both sides were fearfully wasted. A peace at length, in June, 1546, ended a war in which both countries suffered severely, without either attaining any decisive advantage.

The Scottish affairs were now managed almost entirely by Cardinal Beaton, a statesman, as we before observed, of great abilities, but a bigoted Catholic, and a man of a severe and cruel temper. He had gained entire influence over the Regent Arran, and had prevailed upon that fickle nobleman to abandon the Protestant doctrines, reconcile himself to the Church of Rome, and consent to the persecution of the heretics, as the Protestants were still called. Many cruelties were exercised; but that which excited public feeling to the highest degree, was the barbarous death of George Wishart.

This martyr to the cause of Reformation was a man of honorable birth, great wisdom and eloquence, and of primitive piety. He preached the doctrines of the Reformed religion with zeal and with success, and was for some time protected against the efforts of the vengeful Catholics by the barons who had become converts to the Protestant faith. At length, however, he fell into the hands of the Cardinal, being surrendered to him by Lord Bothwell, and was conveyed to the castle of St. Andrews, a strong fortress and palace belonging to the Cardinal as Archbishop, and there thrown into a dungeon. Wishart was then brought to a public trial, for heresy, before the Spiritual Court, where the Cardinal presided. He was accused of preaching heretical doctrine, by two priests, called Lauder and Oliphant, whose outrageous violence was strongly contrasted with the patience and presence of mind shown by the prisoner. He appealed to the authority of the Bible against that of the Church of Rome; but his judges were little disposed to listen to his arguments, and he was condemned to be burnt alive. The place of execution was opposite to the stately castle of the Cardinal, and Beaton himself sat upon the walls, which were hung with tapestry, to behold the death of his heretical prisoner. The spot was also carefully chosen, that the smoke of the pile might be seen as far as possible, to spread the greater terror. Wishart was then brought out, and fastened to a stake with iron chains. He was clad in a buckram garment, and several bags of gunpowder were tied round his body, to hasten the operation of the fire. A quantity of fagots were disposed around the pile. While he stood in expectation of his cruel death, he cast his eyes towards his enemy the Cardinal, as he sat on the battlements of the castle enjoying the dreadful scene.

28th March, 1545.

"Captain," he said to him who commanded the guard, "may God forgive yonder man, who lies so proudly on the wall, — within a few days he shall be seen lying there in as much shame as he now shows pomp and vanity." *

* "The Cardinal seems to have been sensible, that the minds of men would be much agitated by the fate of this amiable sufferer, and even to have apprehended that some attempt might be made to rescue him from the flames. He commanded all the artillery of the fortress to be pointed towards the scene of execution; and, either to watch the ebullitions of popular indignation, to display his contempt of the Reformers, or to satiate himself by contemplating the destruction of a man in

The pile was then fired, the powder exploded, the flames arose, and Wishart was dismissed by a painful death to a blessed immortality in the next world.

Perhaps the last words of Wishart, which seemed to contain a prophetic spirit, incited some men to revenge his death. At any rate, the burning of that excellent person greatly increased the public detestation against the Cardinal, and a daring man stood forth to gratify the general desire, by putting him to death. This was Norman Leslie, called the Master of Rothes, the same who led the men of Fife at the battle of Ancram-moor. It appears, that besides his share of the common hatred to the Cardinal as a persecutor, he had some private feud or cause of quarrel with him. With no more than sixteen men, Leslie undertook to assault the Cardinal in his own castle, amongst his numerous guards and domestics. It chanced that, as many workmen were still employed in laboring upon the fortifications of the castle, the wicket of the castle-gate was open early in the morning, to admit them to their work. The conspirators took advantage of this, and obtained possession of the entrance. Having thus gained admittance, they seized upon the domestics of the Cardinal, and turned them one by one out of the castle, then hastened to the Cardinal's chamber, who had fastened the door. He refused them entrance, until they threatened to apply fire, when, learning that Norman Leslie was without, the despairing prelate at length undid the door, and asked for mercy. Melville, one of the conspirators, told him he should only have such mercy as he

whose grave he hoped that their principles would be buried, he openly, with the prelates who accompanied him, witnessed the melancholy spectacle." — Dr. Cook's *History of the Reformation*, vol. i. p. 291.

had extended to George Wishart, and the other servants of God, who had been slain by his orders. He then, with his sword pointed to his breast, bid the Cardinal say his prayers to God, for his last hour was come. The conspirators now proceeded to stab their victim, and afterwards dragged the dead body to the walls, to show it to the citizens of St. Andrews, his clients and dependents, who came in fury to demand what had become of their bishop. Thus his dead body really came to lie with open shame upon the very battlements of his own castle, where he had sat in triumph to behold Wishart's execution.*

Many persons who disapproved of this most unjustifiable action, were yet glad that this proud cardinal, who had sold the country in some measure to France, was at length removed. Some individuals, who assuredly would not have assisted in the slaughter, joined those who had slain the Cardinal in the defence of the castle. The Regent hastened to besiege the place, which, supplied by England with money, engineers, and provisions, was able to resist the Scottish army for five months. France, however, sent to Scotland a fleet and an army, with engineers better acquainted with the art of attacking strong places than those of the Scottish nation. The castle was, therefore, surrendered. The principal defenders of it were sent to France, and there for some time employed as galley-slaves. The common people made a song upon the event, of which the burden was: —

* "It may now be pronounced, without fear of contradiction, that the assassination of Beaton was no sudden event, arising simply out of indignation for the fate of Wishart, but an act of long-projected murder, encouraged, if not originated, by the English monarch; and, so far as the principal conspirators were concerned, committed from private and mercenary considerations." — TYTLER, vol. v. p. 430.

"Priests, content ye now,
And, priests, content ye now,
Since Norman and his company
Have fill'd the galleys fou." *

Shortly after this tragical incident, King Henry VIII. of England died. But his impatient and angry spirit † continued to influence the counsels of the nation under the Lord Protector, Somerset, who resolved to take the same violent measures to compel the Scots to give their young Queen in marriage to Edward VI. of which Henry had set an example. A chosen and well-disciplined army of eighteen thousand men, well supplied with all necessaries, and supported by an armed fleet, invaded Scotland on the eastern frontier. The Scots assembled a force of

* Knox, folio 77.

† "The savage temper of Henry VIII. nowhere more strongly appears than in the directions, which, on the 10th of April, 1543-4, he transmitted through a despatch of the Privy Council to the Earl of Hertford. After observing that the grand attempt on Scotland was delayed for a season, they command him, in the mean time, to make an inroad into Scotland, 'there to put all to fire and sword, to burn Edinburgh town, and to raze and deface it, when you have sacked it, and gotten what you can out of it, as that it may remain forever a perpetual memory of the vengeance of God lighted upon it for their falsehood and disloyalty. Do what you can, out of hand, and without long tarrying, to beat down and overthrow the castle, sack Holyrood-house, and as many towns and villages about Edinburgh as ye conveniently can; sack Leith, and burn and subvert it, and all the rest, *putting man, woman, and child to fire and sword*, without exception, when any resistance shall be made against you; and this done, pass over to the Fife land, and extend like extremities and destructions in all towns and villages whereunto ye may reach conveniently, not forgetting, amongst all the rest, so to spoil and turn upside down the Cardinal's town of St. Andrews, *as the upper stone may be the nether*, and not one stick stand by another, *sparing no creature alive* within the same, specially such as either in friendship or blood be allied to the Cardinal.'" — *MS. Hamilton Papers*, pp. 44, 45, apud TYTLER, vol. v. pp. 473, 474.

almost double the number of the invaders, but, as usual, unaccustomed to act in union together, or to follow the commands of a single general. Nevertheless, the Scottish leaders displayed at the commencement of the campaign some military skill. They posted their army behind the river Esk, near Musselburgh, a village about six miles from Edinburgh, and there seemed determined to await the advance of the English.

The Duke of Somerset, Regent of England and general of the invading army, was now in a state of difficulty. The Scots were too strongly posted to be attacked with hope of success, and it is probable the English must have retreated with dishonor, had not their enemies, in one of those fits of impatience which caused so many national calamities, abandoned their advantageous position.

Confiding in the numbers of his army, the Scottish Regent (Earl of Arran) crossed the Esk, and thus gave the English the advantage of the ground, they being drawn up on the top of a sloping eminence. The Scots formed in their usual order, a close phalanx. They were armed with broadswords of an admirable form and temper, and a coarse handkerchief was worn in double and triple folds round each man's neck, — "not for cold," says an old historian,* "but for cutting." Especially, each man carried a spear eighteen feet long. When drawn up, they stood close together, the first rank kneeling on one knee, and pointing their spears towards the enemy. The ranks immediately behind stooped a little, and the others stood upright, presenting their lances over the heads of their

* "The Expedicion into Scotlāde, of the Most Woorthcley Fortunate Prince, Edward, Duke of Soomerset, &c. By W. Patten, Londoner," p. 58, ap. DALZELL'S *Fragments of Scottish History*, 4to, Edin. 1798.

comrades, and holding them with the but-end placed against their foot, the point opposed to the breast of the enemy. So that the Scottish ranks were so completely defended by the close order in which they stood, and by the length of their lances, that to charge them seemed to be as rash as to oppose your bare hand to a hedgehog's bristles.

The battle began by the English cavalry, under the Lord Gray, rushing upon the close array of the Scots. They stood fast, menacing the horsemen with their pikes, and calling, "Come on, ye heretics!" The charge was dreadful; but as the spears of the English horse were much shorter than those of the Scottish infantry, they had greatly the worst of the encounter, and were beaten off with the loss of many men. The Duke of Somerset commanded Lord Gray to renew the charge, but Gray replied, he might as well bid him charge a castle-wall. By the advice of the Earl of Warwick, a body of archers and musketeers was employed instead of horsemen. The thick order of the Scots exposed them to insufferable loss from the missiles now employed against them, so that the Earl of Angus, who commanded the vanguard, made an oblique movement to avoid the shot; but the main body of the Scots unhappily mistook this movement for a flight, and were thrown into confusion. The van then fled also, and the English horse returning to the attack, and their infantry pressing forward, the victory was gained with very little trouble. The Scots attempted no further resistance, and the slaughter was very great, because the river Esk lay between the fugitives and any place of safety. Their loss was excessive. For more than five miles the fields were covered with the dead, and with the spears, shields, and swords which the flying soldiers had cast away, that they might run the faster. The day was equally disgraceful and disastrous; so that the field of Pinkie, as it was the last great defeat which the Scots received from the English, was also one of the most calamitous. It was fought on 10th September, 1547.

It seemed to be decreed in those unhappy national wars that the English should often be able to win great victories over the Scots, but that they should never derive any permanent advantage from their successes. The battle of Pinkie, far from paving the way to a marriage between Queen Mary and Edward VI., which was the object of Somerset's expedition, irritated and alarmed the Scots to such a degree, that they resolved to prevent the possibility of such a union, by marrying their young mistress with the Dauphin, that is, the eldest son of the King of France, and sending her to be bred up at the French court. A hasty assent of the Scottish Parliament was obtained to this, partly by the influence of gold, partly by the appearance of the French soldiers, partly, according to the Reformer Knox, by the menaces of the Lord of Buccleuch, whom he describes as "a bloody man, who swore, with many deadly oaths, that they who would not consent should do what they would like worse."

By the match with France the great object of the English government was rendered unattainable. But the Scots had little occasion for triumph. The union with France, which they so hastily and rashly adopted, brought a new and long series of ruinous consequences upon the country.

Scotland, however, enjoyed the immediate advantage of a considerable auxiliary force of French soldiers, under an officer named D'Essé, who rendered material assistance in recovering several forts and castles which had fallen into the hands of the English after the battle of Pinkie, and in which they had left garrisons. The presence of these armed strangers gave great facilities for carrying into accomplishment the treaty with France. The Regent was gratified by the Dukedom of Chatelherault, conferred on him by the French King, with a considerable pension, in order to induce him to consent to the match. The young Queen was embarked on board the French galleys, in July, 1548, accompanied by four young ladies of quality of her own age, destined to be her playfellows in childhood, and her companions when she grew up. They all bore the same name with their mistress, and were called the Queen's Maries.*

The infant Queen being thus transferred to France, her mother, Mary of Guise, the widow of James V., had the address to get herself placed at the head of affairs in Scotland. The Duke of Chatelherault, as we must now term the Earl of Arran, always flexible in his disposition, was prevailed upon to resign the office of Regent, which was occupied by the Queen Dowager, who displayed a considerable degree of wisdom and caution in the administration of the kingdom. Most men wondered at the facility with which the Duke of Chatelherault, himself so near in relation to the throne, had given place to Mary of Guise; but none was so much offended as the Duke's natural brother, who had succeeded Beaton as Archbishop

* "The Queen's Maries were four young ladies of high families in Scotland, viz. Livingston, Fleming, Seatoun, and Beatoun. After their return with the Queen to Scotland, one of them became the subject of a tragic ballad, which has

"'Yestreen the Queen had four Maries,
The night she'll hae but three.'"

—See *The Border Minstrelsy*, SIR W. SCOTT'S *Poetical Works*, vol. iii. p. 294, *et seq.*

of St. Andrews. He exclaimed with open indecency against the mean spirit of his brother, who had thus given away the power of Regent, when there was but a "squalling girl" betwixt him and the crown.

The Queen Regent, thus placed in authority, endeavored to secure herself by diminishing the power of the Scottish nobles and increasing that of the crown. For this purpose, she proposed that a tax should be levied on the country at large, to pay hired soldiers to fight, instead of trusting the defence of the country to the noblemen and their retainers. This proposal was exceedingly ill received by the Scottish Parliament. "We will fight for our families and our country," they said, "better than any hirelings can do, — our fathers did so, and we will follow their example." The Earl of Angus being checked for coming to Parliament with a thousand horse, contrary to a proclamation of the Queen Regent, that none should travel with more than their usual household train, answered jestingly, "That the knaves would not leave him; and that he would be obliged to the Queen, if she could put him on the way of being rid of them, for they consumed his beef and his ale." She had equally bad success, when she endeavored to persuade the Earl to give her up his strong Castle of Tantallon, under pretence of putting a garrison there to defend it against the English. At first he answered indirectly, as if he spoke to a hawk which he held on his wrist, and was feeding at the time, "The devil," said he, "is in the greedy gled [kite]! Will she never be full?" The Queen, not choosing to take this hint, continued to urge her request about the garrison. "The castle, madam," he replied, "is yours at command; but, by St. Bride of Douglas, I must be the captain, and I will keep it for you as well as any one you will put into it."* The other nobles held similar opinions to those of Angus, and would by no means yield to the proposal of levying any hired troops, who, as they feared, might be employed at the pleasure of the Queen Regent to diminish the liberties of the kingdom.

The prevalence of the Protestant doctrines in Scotland strengthened the Scottish nobles in their disposition to make a stand against the Queen Regent's desire to augment her power. Many great nobles, and a still greater proportion of the smaller barons, had embraced the Reformed opinions; and the preaching of John Knox, a man of great courage, zeal, and talents, made converts daily from the Catholic faith.

The Queen Regent, though herself a zealous Catholic, had for some time tolerated, and even encouraged, the Protestant party, because they supported her interest against that of the Hamiltons; but a course of politics had been adopted in France, by her brothers of the House of Guise, which occasioned her to change her conduct in this respect.

* "They tell also how the Queen Regent, when she was discoursing with Angus, told him how the Earl of Huntly had done her very good service, for which she intended to advance him, and make him a duke: to which he answered, 'Why not, madam? We are happy that have such a Princess, that can know and will acknowledge men's service, and is willing to recompense it. But, by the might of God! (this was his oath when he was serious and in anger, at other times it was by Saint *Bride* of Douglas) *if he be a duke, I will be a drake!*' (The common people of Scotland at this day pronounce the female duck as *duke*, the male being, as in England, termed the *drake*.) His meaning was, that in matters of state, he would be above and before him. 'Our predecessors,' says he, 'have done as good service as he or his, for which they have the privilege to be the first of the nobility after those of the blood-royal, and I will not lose it in my time upon any such pretext.' So she desisted from further prosecuting of that purpose." — GODSCROFT, p. 275.

You may remember, that Edward VI. of England succeeded to his father Henry. He adopted the Protestant faith, and completed the Reformation which his father began. But he died early, and was succeeded by his sister Mary of England, daughter of Henry VIII., by his first wife, Catherine of Aragon, whom he divorced under pretext of scruples of conscience. This Mary endeavored to bring back the Catholic religion, and enforced the laws against heresy with the utmost rigor. Many persons were burnt in her reign, and hence she has been called the Bloody Queen Mary. She died, however, after a short and unhappy reign, and her sister Elizabeth ascended the throne, with the general assent of all the people of England. The Catholics of foreign countries, however, and particularly those of France, objected to Elizabeth's title to the crown. Elizabeth was Henry's daughter by his second wife, Anne Bullen. Now, as the Pope had never consented either to the divorce of Queen Catherine, or to the marriage of Anne Bullen, the Catholics urged, that Elizabeth must be considered as illegitimate, and as having, therefore, no lawful right to succeed to the throne, which, as Henry VIII. had no other child, must, they contended, descend upon Queen Mary of Scotland, as the granddaughter of Margaret, Henry's sister, wife of James IV. of Scotland, and the next lawful heir, according to their argument, to her deceased grand-uncle.

The Court of France, not considering that the English themselves were to be held the best judges of the title of their own Queen, resolved, in an evil hour, to put forward this claim of the Scottish Queen to the English crown. Money was coined, and plate wrought, in which Mary, with her husband, Francis the Dauphin, assumed the style, title, and armorial bearings of England, as well as Scotland; and thus laid the first foundation for that deadly hatred between Elizabeth and Mary, which, as you will hear by and by, led to such fatal consequences.

Queen Elizabeth, finding France was disposed to challenge her title to the crown of England, prepared to support it with all the bravery and wisdom of her character. Her first labor was to re-establish the Reformed religion upon the same footing that Edward VI. had assigned to it, and to destroy the Roman Catholic establishments, which her predecessor Mary had endeavored to replace. As the Catholics of France and Scotland were her natural enemies, and attempted to set up the right of Queen Mary as preferable to her own, so she was sure to find friends in the Protestants of Scotland, who could not fail to entertain respect, and even affection, for a princess, who was justly regarded as the protectress of the Protestant cause throughout all Europe.

When, therefore, these changes took place in England, the Queen Regent, at the instigation of her brothers of the House of Guise, began once more to persecute the Protestants in Scotland; while their leaders turned their eyes to Elizabeth for protection, counsel, and assistance; all of which she was easily disposed to render to a party whose cause rested on the same grounds with her own. Thus, while France made a vain pretence of claiming the kingdom of England in the name of Mary, and appealed for assistance to the English Catholics, Elizabeth far more effectually increased the internal dissensions of Scotland, by espousing the cause of the Protestants of that country.

These Scottish Protestants no longer consisted solely of a few studious or reflecting men, whose indulgence in speculation had led them to adopt peculiar opinions in religion, and who could be dragged before the spiritual courts, fined, imprisoned, plundered, banished, or burnt, at pleasure. The Reformed cause had now been adopted by many of the principal nobility; and being the cause, at once, of rational religion and legitimate freedom, it was generally embraced by those who were most distinguished for wisdom and public spirit.

Among the converts to the Protestant faith, was a natural son of the late King James V., who, being designed for the Church, was at this time called Lord James Stewart, the Prior of St. Andrews, but was afterwards better known by the title of the Earl of Murray. He was a young nobleman of great parts, brave and skilful in war, and in peace a lover of justice, and a friend to the liberties of his country. His wisdom, good moral conduct, and the zeal he expressed for the Reformed religion, occasioned his being the most active person amongst the Lords of the Congregation, as the leaders of the Protestant party were now called.

The Queen Regent, more in compliance with the wishes of her brothers than her own inclination, which was gentle and moderate, began the quarrel by commanding the Protestant preachers to be summoned to a court of justice at Stirling, on 10th May, 1559; but such a concourse of friends and favorers attended them, that the Queen was glad to put a stop to the trial, on condition that they should not enter the town. Yet she broke this promise, and had them proclaimed outlaws for not appearing, although they had been stopped by her own command. Both parties then prepared for hostilities; and an incident happened, which heightened their animosity, while it gave to the course of the Reformation a peculiar color of zealous passion.

The Protestants had made their head-quarters at Perth,

where they had already commenced the public exercise of their religion. John Knox, whose eloquence gave him great influence with the people, had pronounced a vehement sermon against the sin of idolatry, in which he did not spare those reproaches which the Queen Regent deserved for her late breach of faith. When his discourse was finished, and while the minds of the hearers were still agitated by its effects, a friar produced a little glass case, or tabernacle, containing the images of saints, which he required the by-standers to worship. A boy who was present, exclaimed, "That was gross and sinful idolatry." The priest, as incautious in his passion as ill-timed in his devotion, struck the boy a blow; and the lad, in revenge, threw a stone, which broke one of the images. Immediately all the people began to cast stones, not only at the images, but at the fine painted windows, and, finally, pulled down the altars, defaced the ornaments of the church, and nearly destroyed the whole building.

The multitude next resolved to attack the splendid convent of the Carthusians. The prior had prepared for defence, his garrison consisting of the Highland tenants belonging to some lands which the convent possessed in the district of Athole. These men were determined to make the most of the occasion, and demanded of the prior, that since they were asked to expose their lives for the good of the Church, they should be assured that if they were killed, their families should retain possession of the lands which they themselves enjoyed. The prior impolitically refused their request. They next demanded refreshments and good liquor, to encourage them to fight. But nothing was served out to them by the sordid churchman, excepting salted salmon and thin drink; so that they had neither heart nor will to fight when it came to the push, and made little defence against the multitude, by whom the stately convent was entirely destroyed.

The example of the Reformers in Perth was followed in St. Andrews and other places; and we have to regret that many beautiful buildings fell a sacrifice to the fury of the lower orders,* and were either totally destroyed, or reduced to piles of shapeless ruins.

The Reformers of the better class did not countenance these extremities, although the common people had some reason for the line of violence they pursued, besides their own natural inclination to tumultuary proceedings. One great point in which the Catholics and Protestants differed was, that the former reckoned the churches as places hallowed and sacred in their own character, which it was a highly a meritorious duty to ornament and adorn with every species of studied beauty of architecture. The Scottish Protestants, on the contrary, regarded them as mere buildings of stone and lime, having no especial claim to respect when the divine service was finished. The defacing, therefore, and even destroying, the splendid Catholic churches, seemed to the early Reformers the readiest mode of testifying their zeal against the superstitions of Popery. There was a degree of policy in pulling down the abbeys and monasteries, with the cells and lodgings made for the accommodation of the monks. "The true way to banish the rooks," said John Knox, "is

* "Of the demolitions at Perth, Knox says that they were the acts of 'the haill multitude convenit, — not of the gentilmen, for the maist parte war gane to denner, nouther of thame that war ernest professouris, *bot of the rascall multitude*, who finding nothing to do in that churche, did rin *without deliberatioun* to the Gray and Black Freiris,'" &c. — *Historie*, p. 128.

to pull down their nests, and the rooks will fly off." But this maxim did not apply to the buildings used for public worship. Respecting these at least, it would have been better to have followed the example of the citizens of Glasgow, who drew out in arms, when the multitude were about to destroy the High Church of that city, and, while they agreed with the more zealous in removing all the emblems of Popish worship, insisted that the building itself should remain uninjured, and be applied to the uses of a Protestant church.

On the whole, however, though many fine buildings were destroyed in Scotland, in the first fury of the Reformation, it is better that the country should have lost these ornaments, than that they should have been preserved entire, with the retention of the corrupt and superstitious doctrines which had been taught in them.

The demolition of the churches and sacred buildings augmented the Queen Regent's displeasure against the Lords of the Congregation, and at length both parties took the field. The Protestant nobles were at the head of their numerous followers; the Queen chiefly relied upon a small but select body of French troops. The war was not very violently carried on, for the side of the Reformers became every day stronger. The Duke of Chatelherault, the first nobleman in Scotland, a second time espoused the cause of the Congregation; and Maitland of Lethington, one of the wisest statesmen in the kingdom, took the same course. At the same time, although the Lords found it easy to bring together large bodies of men, yet they had not the money or means necessary to keep them together for a long time, while the French veteran soldiers were always ready to take advantage when the Reformed leaders were obliged to diminish their forces. Their difficulties became greater when the Queen Regent showed her design to fortify strongly the town of Leith and the adjacent island of Inch-Keith, and placed her French soldiers in garrison there; so that, being in possession of that seaport, she might at all times, when she saw occasion, introduce an additional number of foreigners.

Unskilled in the art of conducting sieges, and totally without money, the Lords of the Congregation had recourse to the assistance of England: and for the first time an English fleet and army approached the territories of Scotland by sea and land, not with the purpose of invasion, as used to be the case of old, but to assist the nation in its resistance to the arms of France, and the religion of Rome.

The English army was soon joined by the Scottish Lords of the Congregation, and advancing to Leith, laid seige to the town, which was most valorously defended by the French soldiers, who displayed a degree of ingenuity in their defence which for a long time resisted every effort of the besiegers. They were, however, blockaded by the English fleet, so that no provisions could be received by sea; and as on land they were surrounded by a considerable army, provisions became so scarce, that they were obliged to feed upon horse-flesh.

In the mean time, their mistress, the Queen Regent, had retired into the castle of Edinburgh, where grief, fatigue, and disappointed expectations, threw her into an illness, of which she died on 10th of June, 1560. The French troops in Leith were now reduced to extremity, and Francis and Mary determined upon making peace in Scotland at the expense of most important concessions to the Reformed party. They agreed that, instead of naming a new Regent, the administration of affairs should be devolved upon a council of government chosen by Parliament; they passed an act of indemnity, as it is called, that is, an act pardoning all offences committed during these wars; and they left the subject of religion to be disposed of as the Parliament should determine, which was, in fact, giving the full power to the Reformed party. All foreign troops, on both sides, were to be withdrawn accordingly.

England, and especially Queen Elizabeth, gained a great point by this treaty, for it recognized, in express terms, the title of that Princess to the throne of England; and Francis and Mary bound themselves to lay aside all claim to that kingdom, together with the arms and emblems of English sovereignty which they had assumed and borne.

The Parliament of Scotland being assembled, it was soon seen that the Reformers possessed the power and inclination to direct all its resolutions upon the subject of religion. They condemned unanimously the whole fabric of Popery, and adopted, instead of the doctrines of the Church of Rome, the tenets contained in a confession, or avowal, of Faith, drawn up by the most popular of the Protestant divines. Thus the whole religious constitution of the Church was at once altered.

There was one particular in which the Scottish Reformers greatly differed from those of England. The English monarch, who abolished the power of the Pope, had established that of the Crown as the visible Head of the Church of England. The meaning of this phrase is, not that the King has the power of altering the religious doctrines of the Church, but only that he should be the chief of the government in Church affairs, as he was always in those of the State. On the contrary, the Reformed ministers of Scotland renounced the authority of any interference of the civil magistrate, whether subject or sovereign, in the affairs of the Church, declaring it should be under the exclusive direction of a court of delegates chosen from its own members, assisted by a certain number of the laity, forming what is called a General Assembly of the Church. The Scottish Reformers disclaimed also the division of the clergy into the various ranks of bishops, deans, prebendaries, and other classes of the clerical order. They discarded this subordination of ranks, though retained in the English Protestant Church, maintaining that each clergyman intrusted with a charge of souls was upon a level in every respect with the rest of his brethren. They reprobated, in particular, the order of Bishop, as holding a place in the National Council, or Parliament; and asserted, that meddling in secular affairs was in itself improper for their office, and naturally led to the usurpation over men's consciences, which had been the chief abomination of the Church of Rome. The laity of Scotland, and particularly the great nobility, saw with pleasure the readiness of the ministers to resign all those pretensions to worldly rank and consequence, which had been insisted upon by the Roman Catholic clergy, and made their self-denying abjuration of titles and worldly business a reason for limiting the subsistence which they were to derive from the funds of the Church, to the smallest possible sum of annual stipend, whilst they appropriated the rest to themselves without scruple.

It remained to dispose of the wealth lately enjoyed by the Catholic clergy, who were supposed to be possessed of half of the revenue of Scotland, so far as it arose from land. Knox and the other Reformed clergy had formed a plan for the decent maintenance of a National Church out of these extensive funds, and proposed that what might be deemed more than sufficient for this purpose should be expended upon hospitals, schools, universities, and places of education. But the lords who had seized the revenues of the Church were determined not to part with the spoil they had obtained; and those whom the preachers had found most active in destroying Popery, were wonderfully cold when it was proposed to them to surrender the lands they had seized upon for their own use. The plan of John Knox was, they said, a "devout imagination," a visionary scheme, which showed the goodness of the preacher's intentions, but which it was impossible to carry into practice. In short, they retained by force the greater part of the Church revenues for their own advantage.

When Francis and Mary, who had now become King and Queen of France, heard that the Scottish Parliament had totally altered the religion, and changed the forms of the National Church from Catholic to Protestant, they were extremely angry; and had the King lived, it is most likely they would have refused to consent to this great innovation, and preferred rekindling the war by sending a new army of French into Scotland. But if they meditated such a measure, it was entirely prevented by the death of Francis II., on the 5th of December, 1560.

During her husband's life, Mary had exercised a great authority in France, for she possessed unbounded influence over his mind. After his death, and the accession of Charles, his brother, that influence and authority were totally ended. It must have been painful to a lofty mind like Mary's thus to endure coldness and neglect in the place where she had met with honor and obedience. She retired, therefore, from the Court of France, and determined to return to her native kingdom of Scotland; a resolution most natural in itself, but which became the introduction to a long and melancholy tale of misfortunes.

CHAPTER XXX.

QUEEN MARY'S RETURN TO SCOTLAND — HAPPY COMMENCEMENT OF HER REIGN — EXPEDITION AGAINST HUNTLY — NEGOTIATIONS WITH ELIZABETH OF ENGLAND CONCERNING A SECOND MARRIAGE — MARRIAGE OF MARY AND DARNLEY.

[1560 — 1565.]

MARY STEWART, the Queen Dowager of France, and the hereditary Queen of Scotland, was, without any exception, the most beautiful and accomplished woman of her time. Her countenance was lovely; she was tall, well-formed, elegant in all her motions, skilled in the exercises of riding and dancing, and possessed of all the female accomplishments which were in fashion at that period. Her education in France had been carefully attended to, and she had profited by the opportunities of instruction she enjoyed. She was mistress of several languages, and understood state affairs, in which her husband had often used her advice. The beauty of Mary was enhanced by her great condescension, and by the good-humor and gayety which she sometimes carried to the verge of excess. Her youth, for she was only eighteen when she returned to Scotland, increased the liveliness of her disposition. The Catholic religion, in which she had been strictly educated, was a great blemish in the eyes of her people; but on the whole the nation expected her return with more hope and joy than Mary herself entertained at the thought of exchanging the fine climate of France and the gayeties of its court, for the rough tempests and turbulent politics of her native country.

Mary set sail from France 15th August, 1561. The English fleet were at sea, and there is great reason to believe that they had a purpose of intercepting the Queen of Scots, as a neighbor whose return was dreaded by Elizabeth. Occupied with anxious forebodings, the Queen remained on the deck of her galley, gazing on the coasts of France. Morning found her in the same occupation; and when they vanished from her eyes, she exclaimed in sorrow, "Farewell, farewell, happy France; I shall never see thee more!"

She passed the English fleet under cover of a mist, and arrived at Leith on the 19th August, where little or no preparation had been made for her honorable reception. Such of the nobles as were in the capital hastened, however, to wait upon their young Queen, and convey her to Holyrood, the palace of her ancestors. Horses were provided to bring her and her train to Edinburgh; but they were wretched ponies, and had such tattered furniture and accoutrements, that poor Mary, when she thought of the splendid palfreys and rich appointments at the court of France, could not forbear shedding tears. The people were, however, in their way, rejoiced to see her; and about two hundred citizens of Edinburgh, each doing his best upon a three-stringed fiddle, played under her window all night, by way of welcome,—a noisy serenade, which deprived her of sleep after her fatigue. She took it as it was meant, nevertheless, and expressed her thanks to the perpetrators of this mistuned and mistimed concert. Mary had immediately after her arrival a specimen of the religious zeal of her Reformed subjects. She had ordered mass to be performed by a Popish ecclesiastic in her own chapel, but the popular indignation was so much excited, that but for the interference of her natural brother, the Prior of St. Andrews, the priest would have been murdered on his own altar.*

Mary behaved with admirable prudence at this early period of her reign. She enchanted the common people by her grace and condescension, and while she sat in council, usually employed in some female work, she gained credit for her wisdom among the statesmen whom she consulted. She was cautious of attempting anything contrary to the religion of her subjects, though different from her own; and using the assistance of the Prior of St. Andrews, and of the sagacious Maitland, she made a rapid progress in the affections of her people. She conferred on the Prior of St. Andrews, who had given up thoughts of the Church, the title and the earldom of Mar, which had been frequently bestowed on branches of the royal family.

With similar prudence, the Queen maintained all the usual intercourse of civility with Elizabeth; and while she refused to abandon her title to the crown of England, in the case of Elizabeth dying without heirs of her body, she expressed her anxious wish to live on the best terms with her sister sovereign, and her readiness to relinquish, during the life of the English Queen, any right of inheri-

* In a month afterwards, "on Sunday, 14th of September," says Randolph to Cecil, "in the Chapel Royal, at Stirling, when her Grace's devout chaplain would, by the good device of Arthur Erskine, have sung a high mass, the Earl of Argyle and the Lord James so disturbed the quire, that some, both priests and clerks, left their places, with broken heads and bloody ears: It was a sport alone for some that were there to behold it; others there were that shed a tear or two, and made no more of the matter." — KEITH'S *History*, p. 190.

tance to the English crown which she might possess to her prejudice. Elizabeth was silenced, if not satisfied; and there continued to be a constant communication of apparent friendship between the two sovereigns, and an exchange of letters, compliments, and occasionally of presents becoming their rank, with much profession of mutual kindness.

But there was one important class of persons to whom Mary's form of religion was so obnoxious that they could not be gained to any favorable thoughts of her. These were the preachers of the Reformed faith, who, recollecting Mary's descent from the family of Guise, always hostile to the Protestant cause, exclaimed against the Queen even in the pulpit, with an indecent violence unfitting that place, and never spoke of her but as one hardened in resistance to the voice of true Christian instruction. John Knox himself introduced such severe expressions into his sermons, that Queen Mary condescended to expostulate with him personally, and to exhort him to use more mild language in the discharge of his duty. Nevertheless, though the language of these rough Reformers was too vehement, and though their harshness was impolitic, as tending unnecessarily to increase the Queen's dislike of them and their form of religion, it must be owned that their suspicions of Mary's sincerity were natural, and in all probability well founded. The Queen uniformly declined to ratify the religious system adopted by the Parliament in 1560, or the confiscation of the church lands. She always seemed to consider the present state of things as a temporary arrangement, to which she was indeed willing to submit for the present, but with the reservation, that it should be subjected to alterations when there was opportunity for them. Her brother, the newly created

Earl of Mar, however, who was at this time her principal counsellor, and her best friend, used his influence with the Protestant clergy in her behalf, and some coldness arose between him and John Knox, on the subject, which continued for more than a year.

The first troublesome affair in Queen Mary's reign seems to have arisen from her attachment to this brother and his interest. She had created him Earl of Mar, as we have said; but it was her purpose to confer on him, instead of this title, that of Earl of Murray, and with it great part of the large estates belonging to that northern earldom, which had become vested in the crown after the extinction of the heirs of the celebrated Thomas Randolph, who enjoyed it in the reign of the great Robert Bruce. The earldom of Murray had afterwards been held by a brother of the Earl of Douglas, but had again been forfeited to the crown on the fall of that great family in James the Second's time.

This exchange, however, could not be made, without giving offence to the Earl of Huntly, often mentioned as head of the most powerful family in the North, who had possessed himself of a considerable part of those domains which had belonged to the earldom of Murray. This Earl of Huntly was a brave man, and possessed of very great power in the northern counties. He was one of the few remaining peers who continued attached to the Catholic religion, and, after the family of Hamilton, was the nearest in connection to the royal family.

It was believed that if the Queen, instead of coming to Leith, had chosen to have landed at Aberdeen, and declared herself determined to reinstate the Catholic religion, the Earl had offered to join her with twenty thousand men for accomplishing that purpose. Mary, however, had declined his proposal, which must have had the immediate consequence of producing a great civil war. The Earl of Huntly was, therefore, considered as hostile to the present government, and to the Earl of Mar, who had the principal management of affairs ; and it was to be supposed, that, possessed as Huntly was of great power, and a very numerous body of dependants and retainers, he would not willingly surrender to his political enemy any part of the domains which he possessed belonging to the earldom of Murray.

The Earl of Mar was, on his part, determined to break the strength of this great opponent; and Queen Mary, who appears also to have feared Huntly's power, and the use which he seemed disposed to make of it, undertook a personal journey to the North of Scotland, to enforce obedience to her commands. About the same time, Sir John Gordon, the Earl of Huntly's son, committed some feudal outrage, for which he was sentenced to temporary confinement. This punishment, though slight, was felt as another mark of disfavor to the house of Gordon, and increased the probability of their meditating resistance. It is difficult, or rather impossible, to say whether there were good grounds for suspecting Huntly of entertaining serious views to take arms against the crown. But his conduct was, to say the least, incautious and suspicious.

The young Queen advanced northward at the head of a small army, encamping in the fields, or accepting such miserable lodgings as the houses of the smaller gentry afforded. It was, however, a scene which awoke her natural courage, and, marching at the head of her soldiery, such was her spirit, that she publicly wished she had been a man, to sleep all night in the fields, and to walk armed with a jack and skull-cap of steel, a good Glasgow buckler at her back, and a broadsword by her side.

Huntly seems to have been surprised by the arrival of his sovereign, and undecided what to do. While he made all offers of submission, and endeavored to prevail on the Queen to visit his house, as that of a dutiful subject, a party of his followers refused her admission into the royal castle of Inverness, and attempted to defend that fortress against her. They were, however, compelled to surrender, and the governor was executed for treason.

Meantime, Sir John Gordon escaped from the prison to which the Queen had sentenced him, and placed himself at the head of the vassals of his house, who were now rising in every direction; while his father, the Earl of Huntly, considering the Queen as guided entirely by his enemy, the Earl of Mar, at length assumed arms in person.

Huntly easily assembled a considerable host, and advanced towards Aberdeen. The purpose of his enterprise was, perhaps, such as Buccleuch had entertained at the field of Melrose, an attack rather upon the Queen's counsellors than on her person. But her brother, who had now exchanged his title of Mar for that of Murray, was as brave and as successful as Angus upon the former occasion, with this advantage, that he enjoyed the confidence of his sovereign. He was, however, in a state of great difficulty. The men on whom he could with certainty rely were few, being only those whom he had brought from the midland counties. He summoned, indeed, the northern barons in his neighborhood, and they came; but with doubtful intentions, full of awe for the house of Gordon, and probably with the private resolution of being guided by circumstances.

Murray, who was an excellent soldier, drew up the men he could trust on an eminence called the Hill of Fare, near Corrichie. He did not allow the northern clans to mix their doubtful succors with this resolute battalion, and the event showed the wisdom of his precaution. Huntly approached, and encountered the northern troops, his allies and neighbors, who offered little or no resistance. They fled tumultuously towards Murray's main body, pursued by the Gordons, who threw away their spears, drew their swords, and advanced in disorder, as to an assured victory. In this tumult they encountered the resistance of Murray's firm battalion of spearmen, who received the attack in close order, and with determined resolution. The Gordons were repulsed in their turn; and those clans who had before fled, seeing they were about to lose the day, returned with sprigs of heather in their caps, which they used to distinguish them, fell upon the Gordons, and completed Murray's victory. Huntly, a bulky man, and heavily armed, fell from horseback in the flight, and was trodden to death, or, as others say, died afterwards of a broken heart. This battle was fought 28th October, 1562. The body of Huntly, a man lately esteemed one of the bravest, wisest, and most powerful in Scotland, was afterwards brought into a court of justice, meanly arrayed in a doublet of coarse canvas, that the sentence of a traitor might be pronounced over the senseless corpse.

Sir John Gordon, the son of the vanquished Earl, was beheaded at Aberdeen, three days after the battle. Murray was placed in possession of the estates belonging to his new earldom, and the Queen returned, after having struck general terror into the minds of such barons as might be thought refractory, by the activity of her measures, and the success of her arms.

Thus far the reign of Mary had been eminently prosperous; but a fatal crisis approached, which was eventually to plunge her into the utmost misery. She had no children by her deceased husband, the King of France, and her subjects were desirous that she should marry a second husband, a purpose which she herself entertained and encouraged. It was necessary, or politic at least, to consult Queen Elizabeth on the subject. That princess had declared her own resolution never to marry, and if she should keep this determination, Mary of Scotland was the next heir to the English crown. In expectation of this rich and splendid inheritance, it was both prudent and natural, that in forming a new marriage, Mary should desire to have the advice and approbation of the princess to whose realm she or her children might hope to succeed, especially if she could retain her favor.

Elizabeth of England was one of the wisest and most sagacious Queens that ever wore a crown, and the English to this day cherish her memory with well-deserved respect and attachment. But her conduct towards her kinswoman Mary, from beginning to end, indicated a degree of envy and deceit totally unworthy of her general character. Determined herself not to marry, it seems to have been Elizabeth's desire to prevent Mary also from doing so, lest she should see before her a lineage, not her own, ready to occupy her throne immediately after her death. She therefore adopted a mean and shuffling policy, recommending one match after another to her kinswoman, but throwing in obstacles whenever any of them seemed likely to take place. At first she appeared desirous that Mary should marry the Earl of Leicester, a nobleman whom, though by no means distinguished by talents or character, she herself admired so much for his personal beauty, as to say, that except for her vow never to marry, she would have chosen him for her own husband. It may be readily believed that she had no design such a match as she hinted at should ever take place, and that if Mary had expressed any readiness to accept of Leicester, Elizabeth would have found ready means to break off the marriage.

This proposal, however, was not at all agreeable to Queen Mary. Leicester, if his personal merit had been much greater, was of too low a rank to pretend to the hand of a Queen of Scotland, and Queen Dowager of France, to whom the most powerful monarchs in Europe were at the same time paying suit.

The Archduke Charles, third son of the Emperor of Germany, was proposed on one side; the hereditary Prince of Spain was offered on another; the Duke of Anjou, who became afterwards Henry II. of France, also presented himself. But if Mary had accepted the hand of a foreign prince, she would in so doing have resigned her chance of succeeding to the English crown: nay, considering the jealousy of her Protestant subjects, she might have endangered her possession of that of Scotland. She was so much impressed by these considerations, that she went so far as to intimate that she might consent to the match with the Earl of Leicester, provided that Elizabeth would recognize her as next heir to the English crown, in case of her own decease without children. This, however, did not suit Elizabeth's policy. She did not desire Mary to be wedded to any one, far less to Leicester, her own personal favorite; and was therefore extremely unlikely to declare her sentiments upon the succession (a subject on which she always observed the most mysterious silence), in order to bring about the union of her rival with the man she herself preferred.

Meantime, the views of Queen Mary turned towards a young nobleman of high birth, nearly connected both with her own family and that of Elizabeth. This was Henry Stewart, Lord Darnley, eldest son of the Earl of Lennox. You may recollect, that after the battle of Flodden the Earl of Angus married the Queen Dowager of Scotland; and, in the tumults which followed, was compelled to retire for a season to London. While Angus resided in England, his wife bore him a daughter, called Lady Margaret Douglas, who, when her parents returned to Scotland, continued to remain at the English court, under the protection of her uncle, King Henry. Again you must remember, that during the regency of the Duke of Chatelherault, the Earl of Lennox attempted to place himself at the head of the English party in Scotland; but his efforts failing through want of power or of conduct, he also was compelled to retire to England, where Henry VIII., in acknowledgment of his unavailing aid, bestowed on him the hand of his niece, Lady Margaret Douglas, who, in right of her mother, Margaret, had a claim of inheritance to the English crown.

The young Lord Darnley's father being of such high rank, and his parents having such pretensions, Mary imagined that in marrying him she would gratify the wishes of Elizabeth, who seemed to point out, though ambiguously, a native of Britain, and one not of royal rank, as her safest choice, and as that which would be most agreeable to herself. Elizabeth seemed to receive the proposal favorably, and suffered the young man, and his father, Lennox, to visit the court of Scotland, in the hope that their presence might embroil matters further; and thinking that, in case the match should be likely to take place, she might easily break it off by recalling them as her subjects; a command which she supposed they would not dare to disobey, as enjoying all their lands and means of living in England.

Young Darnley was remarkably tall and handsome, perfect in all external and showy accomplishments, but unhappily destitute of sagacity, prudence, steadiness of character, and exhibiting only doubtful courage, though extremely violent in his passions. Had this young man possessed a very moderate portion of sense, or even of gratitude, we might have had a different story to tell of Mary's reign,—as it was, you will hear a very melancholy one. Mary had the misfortune to look upon this young nobleman with partiality, and was the more willing to gratify her own inclinations in his favor, that she longed to put an end to the intrigues by which Queen Elizabeth had endeavored to impose upon her, and prevent her marriage. Indeed, while the two Queens used towards each other the language of the most affectionate cordiality, there was betwixt them neither plain dealing nor upright meaning, but great dissimulation, envy, and fear.

Darnley, in the mean time, endeavoring to strengthen the interest which he had acquired in the Queen's affections, had recourse to the friendship of a man, of low rank, indeed, but who was understood to possess particular influence over the mind of Mary. This was an Italian of humble origin, called David Rizzio, who had been promoted from being a menial in the Queen's family to the confidential office of French secretary. His talents for music gave him frequent admission to Mary's presence, as she delighted in that art; and his address, and arts of insinuation, gained him a considerable influence over her mind. It was almost necessary that the Queen should have near her person some confidential officer, skilled at once in languages and in business, through whom she might communicate with foreign states, and with her friends in France in particular. No such agent was likely to be found in Scotland, unless she had chosen a Catholic priest, which would have given more offence to her Protestant subjects than even the employment of a man like Rizzio. Still, the elevation of this person, a stranger, a Catholic, and a man of mean origin, to the rank of a minister of the crown, — and, yet more, the personal familiarity to which the Queen condescended to admit him, and the airs of importance which this low-born foreigner pretended to assume, became the subject of offence to the proud Scottish nobles, and of vulgar scandal among the common people.

Darnley, anxious to strengthen his interest with the Queen on every hand, formed an intimacy with Rizzio, who employed all the arts of flattery and observance to gain possession of his favor, and unquestionably was serviceable to him in advancing his suit. The Queen in the mean while exerted herself to remove the obstacles to her union with Darnley, and with such success, that, with the approbation of far the greater part of her subjects, they were married at Edinburgh on the 29th July, 1565.

CHAPTER XXXI.

THE RUN-ABOUT RAID — MURDER OF RIZZIO — BIRTH OF JAMES VI. — DEATH OF DARNLEY.

[1565 — 1567.]

WHEN Elizabeth received news that this union was determined upon, she gave way to all the weakness of an envious woman. She remonstrated against the match, though, in fact, Mary could scarcely have made a choice less dangerous to England. She recalled Lennox and his son Darnley from Scotland, — a mandate which they refused, or delayed to obey. She committed the Countess of Lennox, the only one of the family within her reach, a prisoner to the Tower of London. Above all, she endeavored to disturb the peace of Scotland, and the government of Mary and her new husband, by stirring up to insurrection those among the Scottish nobility to whom the match with Darnley was distasteful.

The Queen's brother, the Earl of Murray, was by far the most able and powerful of those who were displeased by Mary's marriage. Darnley and he were personal enemies; and, besides, Murray was the principal of the Lords of the Congregation, who affected to see danger to the Protestant religion in Mary's choice of Darnley for a husband, and in the disunion which it was likely to create betwixt Scotland and England. Murray even laid a plan to intercept Darnley, seize his person, and either put him to death, or send him prisoner to England. A body of horse was for this purpose stationed at a pass under the Hill of Bennartey, near Kinross, called the Parrot-well, to intercept the Queen and Darnley as they returned from a Convention of Estates held at Perth; and they only escaped the danger by a hasty march, commenced early in the morning.

After the marriage, Murray and his confederates, who were the Duke of Chatelherault, Glencairn, Argyle, Rothes, and others, actually took up arms. The Queen, in this emergency, assembled her subjects around her. They came in such numbers as showed her popularity. Darnley rode at their head in gilded armor, accompanied by the Queen herself, having loaded pistols at her saddle-bow. Unable to stand their ground, Murray and his accomplices eluded the pursuit of the royal army, and made a sudden march on Edinburgh, where they hoped to find friends. But the citizens not adopting their cause, and the castle threatening to fire on them, the insurgents were compelled to retreat, first to Hamilton, then to Dumfries, until they finally disbanded their forces in despair, and the leaders fled into England. Thus ended an insurrection, which, from the hasty and uncertain manner in which the conspirators posted from one part of the kingdom to another, obtained the popular name of the Run-about Raid (or ride).

Elizabeth, who had encouraged Murray and his associates to rise against Mary, was by no means desirous to have the discredit of having done so, when she saw their attempt was unsuccessful. She caused Murray and the Abbot of Kilwinning to appear before her, in presence of the ambassadors of France and Spain, who, interfering in

Mary's behalf, had accused Elizabeth of fomenting the Scottish disturbances. "How say you," she exclaimed, "my Lord of Murray, and you his companion? Have you had advice or encouragement from me in your late undertaking?" The exiles, afraid to tell the truth, were contented to say, however falsely, that they had received no advice or assistance at her hands. "There you indeed speak truth," replied Elizabeth; "for neither did I, nor any in my name, stir you up against your Queen; your abominable treason may serve for example to my own subjects to rebel against me. Therefore get out of my presence; you are but unworthy traitors!" Mortified and disgraced, Murray and his companions again retired to the Border, where Queen Elizabeth, notwithstanding her pretended resentment, allowed them privately means of support until times should permit them to return into Scotland and renew disturbances there.

Mary had thus overcome her refractory subjects, but she soon found that she had a more formidable enemy in the foolish and passionate husband whom she had chosen. This headstrong young man behaved to his wife with great disrespect, both as a woman and as a Queen, and habitually indulged himself in intoxication, and other disgraceful vices. Although already possessed of more power than fitted his capacity or age, for he was but nineteen, he was importunate in his demands for obtaining what was called in Scotland the Crown Matrimonial; that is, the full equality of royal right in the crown with his consort. Until he obtained this eminence he was not held to be King, though called so in courtesy. He was only the husband of the Queen.

This crown matrimonial had been bestowed on Mary's first husband, Francis, and Darnley was determined to be possessed of the same rank. But Mary, whose bounty had already far exceeded his deserts, as well as his gratitude, was resolved not to make this last concession, at least without the advice and consent of the Parliament.

The childish impatience of Darnley made him regard with mortal hatred whatever interfered with the instant execution of his wishes; and his animosity on this occasion turned against the Italian secretary, once his friend, but whom he now esteemed his deadly foe, because he supposed that Rizzio encouraged the Queen in resisting his hasty ambition. His resentment against the unhappy stranger arose to such a height, that he threatened to poniard him with his own hand; and as Rizzio had many enemies, and no friend save his mistress, Darnley easily procured instruments, and those of no mean rank, to take the execution of his revenge on themselves.

The chief of Darnley's accomplices, on this unhappy occasion, was James Douglas, Earl of Morton, Chancellor of the kingdom, tutor and uncle to the Earl of Angus (who chanced then to be a minor), and administrator, therefore, of all the power of the great house of Douglas. He was a nobleman of high military talent and political wisdom; but although a pretender to sanctity of life, his actions show him to have been a wicked and unscrupulous man. Although Chancellor of the kingdom, and therefore bound peculiarly to respect the laws, he did not hesitate to enter into the young King's cruel and unlawful purpose. Lord Ruthven, a man whose frame was exhausted by illness, nevertheless undertook to buckle on his armor for the enterprise; and they had no difficulty in finding other agents.

It would have been easy to have seized on Rizzio, and disposed of him as the Scottish peers at the Bridge of Lauder used the favorites of James III.* But this would not have accomplished the revenge of Darnley, who complained that the Queen showed this mean Italian more civility than she did to himself, and therefore took the barbarous resolution of seizing him in her very presence. This plan was the more atrocious, as Mary was at this time with child; and the alarm and agitation which such an act of violence was likely to produce, might endanger her life, or that of her unborn offspring.

Whilst this savage plot was forming, Rizzio received several hints of what was likely to happen. Sir James Melville was at pains to explain to him the danger that was incurred by a stranger in any country, who rose so high in the favor of the Prince as to excite the disgust of the natives of the land. A French priest, who was something of an astrologer, warned the Secretary to beware of a bastard. To such counsels he replied, "that the Scots were more given to threaten than to strike; and as for the bastard (by whom he supposed the Earl of Murray to be meant), he would take care that he should never possess power enough in Scotland to do him any harm." Thus securely confident, he continued at court, to abide his fate.

Those lords who engaged in the conspiracy did not agree to gratify Darnley's resentment against Rizzio for nothing. They stipulated, as the price of their assistance, that he should in turn aid them in obtaining pardon and restoration to favor for Murray, and his accomplices in the Run-about Raid; and intimation was despatched to these noblemen, apprising them of the whole undertaking, and desiring them to be at Edinburgh on the night appointed for doing the deed.

* See *ante*, Vol. I. p. 276.

Queen Mary, like her father, James V., was fond of laying aside the state of a sovereign, and indulging in small private parties, quiet, as she termed them, and merry. On these occasions, she admitted her favorite domestics to her table, and Rizzio seems frequently to have had that honor. On the 9th of March, 1566, six persons had partaken of supper in a small cabinet adjoining to the Queen's bedchamber, and having no entrance save through it. Rizzio was of the number. About seven in the evening the gates of the palace were occupied by Morton, with a party of two hundred men; and a select band of the conspirators, headed by Darnley himself, came into the Queen's apartment by a secret staircase. Darnley first entered the cabinet, and stood for an instant in silence, gloomily eyeing his victim. Lord Ruthven followed, in complete armor, looking pale and ghastly, as one scarcely recovered from long sickness. Others crowded in after them, till the little closet was full of armed men. While the Queen demanded the purpose of their coming, Rizzio, who saw that his life was aimed at, got behind her, and clasped the folds of her gown, that the respect due to her person might protect him. The assassins threw down the table, and seized on the unfortunate object of their vengeance, while Darnley himself took hold of the Queen, and forced Rizzio and her asunder. It was their intention, doubtless, to have dragged Rizzio out of Mary's presence, and to have killed him elsewhere; but their fierce impatience hurried them into instant murder. George Douglas, called the postulate of Arbroath, a natural brother of the Earl of Morton, set the example, by snatching Darnley's dagger from his belt, and striking Rizzio with it. He received many other blows. They dragged him through the bedroom and antechamber, and despatched him at the head of the staircase, with no less than fifty-six wounds. Ruthven, after all was over, fatigued with his exertions, sat down in the Queen's presence, and, begging her pardon for the liberty, called for a drink to refresh him, as if he had been doing the most harmless thing in the world.

The witnesses, the actors, and the scene of this cruel tragedy, render it one of the most extraordinary which history records. The cabinet and the bedroom still remain in the same condition in which they were at the time; and the floor near the head of the stair bears visible marks of the blood of the unhappy Rizzio. The Queen continued to beg his life with prayers and tears; but when she learned that he was dead, she dried her tears: "I will now," she said, "study revenge."

The conspirators, who had committed the cruel action entirely or chiefly to gratify Darnley, reckoned themselves, of course, secure of his protection. They united themselves with Murray and his associates, who were just returned from England according to appointment, and agreed upon a course of joint measures. The Queen, it was agreed, should be put under restraint in Edinburgh Castle, or elsewhere; and Murray and Morton were to rule the state under the name of Darnley, who was to obtain the crown matrimonial, which he had so anxiously desired. But all this scheme was ruined by the defection of Darnley himself. As fickle as he was vehement, and as timorous as he had shown himself cruel, Rizzio was no sooner slain than Darnley became terrified at what had been done, and seemed much disposed to deny having given any authority for the crime.

Finding her weak-minded husband in a state between remorse and fear, Mary prevailed on him to take part against the very persons whom he had instigated to the late atrocious proceeding. Darnley and Mary escaped together out of Holyroodhouse, and fled to Dunbar, where the Queen issued a proclamation which soon drew many faithful followers around her. It was now the turn of the conspirators to tremble. That the Queen's conquest over them might be more certain, she pardoned the Earl of Murray, and those concerned in the Run-about Raid, as guilty of more venial offences than the assassins of Rizzio; and thus Murray, Glencairn, and others, were received into favor, while Morton, Ruthven, and his comrades, fled in their turn to England. No Scottish subject, whatever his crime, could take refuge there without finding secret support, if not an open welcome. Such was Elizabeth's constant policy.

Queen Mary was now once more in possession of authority, but much disturbed and vexed by the silly conduct of her husband, whose absurdities and insolences were not abated by the consequences of Rizzio's death; so that the royal pair continued to be upon the worst terms with each other, though disguised under a species of reconciliation.

On the 19th of June, 1566, Mary was delivered of a son, afterwards James VI. When news of this event reached London, Queen Elizabeth was merrily engaged in dancing; but upon hearing what had happened, she left the dance, and sat down, leaning her head on her hand, and exclaiming passionately to her ladies, "Do you not hear how the Queen of Scots is mother of a fair son, while I am but a barren stock!" But next morning she had recovered herself sufficiently to maintain her usual appearance of outward civility, received the Scottish ambassador with much seeming favor, and accepted with thanks the office of godmother to the young Prince, which he proffered to her in Queen Mary's name.*

After a splendid solemnity at christening the heir of Scotland, Queen Mary seems to have turned her mind towards settling the disorders of her nobility; and, sacrificing her own justifiable resentment, she yielded so far as to grant pardon to all those concerned in the murder of Rizzio. Two men of low rank, and no more, had been executed for that crime. Lord Ruthven, the principal actor, had died in England, talking and writing as composedly of "the slaughter of David," as if it had been the most indifferent, if not meritorious, action possible. George Douglas, who struck the first blow, and Ker of Faldonside, another ruffian who offered his pistol at the Queen's bosom in the fray, were exempted from the general pardon. Morton and all the others were permitted to return, to plan new treasons and murders.

We are now come, my dear child, to a very difficult

* "The next morning," says Sir James Melville, "was appointed for me to get audience. At what time my brother and I went by water to Greenwich, and were met by some friends, who told us how sorrowful her Majesty was at my news; but that she had been advised to show a glad and cheerful countenance; which she did, in her best apparel, saying, 'that the joyful news of the Queen her sister's delivery of a fair son, which I had sent her by Secretary Cecil, had recovered her out of a heavy sickness which she had lyen under for fifteen days.' Therefore she welcomed me with a merry volt, and thanked me for the diligence I had used in hasting to give her that welcome intelligence. All this she said before I had delivered unto her my letter of credence. Then I requested her Majesty to be a gossip to the Queen; to which she gladly condescended. 'Your Majesty,' said I, 'will now have a fair occasion to see the Queen, whereof I have heard your Majesty so oft desirous;' whereat she smiled, saying she wished that her estate and affairs might permit her. In the mean time, she promised to send both honorable lords and ladies to supply her room." — *Memoirs*, pp. 138, 139.

period in history. The subsequent events in the reign of Queen Mary are well known; but neither the names of the principal agents in those events, nor the motives upon which they acted, are at all agreed upon by historians. It has, in particular, been warmly disputed, and will probably long continue to be so, how far Queen Mary is to be considered as a voluntary party or actor in the tragical and criminal events of which I am about to tell you; or how far, being innocent of any foreknowledge of these violent actions, she was an innocent victim of the villany of others. Leaving you, my dear child, when you come to a more advanced age, to study this historical point for yourself, I shall endeavor to give you an outline of the facts, as they are admitted and proved on all sides.

James Hepburn, Earl of Bothwell, a man in middle age, had for several years played a conspicuous part in those troubled times. He had sided with the Queen Regent against the Reformed party, and was in general supposed to be attached rather to the reigning Queen than to any of the factions who opposed her. He was head of the powerful family of Hepburn, and possessed great influence in East Lothian and Berwickshire, where excellent soldiers could always be obtained. In his morals Bothwell was wild and licentious, irregular and daring in his ambition; and although his history does not show many instances of personal courage, yet in his early life he had the reputation of possessing it. He had been in danger on the occasion of Rizzio's murder, being supposed, from his regard for the Queen, to have been desirous of preventing that cruel insult to her person and authority. As this nobleman displayed great zeal for Mary's cause, she was naturally led to advance him at court, until many persons, and particularly the preachers of the Reformed religion, thought that she admitted to too great intimacy a man of so fierce and profligate a character; and a numerous party among her subjects accused the Queen as being fonder of Bothwell than she ought to have been, he being a married man, and herself a married woman.

A thoughtless action of Mary's seemed to confirm this suspicion. Bothwell, among other offices of authority, held that of Lord Warden of all the Marches, and was residing at the castle of Hermitage, a royal fortress which belonged to that office, in order to suppress some disorders on the Border. In October, 1566, attempting with his own hand to seize a Border freebooter, called John Elliot of the Park, he was severely wounded in the hand. The Queen, who was then at Jedburgh holding a court of justice, hastened through woods, morasses, and waters, to pay a visit to the wounded Warden; and though the distance was twenty English miles, she went and returned from Hermitage Castle in the same day. This excursion might arise solely from Mary's desire to learn the cause and particulars of a great outrage on her lieutenant; but all those who wished ill to her, who were a numerous body, represented it as expressing her anxiety for the safety of her lover.*

In the mean time, the dissensions between Darnley and the Queen continued to increase; and while he must have been disliked by Mary, from their numerous quarrels, and the affronts he put upon her, as well as from his share in the murder of Rizzio, those who had been concerned with him in that last crime, considered

* See Introduction to the *Border Minstrelsy*, SIR WALTER SCOTT'S *Poetical Works*, vol. i. pp. 133-135.

him as a poor mean-spirited wretch, who, having engaged his associates in so daring an act, had afterwards betrayed and deserted them. His latter conduct showed no improvement in either sense or spirit. He pretended he would leave the kingdom, and by this and other capricious resolutions, hastily adopted and abandoned, he so far alienated the affections of the Queen, that many of the unscrupulous and plotting nobles by whom she was surrounded formed the idea that it would be very agreeable to Mary if she could be freed from her union with this unreasonable and ill-tempered young man.

The first proposal made to her was, that she should be separated from Darnley by a divorce. Bothwell, Maitland, Morton, and Murray, are said to have joined in pressing such a proposal upon Queen Mary, who was then residing at Craigmillar Castle, near Edinburgh; but she rejected it steadily. A conspiracy of a darker kind was then agitated, for the murder of the unhappy Darnley; and Bothwell seems to have entertained little doubt that Mary, thus rid of an unacceptable husband, would choose himself for his successor. He spoke with the Earl of Morton on the subject of despatching Darnley, and represented it as an enterprise which had the approbation of the Queen. Morton refused to stir in a matter of so great consequence, unless he received a mandate under the Queen's hand. Bothwell undertook to procure him such a warrant, but he never kept his word. This was confessed by Morton at his death. When it was asked of him by the clergyman who received his confession, why he had not prevented the conspiracy by making it public, he replied, that there was no one to whom he could confess it with safety. "The Queen," he said, "was herself in the plot; and if I had told Darnley, his folly was so great that I am certain he would have betrayed it to his wife, and so my own destruction would have been assured." But though he did not acknowledge more than I have told you, Morton was always supposed to be one of the active conspirators; and it was universally believed that a daring and profligate relation of his, called Archibald Douglas, parson of Glasgow, was one of the actual murderers.* While these suspicions hung over Morton himself, he seems to have had no reason for believing Mary's guilt, excepting what Bothwell told him; while he admits that Bothwell never showed him any warrant under the Queen's hand, though he promised to do so. It seems probable that Maitland of Lethington also knew the fatal and guilty secret. Morton and he, however, were both men of deep sagacity. They foresaw that Bothwell would render himself, and perhaps the Queen also, odious to the nation by the dark and bloody action which he meditated; and therefore they resolved to let him run on his course, in the hope that he would come to a speedy fall, and that they themselves might succeed to the supreme power.

While these schemes were in agitation against his life, Darnley fell ill at Glasgow, and his indisposition proved to be the small-pox. The Queen sent her physician, and after an interval went herself to wait upon him, and an apparent reconciliation was effected between them. They came together to Edinburgh on the 31st January, 1566–67. The King was lodged in a religious house

* Douglas was, twenty years afterwards, brought to trial for his alleged participation in the murder of Darnley, and acquitted.— See an account of the procedure thereon, in Arnot's *Criminal Trials*, 4to, pp. 7–20.

called the Kirk of Field, just without the walls of the city.* The Queen and the infant Prince were accommodated in the palace of Holyrood. The reason assigned for their living separate was the danger of the child catching the small-pox. But the Queen showed much attention to her husband, visiting him frequently; and they never seemed to have been on better terms than when the conspiracy against Darnley's life was on the eve of being executed. Meanwhile Darnley and his groom of the chamber were alone during the night-time, and separated from any other persons, when measures were taken for his destruction in the following horrible manner: —

On the evening of the 9th February, several persons, kinsmen, retainers, and servants of the Earl of Bothwell, came in secret to the Kirk of Field. They had with them a great quantity of gunpowder; and by means of false keys they obtained entrance into the cellars of the building, where they disposed the powder in the vaults under Darnley's apartment, and especially beneath the spot where his bed was placed. About two hours after midnight upon the ensuing morning, Bothwell himself came, disguised in a riding-cloak, to see the execution of the cruel project. Two of his ruffians went in and took means of firing the powder, by lighting a piece of slow-burning match at one end, and placing the other amongst the gunpowder. They remained for some time watching the event, and Bothwell became so impatient, that it was with difficulty he was prevented from entering the house, to see whether the light had not been extinguished by some accident. One of his accomplices, by looking

* The Kirk of Field stood on part of the site of the College of Edinburgh.

through a window, ascertained that it was still burning. The explosion presently took place, blew up the Kirk of Field, and alarmed the whole city. The body of Darnley was found in the adjoining orchard. The bed in which he lay had preserved him from all action of the fire, which occasioned a general belief that he and his chamber-groom, who was found in the same situation, had been strangled and removed before the house was blown up. But this was a mistake. It is clearly proved, by the evidence of those who were present at the event, that there were no means employed but the gunpowder,— a mode of destruction sufficiently powerful to have rendered any other unnecessary.

CHAPTER XXXII.

MARRIAGE OF MARY AND BOTHWELL — MARY'S SURRENDER TO THE CONFEDERATED LORDS AT CARBERRY — HER IMPRISONMENT IN LOCHLEVEN CASTLE AND ESCAPE THENCE — BATTLE OF LANGSIDE, AND MARY'S FLIGHT TO ENGLAND — UNJUST CONDUCT OF ELIZABETH TOWARDS THE SCOTTISH QUEEN — REGENCY AND MURDER OF MURRAY — CIVIL WARS IN SCOTLAND — REGENCY OF MORTON — HIS TRIAL AND EXECUTION — RAID OF RUTHVEN — AFFAIRS OF JAMES VI. MANAGED BY STEWART, EARL OF ARRAN — DISGRACE AND DEATH OF THIS FAVORITE.

[1567 — 1586.]

THE horrible murder of the unhappy Darnley excited the strongest suspicions and the greatest discontent, in the city of Edinburgh and through the whole kingdom. Bothwell was pointed out by the general voice as the author of the murder; and as he still continued to enjoy the favor of Mary, her reputation was not spared. To have brought this powerful criminal to an open and impartial trial would have been the only way for the Queen to recover her popularity; and Mary made a show of doing this public justice, but under circumstances which favored the criminal.

Lennox, father of the murdered Darnley, had, as was his natural duty, accused Bothwell of the murder of his son. But he received little countenance in prosecuting the accused. Everything seemed to be done as hastily as if it were determined to defeat the operations of justice.

Lennox received information, on the 28th of March, that the 12th of April was appointed for the day of trial; and, at so short warning as fourteen days, he was summoned, as nearest relation of the murdered monarch, to appear as accuser, and to support the charge he had made against Bothwell. The Earl of Lennox complained that the time allowed him to prepare the charge and evidence necessary for convicting so powerful a criminal was greatly too short; but he could not prevail to have it extended.

It was a usual thing in Scotland for persons accused of crimes to come to the bar of a court of justice attended by all their friends, retainers, and dependents, the number of whom was frequently so great that the judges and accusers were overawed, and became afraid to proceed in the investigation; so that the purposes of justice were for the time frustrated. Bothwell, conscious of guilt, was desirous to use this means of protection to the utmost. He appeared in Edinburgh with full five thousand attendants. Two hundred chosen musketeers kept close by his side, and guarded the doors of the court as soon as the criminal had entered. In such circumstances, there could be no chance of a fair trial. Lennox did not appear, saving by one of his vassals, who protested against the proceedings of the day. No charge was made, — no proof of innocence, of course, was required, — and a jury, consisting of nobles and gentlemen of the first rank, acquitted Bothwell of a crime of which all the world believed him to be guilty.

The public mind remained dissatisfied with this mockery of justice; but Bothwell, without regarding the murmurs of the people, hurried forward to possess himself of the situation which he had made vacant by the murder of Darnley. He convened a number of the principal nobility, at a feast given in a tavern, and prevailed on them to sign a bond, in which they not only declared Bothwell altogether innocent of the King's death, but recommended him as the fittest person whom her Majesty could choose for a husband. Morton, Maitland, and others, who afterwards were Mary's bitter enemies and accusers, subscribed this remarkable deed; either because they were afraid of the consequences of a refusal, or that they thought it the readiest and safest course for accomplishing their own purposes, to encourage Bothwell and the Queen to run headlong to their ruin, by completing a marriage which must be disgustful to the whole kingdom.

19th April.

Murray, the most important person in Scotland, had kept aloof from all these proceedings. He was in Fife when the King was murdered, and, about three days before Bothwell's trial, he obtained leave of his sister, the Queen, to travel to France. Probably he did not consider that his own person would be safe, should Bothwell rise to be King.

The Earl of Bothwell, thus authorized by the apparent consent of the nobility, and, no doubt, thinking himself secure of the Queen's approbation, suddenly appeared at the Bridge of Cramond, with a thousand horse, as Mary arrived there on her return from Stirling to Edinburgh. Bothwell took the Queen's horse by the bridle, and surrounding and disarming her attendants, he led her, as if by an appearance of force, to the strong castle of Dunbar, of which he was governor. On this occasion, Mary seems neither to have attempted to resist, nor to have expressed that feeling of anger and shame which would have been proper to her character as a queen or as a woman. Her attendants were assured by the officers of Bothwell, that she was carried off in consequence of her own consent;

and, considering that such an outrage was offered to a sovereign of her high rank and bold spirit, her tame submission and silence under it seem scarce otherwise to be accounted for. They remained at Dunbar ten days, after which they again appeared in Edinburgh, apparently reconciled; the Earl carefully leading the Queen's palfrey, and conducting her up to the castle of Edinburgh, the government of which was held by one of his adherents.

Whilst these strange proceedings took place, Bothwell had been able to procure a sentence of divorce against his wife, a sister of the Earl of Huntly. On the 12th of May the Queen made a public declaration that she forgave Bothwell the late violence which he had committed, and that, although she was at first highly displeased with him, she was now resolved not only to grant him her pardon, but also to promote him to further honors. She was as good as her word, for she created him Duke of Orkney; and on the 15th of the same month did Mary, with unpardonable indiscretion, commit the great folly of marrying this ambitious and profligate man, stained as he was with the blood of her husband.*

The Queen was not long in discovering that by this unhappy marriage she had gotten a more ruthless and wicked husband than she had in the flexible Darnley. Bothwell used her grossly ill; and, being disappointed in his plans of getting the young Prince into his keeping, used such upbraiding language to Mary, that she prayed for a knife with which to stab herself, rather than endure his ill-treatment.

In the mean time, the public discontent rose high, and

* "As a sad presage of what was quickly to follow, this phrase of Ovid was found affixt on the palace gate, the night of the marriage: '*Mense malas Maio nubere vulgus ait.*'" — KEITH, p. 386.

Morton, Maitland, and others, who had been themselves privy to the murder of Darnley, placed themselves, notwithstanding, at the head of a numerous party of the nobility, who resolved to revenge his death and remove Bothwell from his usurped power. They took arms hastily, and had nearly surprised the Queen and Bothwell, while feasting in the castle of the Lord Borthwick, from whence they fled to Dunbar, the Queen being concealed in the disguise of a page.

The confederated lords marched towards Dunbar, and the Queen and Bothwell, having assembled an army, advanced to the encounter, and met them on Carberry Hill, not far from the place where the battle of Pinkie was fought. This was on the 15th of June, 1567. Mary would have acted more wisely in postponing the threatened action, for the Hamiltons, in great force, were on their way to join her. But she had been accustomed to gain advantages by rapid and ready movements, and was not at first sufficiently aware what an unfavorable impression existed against her even in her own army. Many, if not most, of those troops who had joined the Queen, had little inclination to fight in Bothwell's cause. He himself, in a bravado, offered to prove his innocence of Darnley's murder, by a duel in the lists with any of the opposite lords who should affirm his guilt. The valiant Kirkaldy of Grange, Murray of Tullibardin, and Lord Lindsay of the Byres, successively undertook the combat; but Bothwell found exceptions to each of them; and finally it appeared that this wicked man had not courage to fight with any one in that quarrel. In the mean time, the Queen's army began to disband, and it became obvious that they would not fight in her cause, while they considered it as the same with that of Bothwell. She therefore recommended to him to fly from the field of action; an advice which he was not slow in following, riding to Dunbar as fast as he could, and from thence escaping by sea.

Mary surrendered herself, upon promise of respect and kind treatment, to the Laird of Grange, and was conducted by him to the head-quarters of the confederate army. When she arrived there, the lords received her with silent respect; but some of the common soldiers hooted at and insulted her, until Grange, drawing his sword, compelled them to be silent. The lords adopted the resolution of returning to the capital, and conveying Mary thither, surrounded by their troops.

As the unhappy Queen approached Edinburgh, led as it were in triumph by the victors, the most coarse and insulting behavior was used towards her by the lower classes. There was a banner prepared for this insurrection, displaying, on the one side, the portrait of Darnley, as he lay murdered under a tree in the fatal orchard, with these words embroidered, "Judge and avenge my cause, O Lord!" and on the other side, the little Prince on his knees, holding up his hands, as if praying to Heaven to punish his father's murderers. As the Queen rode through the streets, with her hair loose, her garments disordered, covered with dust, and overpowered with grief, shame, and fatigue, this fatal flag was displayed before her eyes, while the voices of the rude multitudes upbraided her with having been an accomplice in Darnley's murder. The same cries were repeated, and the same insulting banner displayed, before the windows of the Lord Provost's house, to which she was for a few hours committed as if a prisoner. The better class of craftsmen and citizens were at length moved by her sorrows, and showed such a desire to take her part, that the lords determined to remove her from the city, where respect to her birth and misfortune seemed likely to create partisans, in spite of her own indiscretions, and the resentment of her enemies. Accordingly, on the next evening, being 16th June, 1567, Mary, in disguised apparel, and escorted by a strong armed force, was conveyed from Holyrood to the castle of Lochleven, which stands on a little island, surrounded by the lake of the same name, and was there detained a prisoner.

The insurgent lords now formed themselves into a Secret Council, for managing the affairs of the nation. Their first attention was turned to securing Bothwell, although, perhaps, there may have been some even among their own number — Morton, for example, and Maitland — who had been participant with him in the murder of Darnley, who could not be very desirous that he should be produced on a public trial. But it was necessary to make a show of pursuing him, and many were sincerely desirous that he should be taken.

Kirkaldy of Grange followed Bothwell with two vessels, and had nearly surprised him in the harbor of Lerwick, the fugitive making his escape at one issue of the bay, while Grange entered at another; and Bothwell might even then have been captured, but that Grange's ship ran upon a rock, and was wrecked, though the crew escaped. Bothwell was only saved for a more melancholy fate. He took to piracy in the Northern Seas, in order to support himself and his sailors. He was in consequence assaulted and taken by some Danish ships of war. The Danes threw him into the dungeons of the castle of Malmay, where he died in captivity, about the end of the year 1576. It is said, that this atrocious criminal confessed at his death, that he had conducted the murder of Darnley, by the assistance of Murray, Maitland, and Morton, and that Mary was altogether guiltless of that crime. But there is little reliance to be placed on the declaration of so wicked a man, even if it were certain he had made it.

Meantime poor Mary reaped the full consequences of Bothwell's guilt, and of her own infatuated attachment to him. She was imprisoned in a rude and inconvenient tower, on a small islet, where there was scarce room to walk fifty yards; and not even the intercession of Queen Elizabeth, who seems for the time to have been alarmed at the successful insurrection of subjects against their sovereign, could procure any mitigation of her captivity. There was a proposal to proceed against the Queen as an accomplice in Darnley's murder, and to take her life under that pretence. But the lords of the Secret Council resolved to adopt somewhat of a gentler course, by compelling Mary to surrender her crown to her son, then an infant, and to make the Earl of Murray Regent during the child's minority. Deeds to this purpose were drawn up, and sent to the castle of Lochleven, to be signed by the Queen. Lord Lindsay, the rudest, most bigoted, and fiercest of the confederated lords, was deputed to enforce Mary's compliance with the commands of the Council. He behaved with such peremptory brutality as had perhaps been expected, and was so unmanly as to pinch with his iron glove the arm of the poor Queen, to compel her to subscribe the deeds.*

* "The signature of the three instruments by the Queen," says Chalmers, "whether voluntary or involuntary, was not, it seems, deemed sufficiently constitutional without the Privy Seal. The same brutal Lord Lindsay brought these instruments to Thomas Sinclair, who acted as deputy-keeper of that seal, from 1555 to 1574, and who appears to have been, in a vicious age, an honest and spirited man. He refused to affix the seal to such instruments, *the Queen being in*

If Mary had any quarter to which, in her disastrous condition, she might look for love and favor, it was to her brother Murray. She may have been criminal,—she had certainly been grossly infatuated,—yet she deserved her brother's kindness and compassion. She had loaded him with favors, and pardoned him considerable offences. Unquestionably she expected more favor from him than she met with. But Murray was ambitious; and ambition breaks through the ties of blood, and forgets the obligations of gratitude. He visited his imprisoned sister and benefactress in Lochleven Castle, but it was not to bring her comfort: on the contrary, he pressed all her errors on her with such hard-hearted severity, that she burst into floods of tears, and abandoned herself to despair.

Murray accepted of the Regency, and in doing so broke
22d Aug., 1567. all remaining ties of tenderness betwixt himself and his sister. He was now at the head of the ruling faction, consisting of what were called the King's Lords; while such of the nobility as desired that Mary, being now freed from the society of Bothwell, should be placed at liberty, and restored to the administration of the kingdom, were termed the Queen's Party. The strict and sagacious government of Murray imposed silence and submission for a time upon this last-named faction; but a singular incident changed the face of things for a moment, and gave a gleam of hope to the unfortunate captive.

Sir William Douglas, the Laird of Lochleven, owner

ward. Lord Lindsay, therefore, with a company of folks, *compelled* Sinclair to affix the seal, the officer protesting against this violence, which he could not resist." — *Life of Queen Mary*, 4to, vol. i. pp. 248, 249.

of the castle where Mary was imprisoned, was a half-brother, by the mother's side, of the Regent Murray. This baron discharged, with severe fidelity, the task of Mary's jailor; but his youngest brother, George Douglas, became more sensible to the Queen's distress, and perhaps to her beauty, than to the interests of the Regent, or of his own family. A plot laid by him for the Queen's deliverance was discovered, and he was expelled from the island in consequence. But he kept up a correspondence with a kinsman of his own, called Little Douglas, a boy of fifteen or sixteen, who had remained in the castle. On Sunday, the 2d May, 1568, this little William Douglas contrived to steal the keys of the castle while the family were at supper. He let Mary and her attendant out of the tower when all had gone to rest, — locked the gates of the castle to prevent pursuit, — placed the Queen and her waiting-woman in a little skiff, and rowed them to the shore, throwing the keys of the castle into the lake in the course of their passage. Just when they were about to set out on this adventurous voyage, the youthful pilot had made a signal, by a light in a particular window, visible at the upper end of the lake, to intimate that all was safe. Lord Seaton and a party of the Hamiltons were waiting at the landing-place. The Queen instantly mounted, and hurried off to Niddry, in West Lothian, from which place she went next day to Hamilton. The news flew like lightning throughout the country, and spread enthusiasm everywhere. The people remembered Mary's gentleness, grace, and beauty, — they remembered her misfortunes also, — and if they reflected on her errors, they thought they had been punished with sufficient severity. On Sunday, Mary was a sad and helpless captive in a lonely tower. On the Saturday following, she was at the head of a powerful confederacy, by which nine earls, nine bishops, eighteen lords, and many gentlemen of high rank, engaged to defend her person and restore her power. But this gleam of success was only temporary.

It was the Queen's purpose to place her person in security in the castle of Dunbarton, and her army, under the Earl of Argyle, proposed to carry her thither in a species of triumph. The Regent was lying at Glasgow with much inferior forces; but, with just confidence in his own military skill, as well as the talents of Morton, and the valor of Kirkaldy and other experienced soldiers, he determined to meet the Queen's lords in their proposed march, and to give them battle.

On 13th May, 1568, Murray occupied the village of Langside, which lay full in the march of the Queen's army. The Hamiltons, and other gentlemen of Mary's troop, rushed forth with ill-considered valor to dispute the pass. They fought, however, with obstinacy, after the Scottish manner; that is, they pressed on each other front to front, each fixing his spear in his opponent's target, and then endeavoring to bear him down, as two bulls do when they encounter each other. Morton decided the battle, by attacking the flank of the Hamiltons, while their column was closely engaged in the front. The measure was decisive, and the Queen's army was completely routed.

Queen Mary beheld this final and fatal defeat from a castle called Crookstane, about four miles from Paisley, where she and Darnley had spent some happy days after their marriage, and which, therefore, must have been the scene of bitter recollections. It was soon evident that there was no resource but in flight, and, escorted by Lord Herries and a few faithful followers, she rode sixty miles before she stopped at the Abbey of Dundrennan, in Galloway. From this place she had the means of retreating either to France or England, as she should ultimately determine. In France she was sure to have been well received; but England afforded a nearer, and, as she thought, an equally safe place of refuge.

Forgetting, therefore, the various causes of emulation which existed betwixt Elizabeth and herself, and remembering only the smooth and flattering words which she had received from her sister sovereign, it did not occur to the Scottish Queen that she should incur any risk by throwing herself upon the hospitality of England. It may also be supposed that poor Mary, amongst whose faults want of generosity could not be reckoned, judged of Elizabeth according to the manner in which she would herself have treated the Queen of England in the same situation. She therefore resolved to take refuge in Elizabeth's kingdom, in spite of the opposition of her wiser attendants.* They kneeled and entreated in vain. She entered the fatal boat, crossed the Solway, and delivered herself up to a gentleman named Lowther, the English

* "This resolution unwisely taken, Lord Herries wrote on Saturday the 15th of May, to Lowther, the deputy-captain of Carlisle, informing him of the Queen's misfortune, and desiring to know, if she should be reduced to the necessity of seeking refuge in England, she might come safely to Carlisle. Lowther wrote a doubtful answer, saying that Lord Scroope, the warden of that march, was at London, to whom he had written; but if the Queen should be pressed by necessity to pass the Borders, he would meet and protect her till his mistress's pleasure were known. Without waiting, however, for this answer, which was promptly written, the Queen, with sixteen attendants, the chief of whom was the gallant Lord Herries, embarked in a fishing-boat, and on the evening of Sunday, 16th May, 1568, arrived safe at Workington. On this occasion the unfortunate Queen had not a second habit—nor a shilling in her pocket."—CHALMERS, vol. i. p. 281.

deputy-warden. Much surprised, doubtless, at the incident, he sent express to inform Queen Elizabeth; and, receiving the Scottish Queen with as much respect as he had the means of showing, lodged her in Carlisle Castle.

Queen Elizabeth had two courses in her power, which might be more or less generous, but were alike just and lawful. She might have received Queen Mary honorably, and afforded her the succor she petitioned for; or, if she did not think that expedient, she might have allowed her to remain in her dominions, at liberty to depart from them freely, as she had entered them voluntarily.

But Elizabeth, great as she was upon other occasions of her reign, acted on the present from mean and envious motives. She saw in the fugitive who implored her protection, a princess who possessed a right of succession to the crown of England, which, by the Catholic part of her subjects at least, was held superior to her own. She remembered that Mary had been led to assume the arms and titles of the English monarchy, or rather that the French had assumed them in her name, when she was in childhood. She recollected that Mary had been her rival in accomplishments; and certainly she did not forget that she was her superior in youth and beauty; and had the advantage, as she had expressed it herself, to be the mother of a fair son, while she remained a barren stock. Elizabeth, therefore, considered the Scottish Queen, not as a sister and friend in distress, but as an enemy, over whom circumstances had given her power, and determined upon reducing her to the condition of a captive.

In pursuance of the line of conduct to which this mean train of reasoning led, the unfortunate Mary was surrounded by English guards; and, as Elizabeth reasonably doubted that if she were left upon the Border, the fugitive Queen might obtain aid from her adherents in Scotland, she was removed to Bolton Castle, in Yorkshire. But some pretext was wanting for a conduct so violent, so ungenerous, and so unjust, and Elizabeth contrived to find one.

The Regent Murray, upon Mary's flight to England, had endeavored to vindicate his conduct in the eyes of Queen Elizabeth, by alleging that his sister had been accessory to the murder of her husband, Darnley, in order that she might marry her paramour, Bothwell. Now, although this, supposing it to be true, was very criminal conduct, yet Elizabeth had not the least title to constitute herself judge in the matter. Mary was no subject of hers, nor, according to the law of nations, had the English Queen any right to act as umpire in the quarrel between the Scottish sovereign and her subjects. But she extorted in the following manner a sort of acquiescence in her right to decide, from the Scottish Queen.

The messengers of Queen Elizabeth informed Mary that their mistress regretted extremely that she could not at once admit her to her presence, nor give her the affectionate reception which she longed to afford her, until her visitor stood clear, in the eyes of the world, of the scandalous accusations of her Scottish subjects. Mary at once undertook to make her innocence evident to Elizabeth's satisfaction; and this the Queen of England pretended to consider as a call upon herself to act as umpire in the quarrel betwixt Mary and the party by which she had been deposed and exiled. It was in vain that Mary remonstrated, that, in agreeing to remove Elizabeth's scruples, she acted merely out of respect to her opinion, and a desire to conciliate her favor, but not with the purpose of constituting the English Queen her judge in a formal trial. Elizabeth was determined to keep the advantage which she had attained, and to act as if Mary had, of her full free-will, rendered her rival the sole arbiter of her fate.

The Queen of England accordingly appointed commissioners to hear the parties, and consider the evidence which was to be laid before them by both sides. The Regent Murray appeared in person before these commissioners, in the odious character of the accuser of his sister, benefactress, and sovereign. Queen Mary also sent the most able of her adherents, the Bishop of Ross, Lord Herries, and others, to plead the case on her side.

The Commission met at York in October, 1568. The proceedings commenced with a singular attempt to establish the obsolete question of the alleged supremacy of England over Scotland. "You come hither," said the English commissioners to the Regent and his assistants, "to submit the differences which divide the kingdom of Scotland to the Queen of England, and therefore I first require you to pay her Grace the homage due to her." The Earl of Murray blushed, and was silent. But Maitland of Lethington answered with spirit: "When Elizabeth restores to Scotland the earldom of Huntingdon, with Cumberland, Northumberland, and such other lands as Scotland did of old possess in England, we will do such homage for these territories as was done by the ancient sovereigns of Scotland who enjoyed them. As to the crown and kingdom of Scotland, they are more free than those of England, which lately paid Peter-pence to Rome."

This question being waived, they entered on the proper business of the Commission. It was not without hesitation that Murray was induced to state his accusation in explicit terms, and there was still greater difficulty in obtaining from him any evidence in support of the odious charges of matrimonial infidelity, and accession to the murder of her husband, with which that accusation charged Mary. It is true, the Queen's conduct had been unguarded and imprudent, but there was no arguing from thence that she was guilty of the foul crime charged. Something like proof was wanted, and at length a box of letters and papers was produced, stated to have been taken from a servant of Bothwell, called Dalgleish. These letters, if genuine, certainly proved that Mary was a paramour of Bothwell while Darnley was yet alive, and that she knew and approved of the murder of that ill-fated young man. But the letters were alleged by the Queen's commissioners to be gross forgeries, devised for the purpose of slandering their mistress. It is most remarkable, that Dalgleish had been condemned and executed without a word being asked him about these letters, even if it had been only to prove that they had been found in his possession. Lord Herries and the Bishop of Ross did not rest satisfied with defending the Queen; they charged Murray himself with having confederated with Bothwell for the destruction of Darnley.

At the end of five months' investigation, the Queen of England informed both parties that she had, on the one hand, seen nothing which induced her to doubt the worth and honor of the Earl of Murray, while, on the other hand, he had, in her opinion, proved nothing of the criminal charges which he had brought against his sovereign. She was therefore, she said, determined to leave the affairs of Scotland as she had found them.

To have treated both parties impartially, as her sentence seemed intended to imply her desire to do, the

Queen ought to have restored Mary to liberty. But while Murray was sent down with the loan of a large sum of money, Mary was retained in that captivity which was only to end with her life.

Murray returned to Scotland, having had all the advantage of the conference at York. His coffers were replenished, and his power confirmed, by the favor of Queen Elizabeth; and he had little difficulty in scattering the remains of the Queen's lords, who, in fact, had never been able to make head since the battle of Langside, and the flight of their mistress.

In the mean time, some extraordinary events took place in England. The Duke of Norfolk had formed a plan to restore Queen Mary to liberty, and was in recompense to be rewarded with her hand in marriage. The Regent Murray had been admitted into the secret of this plot, although it may be supposed the object was not very acceptable to him. Many of the great nobles had agreed to join in the undertaking, particularly the powerful Earls of Westmoreland and Northumberland. The plot of Norfolk was discovered and proved against him, chiefly by the declarations of Murray, who meanly betrayed the secret intrusted to him; and he was seized upon, committed to confinement, and, in a few months afterwards, upon the discovery of some new intrigues, was tried and executed.

But before this catastrophe, Northumberland and Westmoreland rushed into a hasty rebellion, which they were unable to conduct with sufficient vigor. Their troops dispersed without a battle before the army which Queen Elizabeth sent against them. Westmoreland found a secure refuge among the Scottish Borderers, who were favorable to the cause of Mary. They assisted him in his escape to the sea-coast, and he finally made his way to

Flanders, and died in exile. Northumberland was less fortunate. A Borderer, named Hector Armstrong of Harlaw, treacherously betrayed him to the Regent Murray, who refused indeed to deliver him up to Queen Elizabeth, but detained him prisoner in that same lonely castle of Lochleven, which had been lately the scene of Mary's captivity.

All these successive events tended to establish the power of Murray, and to diminish the courage of such lords as remained attached to the opposite party. But it happens frequently, that when men appear most secure of the object they have been toiling for, their views are suddenly and strangely disappointed. A blow was impending over Murray from a quarter, which, if named to the haughty Regent, he would probably have despised, since it originated in the resentment of a private man.

After the battle of Langside, six of the Hamiltons, who had been most active on that occasion, were sentenced to die, as being guilty of treason against James VI., in having espoused his mother's cause. In this doom there was little justice, considering how the country was divided between the claims of the mother and the son. But the decree was not acted upon, and the persons condemned received their pardon through the mediation of John Knox with the Regent.

One of the individuals thus pardoned was Hamilton of Bothwellhaugh, a man of a fierce and vindictive character. Like others in his condition, he was punished by the forfeiture of his property, although his life was spared. His wife had brought him, as her portion, the lands of Woodhouselee, near Roslin, and these were bestowed by Murray upon one of his favorites. This person exercised the right so rudely, as to turn Hamilton's wife out of her own house undressed, and unprotected from the fury of the weather. In consequence of this brutal treatment, she became insane, and died. Her husband vowed revenge, not on the actual author of his misfortune, but upon the Regent Murray, whom he considered as the original cause of it, and whom his family prejudices induced him to regard as the usurper of the sovereign power, and the oppressor of the name and house of Hamilton. There is little doubt that the Archbishop of St. Andrews, and some others of his name, encouraged Bothwellhaugh in this desperate resolution.

The assassin took his measures with every mark of
23d Jan., deliberation. Having learned that the Regent was
1570. to pass through Linlithgow on a certain day, he secretly introduced himself into an empty house belonging to the Archbishop of St. Andrews, which had in front a wooden balcony looking upon the street. Bothwellhaugh hung a black cloth on the wall of the apartment where he lay, that his shadow might not be seen from without, and spread a mattress on the floor, that the sound of his feet might not be heard from beneath. To secure his escape he fastened a fleet horse in the garden behind the house, and pulled down the lintel stones from the posts of the garden door, so that he might be able to pass through it on horseback. He also strongly barricaded the front door of the house, which opened to the street of the town. Having thus prepared all for concealment until the deed was done, and for escape afterwards, he armed himself with a loaded carabine, shut himself up in the lonely chamber, and waited the arrival of his victim.

Some friend of Murray transmitted to him a hint of the danger which he might incur, in passing through the street of a place in which he was known to have enemies, and advised that he should avoid it by going round on the outside of the town; or, at least, by riding hastily past the lodging which was more particularly suspected, as belonging to the Hamiltons. But the Regent, thinking that the step recommended would have an appearance of timidity, held on his way through the crowded street. As he came opposite the fatal balcony, his horse being somewhat retarded by the number of spectators, Bothwellhaugh had time to take a deliberate aim. He fired the carabine, and the Regent fell, mortally wounded. The ball, after passing through his body, killed the horse of a gentleman who rode on his right hand. His attendants rushed furiously at the door of the house from which the shot had issued; but Bothwellhaugh's precautions had been so securely taken that they were unable to force their entrance till he had mounted his good horse, and escaped through the garden gate. He was, notwithstanding, pursued so closely, that he had very nearly been taken; but after spur and whip had both failed, he pricked his horse with his dagger, compelled him to take a desperate leap over a ditch, which his pursuers were unable to cross, and thus made his escape.

The Regent died in the course of the night, leaving a character which has been, perhaps, too highly extolled by one class of authors, and too much depreciated by another, according as his conduct to his sister was approved or condemned.

The murderer escaped to France. In the civil wars of that country, an attempt was made to engage him, as a known desperado, in the assassination of the Admiral Coligni; but he resented it as a deadly insult. He had slain a man in Scotland, he said, from whom he had sustained a mortal injury; but the world could not engage him to attempt the life of one against whom he had no personal cause of quarrel.

The death of Murray had been an event expected by many of Queen Mary's adherents. The very night after it happened, Scott of Buccleuch and Ker of Fairniehirst broke into England, and ravaged the frontier with more than their wonted severity. When it was objected by one of the sufferers under this foray, that the Regent would punish the party concerned in such illegal violence, the Borderer replied contemptuously, that the Regent was as cold as his bridle-bit. This served to show that their leaders had been privy to Bothwellhaugh's action, and now desired to take advantage of it, in order to give grounds for war between the countries. But Queen Elizabeth was contented to send a small army to the frontier, to burn the castles and ravage the estates of the two clans which had been engaged in the hostile inroad; a service which they executed with much severity on the clans of Scott and Ker, without doing injury to those other Borderers against whom their mistress had no complaint.

Upon the death of Murray, Lennox was chosen Regent. He was the father of the murdered Darnley, yet showed no excessive thirst of vengeance. He endeavored to procure a union of parties, for the purpose of domestic peace. But men's minds on both sides had become too much exasperated against each other. The Queen's party was strengthened by Maitland of Lethington and Kirkaldy of Grange joining that faction, after having been long the boast of that of the King. Lethington we have often mentioned as one of the ablest men in Scotland, and Kirkaldy was certainly one of the bravest. He was, besides, Governor of Edinburgh Castle, and his declaring that he held that important place for the Queen, gave great spirit to Mary's adherents. At the same time, they were deprived of a stronghold of scarcely inferior consequence, by the loss of Dunbarton Castle in the following extraordinary manner. April, 1571.

This fortress is one of the strongest places in the world. It is situated on a rock, which rises almost perpendicularly from a level plain to the height of several hundred feet. On the summit of this rock the buildings are situated, and as there is only one access from below, which rises by steps, and is strongly guarded and fortified, the fort might be almost held to be impregnable, that is, impossible to be taken. One Captain Crawford of Jordanhill, a distinguished adherent of the King's party, resolved, nevertheless, to make an attempt on this formidable castle.

He took advantage of a misty and moonless night to bring to the foot of the castle-rock the scaling-ladders which he had provided, choosing for his terrible experiment the place where the rock was highest, and where, of course, less pains were taken to keep a regular guard. This choice was fortunate; for the first ladder broke with the weight of the men who attempted to mount, and the noise of the fall must have betrayed them, had there been any sentinel within hearing. Crawford, assisted by a soldier, who had deserted from the castle, and was acting as his guide, renewed the attempt in person, and having scrambled up to a projecting ledge of rock, where there was some footing, contrived to make fast the ladder, by tying it to the roots of a tree, which grew about midway up the rock. Here they found a small flat surface, sufficient, however, to afford footing to the whole party, which was, of course, very few in number. In scaling the second precipice, another accident took place: One of the party, subject to epileptic fits, was seized by one of these attacks, brought on perhaps by terror, while he was in the act of climbing up the ladder. His illness made it impossible for him either to ascend or descend. To have slain the man would have been a cruel expedient, besides that the fall of his body from the ladder might have alarmed the garrison. Crawford caused him, therefore, to be tied to the ladder; then all the rest descending, they turned the ladder, and thus mounted with ease over the belly of the epileptic person. When the party gained the summit, they slew the sentinel ere he had time to give the alarm, and easily surprised the slumbering garrison, who had trusted too much to the security of their castle to keep good watch. This exploit of Crawford may compare with anything of the kind which we read of in history.

Hamilton, the Archbishop of Saint Andrews, was made prisoner in Dunbarton, where he had taken refuge, as he was particularly hated by the King's party. He was now in their hands, and, as they had formerly proclaimed him a traitor, they now without scruple put him to death as such. This cruel deed occasioned other violences, by way of retaliation, which, in turn, led to fresh acts of bloodshed. All natural ties were forgotten in the distinction of Kingsmen and Queensmen; and, as neither party gave quarter to their opponents, the civil war assumed a most horrible aspect. Fathers, and sons, and brothers, took opposite sides, and fought against each other. The very children of the towns and villages formed themselves into bands for King James or Queen Mary, and fought inveterately with stones, sticks, and knives.

In the midst of this confusion, each party called a Parliament, which was attended only by the lords of their own side. The Queen's Parliament met at Edinburgh, under protection of the castle, and its governor Kirkaldy. The King's faction had a much more numerous assembly, assuming the same denomination, at Stirling, where they produced the young King, to give authority to their proceedings. The boy, with natural childishness, taking notice of a rent in the carpet which covered the table at which the clerks sat, observed, "there was a hole in the Parliament." These words were remarked afterwards, as if they had contained a sort of prophecy of the following singular event: —

Kirkaldy devised an enterprise, by which, if successful, he would have put a complete stop to the proceedings of the King's Parliament, nay, to the civil war itself. He sent for Buccleuch and Fairniehirst, already noticed as zealous partisans of Mary, desiring them to bring a large party of their best horsemen, and joined with them the Lord Claud Hamilton, with a detachment of infantry. The whole was guided by a man of the name of Bell, who knew the town of Stirling, being a native of that place. On the 4th of September, 1571, he introduced the party, consisting of about five hundred men, into the middle of the town, at four in the morning, without even a dog barking at them. They then raised the alarm, crying out, "God and the Queen! think on the Archbishop of Saint Andrews! all is our own!" According to the directions they had received, they sent parties to the different houses of which the King's lords had taken possession, and made them prisoners without resistance, except on the part of Morton, whose obstinate valor obliged them to set fire to his lodgings. He then reluctantly surrendered himself to Buccleuch, who was his near connection.

But his resistance had gained some time, and the assailants had scattered themselves in quest of plunder. At this moment, Mar brought a party of musketeers out of the castle, and placing them behind the walls of a house which he had commenced building on the castle-hill, he opened a heavy and unexpected fire upon the Queensmen. These being already in disorder, were struck with panic in the moment of victory, and began to fly. The scene was now completely changed, and they who had been triumphant the moment before, were glad to surrender to their own captives. Lennox the Regent had been mounted behind Spens of Wormeston, who had made him captive. He was a particular object of vengeance to the Hamiltons, who longed to requite the death of the Archbishop of Saint Andrews. He was killed, as was believed, by Lord Claud Hamilton's orders, and Spens, who most honorably endeavored to protect his prisoner, was slain at the same time. The Queen's party retreated out of Stirling without much loss, for the Borderers carried off all the horses, upon which the opposite party might have followed the chase. Kirkaldy received the news of the Regent's death with much dissatisfaction, abusing those who commanded the party as disorderly beasts, who neither knew how to gain a victory, nor how to use it. Had he placed himself at the head of the detachment, as he had earnestly desired to do, it is probable that the Raid of Stirling might have ended the war. As it fell out, the quarrel was only embittered, if possible, by the death of Lennox.

The Earl of Mar was named Regent on the King's side. He was a man of fair and moderate views, and so honorably desirous of restoring the blessing of peace to his country, that the impossibility of attaining his object is said to have shortened his life. He died 29th October, 1572, having been Regent little more than one year.*

The Earl of Morton was next made Regent. We have seen that this nobleman, however respectable for courage and talents, was nevertheless of a fierce, treacherous, and cruel disposition. He had been concerned in Rizzio's murder, and was at least acquainted with that of Darnley. It was to be expected that he would continue the war with the same ferocious cruelty by which it had been distinguished, instead of laboring, like Mar, to diminish its violence. This fell out accordingly. Each party continued to execute their prisoners; and as skirmishes were daily fought, the number of persons who fell by the sword, or died upon the gibbet, was fearfully great. From the family name of Morton, these were called the Douglases' wars.

After these hostilities had existed for about five years, the Duke of Chatelherault and the Earl of Huntly, the two principal nobles who had supported the Queen's cause, submitted themselves to the King's authority, and to the sway of the Regent. Kirkaldy of Grange, assisted by the counsels of Maitland of Lethington, continued to maintain the castle of Edinburgh against Morton. But Queen Elizabeth, who became now desirous of ending the Scottish dissensions, sent Sir William Drury from Berwick with a considerable number [1,500] of regular forces, and, what was still more needful, a large train of artillery, which formed a close siege around the castle of

* "He was, perhaps, the only person in the kingdom who could have enjoyed the office of Regent without envy, and have left it without loss of reputation. Notwithstanding their mutual animosities, both parties acknowledged his views to be honorable, and his integrity to be uncorrupted." — WOOD'S *Peerage*, vol. ii. p. 212.

Edinburgh. The garrison were, however, much more distressed for provisions than by the shot of the English batteries. It was not till after a valiant defence, in the course of which one of the springs which supplied the fortress with water was dried up, and the other became choked with ruins, that the gallant Kirkaldy was compelled to capitulate.

After a siege of thirty-three days he surrendered to the English general, who promised that his mistress should intercede with the Regent for favorable treatment to the governor and his adherents. This might the rather have been expected, because Morton and Kirkaldy had been at one time great friends. But the Regent was earnest in demanding the life of his valorous opponent; and Elizabeth, with little regard to her general's honor or her own, abandoned the prisoners to Morton's vengeance. Kirkaldy and his brother were publicly executed, to the great regret even of many of the King's party themselves. Maitland of Lethington, more famed for talents than integrity, despaired of obtaining mercy where none had been extended to Kirkaldy, and put a period to his existence by taking poison. Thus ended the civil wars of Queen Mary's reign, with the death of the bravest soldier, and of the ablest statesman, in Scotland; for such were Kirkaldy and Maitland.

From the time of the surrender of Edinburgh Castle, 29th May, 1573, the Regent Morton was in complete possession of the supreme power in Scotland. As Queen Elizabeth had been his constant friend during the civil wars, he paid devoted attention to her wishes when he became the undisputed ruler of the kingdom.

Morton even went so far as to yield up to the justice, or the revenge, of the English Queen, that unfortunate

Earl of Northumberland, who, as I formerly mentioned, had raised a rebellion in England, and flying into Scotland, had been confined by the Regent Murray 1569.
in Lochleven Castle. The surrender of this unfortunate nobleman to England was a great stain, not only on the character of Morton, but on that of Scotland in general, which had hitherto been accounted a safe and hospitable place of refuge for those whom misfortune or political faction had exiled from their own country. It was the more particularly noticed, because when Morton himself had been forced to fly to England, on account of his share in Rizzio's murder, he had been courteously received and protected by the unhappy nobleman whom he had now delivered up to his fate. It was an additional and aggravating circumstance, that it was a Douglas who betrayed a Percy; and when the annals of their ancestors were considered, it was found that while they presented many acts of open hostility, many instances of close and firm alliance, they never till now had afforded an example of any act of treachery exercised by the one family against the other. To complete the infamy of the transaction, a sum of money was paid to the Regent on this occasion, which he divided with Douglas of Lochleven. Northumberland was beheaded at York, 1572.

In other respects, Scotland derived great advantage from the peace with England, as some degree of repose was highly necessary to this distracted country. The peace now made continued, with little interruption, for thirty years and upwards.

On one occasion, however, a smart action took place betwixt the Scots and English, which, though of little consequence, I may here tell you of, chiefly because it was the last considerable skirmish,—with the exception of a deed of bold daring, of which I shall speak by and by,—which the two nations had, or, it is to be hoped, ever will have, with each other.

It was the course adopted for preserving peace upon the Border, that the wardens on each side used to meet on days appointed, and deliver up to each other the malefactors who had committed aggressions upon either country, or else make pecuniary reparation for the trespasses which they had done. On the 7th July, 1575, Carmichael, as warden for the Scottish Middle Marches, met Sir John Foster, the English officer, on the opposite frontier, each being, as usual, accompanied by the guards belonging to their office, as well as by the armed clans inhabiting their jurisdiction. Foster was attended by the men of Tynedale, in greater numbers than those of the Scottish Borderers, all well armed with jack and spear, as well as bows and arrows. The meeting was at first peaceful. The wardens commenced their usual business of settling delinquencies; and their attendants began to traffic with each other, and to engage in sports and gaming. For, notwithstanding their habitual incursions, a sort of acquaintance was always kept up between the Borderers on both sides, like that which takes place betwixt the outposts of two contending armies.

During this mutual friendly intercourse, a dispute arose between the two wardens, Carmichael desiring delivery of an English depredator, for whom Foster, on the other hand, refused to be responsible. They both arose from their seats as the debate grew warm, and Sir John Foster told Carmichael, contemptuously, he ought to match himself with his equals. The English Borderers immediately raised their war-cry of "To it, Tynedale!" and without further ceremony, shot a flight of arrows among the Scots, who, few in number, and surprised, were with difficulty able to keep their ground. A band of the citizens of Jedburgh arrived just in time to support their countrymen, and turn the fate of the day; for most of them having fire-arms, the old English long-bow no more possessed its ancient superiority. After a smart action, the English were driven from the field; Sir John Foster, with many of the English gentlemen, being made prisoners, were sent to be at the Regent Morton's disposal. Sir George Heron of Chipchase, and other persons of condition, were slain on the English side. The Scots lost but one gentleman of name.

Morton, afraid of Queen Elizabeth's displeasure, though the offence had been given by the English, treated the prisoners with distinction, and dismissed them, not only without ransom, but with presents of falcons, and other tokens of respect. "Are you not well treated?" said a Scotsman to one of these liberated prisoners, "since we give you live hawks for dead herons?"

This skirmish, called the Raid of the Redswair,* took place on the mountainous ridge of the Carter. It produced no interruption of concord between the two countries, being passed over as a casual affray. Scotland, therefore, enjoyed the blessings of peace and tranquillity during the greater part of Morton's regency.

But the advantages which the kingdom derived from peace were in some measure destroyed by the corrupt and oppressive government of Morton, who turned his thoughts almost entirely to amassing treasure, by every means in his power. The extensive property, which formerly belonged to the Roman Catholic Church, was a

* See "The Raid of the Reidswire," SIR WALTER SCOTT'S *Poetical Works*, vol. ii. pp. 15-31.

mine out of which the Regent and the other great nobles contrived to work for themselves a great deal of wealth. This they did chiefly by dealing with those who were placed in the room of the abbots and priors as commendators, by which word the Scots distinguished a layman who obtained possession of an ecclesiastical benefice. To these commendators the nobles applied, and, by fair means or force, compelled them to make over and transfer to them the property of the abbacies, or at least to grant it to them in long leases for a trifling rent. That you may understand how this sort of business was managed, I will give you a curious instance of it:—

In August, 1570, Allan Stewart, commendator of the abbacy in Crossraguel, in Ayrshire, was prevailed on to visit the Earl of Cassilis, who conveyed him, partly against his will, to a lonely tower, which overhangs the sea, called the Black Vault of Denure, the ruins of which are yet visible. He was treated for some time kindly; but as his arms and servants were removed from him, he soon saw reason to consider himself less as a friendly guest than as a prisoner, to whom some foul play was intended. At length, the Earl conveyed his guest into a private chamber, in which there was no furniture of any kind, excepting a huge clumsy iron grate or gridiron, beneath which was a fire of charcoal. "And now, my lord abbot," said the Earl of Cassilis, "will you be pleased to sign these deeds?" And so saying, he laid before him leases and other papers, transferring the whole lands of the abbacy of Crossraguel to the Earl himself. The commendator refused to yield up the property, or to subscribe the deeds. A party of ruffians then entered, and seizing the unhappy man, stripped him of his clothes, and forcibly stretched him on the iron bars, where he lay, scorched by the fire beneath, while they basted him with oil, as a cook bastes the joint of meat which she roasts upon a spit. The agony of such torture was not to be endured. The poor man cried pitifully, begging they would put him to instant death, rather than subject him to this lingering misery, and offered his purse, with the money it contained, to any who would in mercy shoot him through the head. At length he was obliged to promise to subscribe whatever the Earl wished, rather than endure the excessive torture any longer. The letters and leases being then presented to him, he signed them with his half-roasted hand, while the Earl all the while exclaimed, with the most impudent hypocrisy, "Benedicite! you are the most obstinate man I ever saw, to oblige me to use you thus; I never thought to have treated any one as your stubbornness has made me treat you." The commendator was afterwards delivered by a party commanded by Hamilton of Bargany, who attacked the Black Vault of Denure for the purpose of his liberation.* But the wild, savage, and ferocious conduct of the Earl shows in what manner the nobles obtained grants of the church lands from those who had possession of them for the time.

The Earl of Morton, however, set the example of another and less violent mode of appropriating church revenues to his own purposes. This was by reviving the order of bishops, which had been discarded from the Presbyterian form of church government. For example, on the execution of the Archbishop of Saint Andrews, he caused Douglas, Rector of Saint Andrews, to be made archbishop in his place; but then he allowed this nominal prelate only a small pension out of the large revenues of the bishopric, and retained possession of all the rest of the

* See note to "Ivanhoe," *Waverley Novels*, vol. xvi. pp. 329-337.

income for his own advantage, though the rents were levied in the bishop's name.

These and other innovations gave great distress to John Knox, the bold and inflexible father of the Scottish Reformation. He saw with pain that the Protestant nobles were likely to diminish even the scanty subsistence which had hitherto been supplied to the Scottish clergy, out of the ample funds belonging originally to the Church of Rome. He was also jealous of the republican equality of the clergy, when he beheld the Church of Scotland innovated upon by this new introduction of bishops, though with limited incomes and diminished power. For these and other reasons he had more than once bitterly rebuked
24th Nov., 1672. the Regent Morton; but when this remarkable man died, the Regent, who attended his funeral, pronounced over his coffin an eulogium never to be forgotten. "There lies he," said Morton, "who never feared the face of man."

In the state as in the church, the Regent displayed symptoms of a vindictive, avaricious, and corrupt disposition. Although the civil wars were ended, he resolved to avenge upon the Hamiltons the continued support which that powerful family had given to the Queen's party, and the obstacles which they had thrown in the way of his own exaltation. He proceeded to act against them as public enemies, drove them out of Scotland, and seized upon their estates. The Earl of Arran, eldest brother of the family, to whom the estates actually belonged, was insane, and in a state of confinement; but this did not prevent Morton from declaring that the earldom and the lands belonging to it were forfeited, — an abuse of law which scandalized all honest men.

It was not only by confiscation that Morton endeavored

to amass wealth. He took money for the offices which he had it in his power to bestow. Even in administering justice his hands were not pure from bribes; although to dispense the behests of law from favor or love of gain, is one of the greatest crimes of which a public man can be guilty.

It is told of Earl Morton, in a history of the family of Somerville, that a nobleman of that house having a great and important cause to be decided, in which the influence of the Regent might assuredly occasion it to be determined as he himself should think fit, he followed, by the advice of an ancient and experienced acquaintance of the Regent the following singular course: Lord Somerville waited on the Earl of Morton, and recommended his case to his favorable opinion, — a kind of personal solicitation which was then much in use. Having spoken with the Regent for a short time, he turned to depart, and opening his purse, as if to take out some money to give to the ushers and attendants, as was the custom upon such occasions, he left the purse on the table as though he had forgot it. Morton called after him: — "My lord, your purse, — you have forgotten your purse!" — but Lord Somerville hastened away without turning back. He heard nothing more of the purse, which he had taken care should be pretty full of gold; but Lord Morton that day decided the cause in his favor.* 18th Dec., 1577.

Instances of such greedy profligacy by degrees alienated from Morton even the affection and inclination of his best friends,† and his government at length became

* Memorie of the Somervilles, vol. i. pp. 449 – 453.

† Godscroft, the partial historian of the house of Douglas, admits, "that many of Morton's public measures were rather pretexts for extorting money than for any other good use or end," and adds, "his attendants were not altogether void of envie, for their great wealth,

so unpopular, that a universal wish was entertained that the King would put an end to the Regency by assuming the government into his own hands.

These opinions prevailed so generally, that Morton, on the 12th March, 1578, resigned his office of Regent, and retired to reside in his castle of Dalkeith, as a private man, leaving the government to be administered by a council of nobles, twelve in number. But, accustomed to be at the head of the government, he could not long remain inactive. He burst from his seclusion in the gloomy fortress, which the people called the Lion's Den, and, using a mixture of craft and force, expelled the new counsellors; and once more, after the old Douglas fashion, obtained the supreme management of public affairs. But the sovereign was no longer a child. He was now beginning to think and act for himself; and it is necessary you should know something of his character.

James VI. was but an infant when he was placed on the throne of his mother. He was now only a boy of fourteen, very good-natured, and with as much learning as two excellent schoolmasters could cram him with. In fact, he had more learning than wisdom; and yet, in the course of his future life, it did not appear that he was without good sense so much, as that he was destitute of the power to form manly purposes, and the firmness necessary to maintain them. A certain childishness and meanness of mind rendered his good sense useless, and his learning ridiculous. Even from his infancy he was passionately addicted to favorites, and already, in his

nor of hatred, in regard of the way men thought they got it, which was by receiving and taking bribes from such as had suits to him, for obtaining accesse to him or his favour, by their means, and some such indirect wayes."—*History*, fol. 335.

thirteenth or fourteenth year, there were two persons so high in his good graces that they could bring him to do anything they pleased.

The first was Esme Stewart of Aubigny, a nephew of the late Earl of Lennox, and his heir. The King not only restored this young man to the honors of his family, but created him Duke of Lennox, and raised him with too prodigal generosity to a high situation in the state. There was nothing in the character of this favorite, either to deserve such extreme preferment, or to make him unworthy of it. He was a gallant young gentleman, who was deeply grateful to the King for his bounty, and appears to have been disposed to enjoy it without injuring any one.

Very different was the character of the other favorite of James VI. This was Captain James Stewart, a second son of the family of Ochiltree. He was an unprincipled, abandoned man, without any wisdom except cunning, and only distinguished by the audacity of his ambition, and the boldness of his character.

The counsels of these two favorites increased the King's natural desire to put an end to the sway of Morton, and Stewart resolved that the pretext for his removal should also be one which would bring him to the block. The grounds of accusation were artfully chosen. The Earl of Morton, when he resigned the regency, had obtained a pardon under the great seal for all crimes and offences which he had or might have committed against the King; but there was no mention, in that pardon, of the murder of Henry Darnley, the King's father; and in counselling, if not in committing that murder, the Earl of Morton had certainly participated. The favorite Stewart took the office of accuser upon himself; and entering the

King's chamber suddenly when the Privy Council were assembled, he dropped on his knees before James, and accused the Earl of Morton of having been concerned in the murder of the King's father. To this Morton, with a haughty smile, replied, that he had prosecuted the perpetrators of that offence too severely to make it probable that he himself was one of them. All he demanded was a fair inquiry.

Upon this public accusation, the Earl, so lately the most powerful man in Scotland, was made prisoner, and appointed to abide a trial. The friends he had left earnestly exhorted him to fly. His nephew, the Earl of Angus, offered to raise his men, and protect him by force. Morton refused both offers, alleging he would wait the event of a fair investigation. The Queen of England interfered in Morton's behalf with such partial eagerness, as perhaps prejudiced James still more against the prisoner, whom he was led to believe to be more attached to Elizabeth's service than to his own.

Meantime the accuser, Stewart, was promoted to the earldom of Arran, vacant by the forfeiture of the Hamiltons. Morton, who had no knowledge of this preferment, was astonished when he heard that the charge ran against him in the name of James, Earl of Arran. When it was explained to him who it was that now enjoyed the title, he observed, "Is it even so? then I know what I have to expect." It was supposed that he recollected an old prophecy, which foretold "that the Bloody Heart" (the cognizance of the Douglases) "should fall by the mouth of Arran;" and it was conjectured that the fear of some one of the Hamiltons accomplishing that prophecy had made him the more actively violent in destroying that family. If so, his own tyrannical oppression only opened the way for the creation of an Arran different from those whom he had thought of.

The trial of Morton appears to have been conducted with no attention to the rules of impartial justice; for the servants of the accused person were apprehended, and put to the torture, in order to extort from them confessions which might be fatal to their master. Morton protested against two or three persons who were placed upon his jury, as being his mortal enemies; but they were nevertheless retained. They brought in a verdict, finding that he was guilty, art and part, of the murder of Henry Darnley. A man is said to be art and part of a crime, when he contrives the manner of the deed, and concurs with and encourages those who commit the crime, although he does not put his own hand to the actual execution. Morton heard the verdict with indignation, and struck his staff against the ground as he repeated the words, "Art and part! art and part! God knoweth the contrary." On the morning after his sentence he awoke from a profound sleep: "On former nights," he said, "I used to lie awake, thinking how I might defend myself; but now my mind is relieved of its burden." Being conjured by the clergymen who attended him to confess all he knew of Henry Darnley's murder, he told them, as we have noticed elsewhere, that a proposal had been made to him by Bothwell to be accessory to the deed, but that he had refused to assent to it without an order under the Queen's hand, which Bothwell promised to procure, but could not, or at least did not, do so. Morton admitted that he had kept the secret, not knowing, he said, to whom to discover it. For if he had told it to Queen Mary, she was herself one of the conspirators; if to Darnley, he was of a disposition so fickle that the Queen would work it out of him, and then he, Morton, was equally undone. He also admitted that he knew that his friend, dependent, and kinsman, Archibald Douglas, was present at the murder, whom, notwithstanding, he never brought to justice, but, on the contrary, continued to favor. Upon the whole, he seems to allow that he suffered justly for concealing the crime, though he denied having given counsel or assistance to its actual execution. "But it is all the same," he said; "I should have had the same doom, whether I were as innocent as St. Stephen, or as guilty as Judas."

As they were about to lead the Earl to execution, Captain Stewart, his accuser, now Earl of Arran, came to urge his subscribing a paper containing the purport of his confession. Morton replied, "I pray you trouble me not; I am now to prepare for death, and cannot write in the state in which I am." Arran then desired to be reconciled to him, pretending he had only acted from public and conscientious motives. "It is no time to count quarrels now," said the Earl; "I forgive you and all others."

This celebrated man died by a machine called the *Maiden*, which he himself had introduced into Scotland 2d June, 1581. from Halifax, in Yorkshire. The criminal who suffered by this engine, was adjusted upon planks, in a prostrate state, his neck being placed beneath a sharp axe, heavily loaded with lead, which was suspended by a rope brought over a pulley. When the signal was given, the rope was cast loose, and the axe, descending on the neck of the condemned person, severed, of course, the head from the body. Morton submitted to his fate with the most Christian fortitude; and in him died the last of those terrible Douglases, whose talents and courage rendered them the pride of their country, but whose ambition was often its scourge. No one could tell what became of the treasures he had amassed, and for the sake of which he sacrificed his popularity as a liberal, and his conscience as an honest man. He was, or seemed to be, so poor, that, when going to the scaffold, he borrowed money from a friend, that he might bestow a parting alms upon the mendicants who solicited his charity. Some have thought that his mass of wealth lies still concealed among the secret vaults of his castle of Dalkeith, now belonging to the Duke of Buccleuch. But Hume of Godscroft, who writes the history of the Douglas family, says that large sums were expended by the Earl of Angus, the nephew of Morton, in maintaining a number of exiles, who, like the Earl himself, were banished from Scotland, and at length, when paying away some money for this purpose, he was heard to say, "The last of it is now gone, and I never looked that it should have done so much good." This Godscroft believed to allude to the final expenditure of the treasures of the Regent Morton.

After the death of Morton, his faults and crimes were in a great measure forgotten, when it was observed that Arran (that is, Captain Stewart) possessed all the late Regent's vices of corruption and oppression, without his wisdom or his talents. Lennox, the King's other favorite, was also unpopular, chiefly because he was unacceptable to the clergy, who, although he avowedly professed the Protestant religion, were jealous of his retaining an attachment to the Catholic faith. This suspicion arose from his having been educated in France. They publicly preached against him as "a great Champion, called his Grace, who, if he continued to oppose himself to religion, should have little grace in the end."

A plot was formed among the discontented nobles to remove the King's favorites from the court; and this was to be accomplished by forcibly seizing on the person of the King himself, which, during the minority of the Prince, was the ordinary mode of changing an administration in the kingdom of Scotland.

On the 23d August, 1582, the Earl of Gowrie invited the King to his castle at Ruthven, under pretext of hunting; he was joined by the Earl of Mar, Lord Lindsay, the Tutor of Glamis, and other noblemen, chiefly such as had been friendly to the Regent Morton, and who were, like him, attached to Queen Elizabeth's faction. When the King saw so many persons gather round him whom he knew to be of one way of thinking, and that hostile to his present measures, he became apprehensive of their intentions, and expressed himself desirous of leaving the castle.

The nobles gave him to understand that he would not be permitted to do so; and when James rose and went towards the door of the apartment, the Tutor of Glamis, a rude, stern man, placed his back against it, and compelled him to return. Affronted at this act of personal restraint and violence, the King burst into tears. "Let him weep on," said the Tutor of Glamis, fiercely; "better that bairns (children) weep, than bearded men." These words sank deep into the King's heart, nor did he ever forget or forgive them.

The insurgent lords took possession of the government, and banished the Duke of Lennox to France, where he died broken-hearted at the fall of his fortunes. James afterwards recalled his son to Scotland, and invested him with his father's fortunes and dignities. Arran, the King's much less worthy favorite, was thrown into prison, and closely guarded. The King himself, reduced to a state of captivity, like his grandfather, James V., when in the hands of the Douglases, temporized, and watched an opportunity of escape. His guards consisted of a hundred gentlemen, and their commander, Colonel Stewart, a relation of the disgraced and imprisoned Arran, was easily engaged to do what the King wished.

James, with the purpose of recovering his freedom, made a visit to Saint Andrews, and, when there, affected some curiosity to see the castle. But no sooner had he entered it than he caused the gates to be shut, and excluded from his presence the nobles who had been accessory to what was called the Raid of Ruthven. 25th June, 1583.

The Earl of Gowrie and his accomplices, being thus thrust out of office, and deprived of the custody of the King's person, united in a fresh plot for regaining the power they had lost, by a new insurrection. In this, however, they were unsuccessful. The King advanced against them with considerable forces; Gowrie was made prisoner, tried and executed at Stirling, 4th May, 1584.* Angus and the other insurgents fled to England, the ordinary refuge of Scottish exiles. The execution of Gowrie gave rise long afterwards to that extraordinary event in Scottish history, called the Gowrie Conspiracy, of which I shall give you an account by and by.

The upstart Earl of Arran was now restored to power,

* "Sentence was given that he should be taken to the market-cross, have his head cut off, and be dismembered as a traitor. The last part thereof was dispensed, and he in the evening beheaded. This was the end of that nobleman who, in his life, was much honored and employed in the chief offices of court; a man wise, but said to have been too curious, and to have consulted with wizards touching the state of things in future times." — "He was heard to make that common regret which many great men have done in such misfortunes, 'That if he had served God as faithfully as he had done the King, he had not come to that end.'" — SPOTSWOOD, pp. 332, 333.

and indeed raised higher than ever, by that indiscriminate affection which on this and other occasions induced James to heap wealth and rank without bounds upon his favorites. This worthless minister governed everything at court and throughout the kingdom; and, though ignorant as well as venal and profligate, he was raised to the dignity of Lord Chancellor, the highest law-office in the state, and that in which sagacity, learning, and integrity were chiefly required.

One day when the favorite was bustling into the Court of Justice, at the head of his numerous retinue, an old man, rather meanly dressed, chanced to stand in his way. As Arran pushed rudely past him, the man stopped him, and said, "Look at me, my lord, — I am Oliver Sinclair!" Oliver Sinclair, you remember, was the favorite of James V., and had exercised during his reign as absolute a sway in Scotland as Arran now enjoyed under his grandson, James VI. In presenting himself before the present favorite in his neglected condition, he gave Arran an example of the changeful character of court favor. The lesson was a striking one; but Arran did not profit by it.

The favorite's government became so utterly intolerable,* that, in the year 1585, the banished lords found a welcome reception in Scotland, and marching to Stirling at the head of ten thousand men, compelled James to

* "The public," says Dr. Robertson, "beheld with astonishment and indignation, a man educated as a soldier of fortune, ignorant of law, and a contemner of justice, appointed to preside in Parliament, in the Privy Council, in the Court of Session, and intrusted with the supreme disposal of the property of his fellow-subjects. He was, at the same time, governor of the castles of Stirling and Edinburgh, the two principal forts in Scotland; Provost of the city of Edinburgh; and, as if by all these accumulated dignities his merits were not sufficiently recompensed, he had been created Lieutenant-General over the whole kingdom. His venality as a judge was scandalous — his rapa-

receive them into his counsels; and, by using their victory with moderation, were enabled to maintain the power which they had thus gained. Arran, stripped of his earldom and ill-gotten gains, and banished from the court, was fain to live privately and miserably among the wilds of the northwest of Ayrshire, afraid of the vengeance of his numerous enemies.

The fate which he apprehended from their enmity befell him at length; for, in 1596, seeing, or thinking he saw, some chance of regaining the King's favor, and listening, as he said, to the words of some idle soothsayer, who pretended that his head was about to be raised higher than ever, Stewart (for he was an earl no longer) ventured into the southern county of Dumfries. Here he received a hint to take care of his safety, since he was now in the neighborhood of the Douglases, whose great leader, the Earl of Morton, he had been the means of destroying; and in particular, he was advised to beware of James Douglas of Torthorwald, the Earl's near kinsman [nephew]. Stewart replied haughtily, he would not go out of his road for him, or all of the name of Douglas. This was reported to Torthorwald, who, considering the expression as a defiance, immediately mounted, with three servants, and pursued the disgraced favorite. When they overtook him, they thrust a spear through his body, and killed him* on the spot, without resistance. His head

ciousness as a minister was insatiable — his spies and informers filled the whole country. The nearest neighbors distrusted and feared each other. All familiar society was at an end. There is not perhaps in history an example of a minister so universally detestable to a nation, or who more justly deserved its detestation." — *History*, chap. vii.

* "Sir James Douglas was killed on the High Street of Edinburgh, 1608, by Captain William Stewart, a nephew of the Chancellor, who run him through the body to revenge his uncle's death." — WOOD, vol. i. p. 123.

was cut off, placed on the point of a lance, and exposed from the battlements of the tower of Torthorwald; and thus, in some sense, the soothsayer's prophecy was made good, as his head was raised higher than before, though not in the way he had been made to hope. His body was left for several days on the place where he was killed, and was mangled by dogs and swine. So ended this worthless minion, by a death at once bloody and obscure.

CHAPTER XXXIII.

SEVERITIES TO WHICH MARY WAS SUBJECTED IN HER CAPTIVITY — BABINGTON'S CONSPIRACY — TRIAL OF MARY — HER SENTENCE AND EXECUTION — REIGN OF JAMES VI. — FEUDS OF THE NOBLES, AND BLOODTHIRSTY SPIRIT OF THE TIMES — THE RESCUE OF KINMONT WILLIE FROM CARLISLE CASTLE BY BUCCLEUCH — THE GOWRIE CONSPIRACY — JAMES'S ACCESSION TO THE THRONE OF ENGLAND.

[1586 — 1603.]

I DARE say you are wondering all this time what became of Queen Mary. We left her, you know, in the hands of Queen Elizabeth, who had refused to decide anything on the question of her guilt or innocence. This was in 1568 – 9, and undoubtedly, by every rule of law or justice, Mary ought then to have been set at liberty. She had been accused of matters which Elizabeth herself had admitted were not brought home to her by proof, and of which, even if they had been proved, the Queen of England had no right to take cognizance. Nevertheless, Elizabeth continued to treat Mary as guilty, though she declined to pronounce her so, and to use her as her subject, though she was an independent sovereign, who had chosen England for a retreat, in the hope of experiencing that hospitable protection which would have been given to the meanest Scottish subject, who, flying from the laws of his own country, sought refuge in the sister kingdom. When you read English history, you will see that Elizabeth was a great and glorious Queen, and well deserved the title of the Mother of her Country; but her conduct towards Queen Mary casts a deep shade over her virtues, and leads us to reflect what poor frail creatures even the wisest of mortals are, and of what imperfect materials that which we call human virtue is found to consist.

Always demanding her liberty, and always having her demand evaded or refused, Mary was transported from castle to castle,* and placed under the charge of various keepers, who incurred Elizabeth's most severe resentment, when they manifested any of that attention to soften the rigors of the poor Queen's captivity, which mere courtesy and compassion for fallen greatness sometimes prompted. The very furniture and accommodations of her apartments were miserably neglected, and the expenses of her household were supplied as grudgingly as if she had been an unwelcome guest, who could depart at pleasure, and whom, therefore, the entertainer endeavors to get rid of by the coldness and discomfort of the reception afforded. It was, upon one occasion, with difficulty that the Queen Dowager of France, and actual Queen of Scotland, obtained the accommodation of a down bed, which a complaint in her limbs, the consequence of damp and confinement, rendered a matter of needful accommodation rather than of luxury. When she was permitted to take exercise, she was always strongly guarded, as if

* On her own soliciting, towards recovery of health, Mary was allowed visits to Buxton; but all the while a prisoner; the waters there were of little avail, when air, exercise, and amusement were denied. Her forced removals were, in 1568, from Carlisle to Bolton, — 1569, to Tutbury, Wingfield, Tutbury, Ashby-de-la-Zouche, Coventry, — 1570, to Tutbury, Chatsworth, Sheffield, — 1577, to Chatsworth, — 1578, to Sheffield, — 1584, to Wingfield, — 1585, to Tutbury, Chartley, Tixhall, Chartley, — 1586 (25th September) to Fotheringay.

she had been a criminal; and if any one offered her a compliment, or token of respect, or any word of comfort, Queen Elizabeth, who had her spies everywhere, was sure to reproach those who were Mary's guardians for the time, with great neglect of their duty, in permitting such intercourse.

During this severe captivity on the one part, and the greatest anxiety, doubt, and jealousy, on the other, the two Queens still kept up a sort of correspondence. In the commencement of this intercourse, Mary endeavored, by the force of argument, by the seductions of flattery, and by appeals to the feelings of humanity, to soften towards her the heart of Elizabeth. She tried also to bribe her rival into a more humane conduct towards her, by offering to surrender her crown and reside abroad, if she could but be restored to her personal freedom. But Elizabeth had injured the Queen of Scotland too deeply to venture the consequences of her resentment, and thought herself, perhaps, compelled to continue the course she had commenced, from the fear that, once at liberty, Mary might have pursued measures of revenge, and that she herself would find it impossible to devise any mode of binding the Scottish Queen to perform, when at large, such articles as she might consent to when in bondage.

Despairing at length of making any favorable impression upon Elizabeth, Mary, with more wit than prudence, used her means of communicating with the Queen of England, to irritate and provoke her; yielding to the not unnatural, though certainly the rash and impolitic purpose of retaliating some part of the pain to which she was herself subjected, upon the person whom she justly considered as the authoress of her calamities.

Being for a long time under the charge of the Earl of

Shrewsbury, whose lady was a woman of a shrewish disposition, Mary used to report to Elizabeth, that the Countess had called her old and ugly; had said she was grown as crooked in her temper as in her body, with many other scandalous and abusive expressions, which must have given exquisite pain to any woman, and more especially to a Queen so proud as Elizabeth, and desirous, even in old age, of being still esteemed beautiful. Unquestionably, these reproaches added poignancy to the hatred with which the English sovereign regarded Queen Mary.

But, besides these female reasons for detesting her prisoner, Elizabeth had cause to regard the Queen of Scots with fear, as well as envy and hatred. The Catholic party in England were still very strong, and they considered the claim of Mary to the throne of England, as descended from the Princess Margaret, daughter of Henry VII., to be preferable to that of the existing Queen, who was, in their judgment, illegitimate, as being the heir of an illegal marriage betwixt Henry VIII. and Anne Bullen. The Popes also, by whom Elizabeth was justly regarded as the great prop of the Reformed religion, endeavored to excite against her such of her subjects as still owned obedience to the See of Rome. At length, in 1570–71, Pius V., then the reigning Pope, published a bull, or sentence of excommunication, by which he deprived Queen Elizabeth (as far as his sentence could) of her hopes of heaven, and of her kingdom upon earth, excluded her from the privileges of Christians, and delivered her over as a criminal to whomsoever should step forth to vindicate the Church, by putting to death its greatest enemy. The zeal of the English Catholics was kindled by this warrant from the Head of their Church. One of them [named Felton] was found bold enough to fix a copy of the sentence of excommunication upon the door of the Bishop of London, and various plots were entered into among the Papists for dethroning Elizabeth, and transferring the kingdom of England to Mary, a sovereign of their own religion, and in their eyes the lawful successor to the crown.

As fast as one of these conspiracies was dicovered, another seemed to form itself; and as the Catholics were promised powerful assistance from the King of Spain, and were urged forward by the impulse of enthusiasm, the danger appeared every day more and more imminent. It cannot be doubted that several of these plots were communicated to Mary in her imprisonment; and, considering what grounds she had to complain of Elizabeth, it would have been wonderful if she had betrayed to her jailer the schemes which were formed to set her at liberty. But these conspiracies coming so closely the one after the other, produced one of the most extraordinary laws that was ever passed in England; declaring, that if any rebellion, or any attempt against Queen Elizabeth's person, should be meditated by, or for, any person pretending a right to the crown, the Queen might grant a commission to twenty-five persons, who should have power to examine into, and pass sentence upon such offences; and, after judgment given, a proclamation was to be issued, depriving the persons in whose behalf the plots or rebellion had been made, of all right to the throne; and it was enacted that they might be prosecuted to the death. The hardship of this enactment consisted in its rendering Mary, against whom it was levelled, responsible for the deeds of others, as well as for her own actions; so that if the Catholics arose in rebellion, although without warrant from Mary, or even against her inclination, she was nevertheless rendered liable to lose her right of succession to the crown, and, indeed, to forfeit her life. Nothing short of the zeal of the English Government for the Reformed religion, and for the personal safety of Elizabeth, could have induced them to consent to a law so unjust and so oppressive.

This act was passed in 1585, and in the following year, a pretext was found for making it the ground of proceedings against Mary. Anthony Babington, a young gentleman of fortune and of talents, but a zealous Catholic, and a fanatical enthusiast for the cause of the Scottish Queen, had associated with himself five resolute friends and adherents, all men of condition, in the desperate enterprise of assassinating Queen Elizabeth, and setting Mary at liberty. But their schemes were secretly betrayed to Walsingham, the celebrated Minister of the Queen of England. They were suffered to proceed as far as was thought safe, then seized, tried, and executed.

It was next resolved upon, that Mary should be brought to trial for her life, under pretence of her having encouraged Babington and his companions in their desperate
25th Sept., 1586. purpose. She was removed to the castle of Fotheringay, and placed under two keepers, Sir Amias Paulet and Sir Drew Drury, whose well-known hatred of the Catholic religion was supposed to render them inclined to treat their unfortunate captive with the utmost rigor. Her private cabinet was broken open and stripped of its contents, her most secret papers were seized upon and examined, her principal domestics were removed from her person, her money and her jewels were taken from her. Queen Elizabeth then proceeded to name commissioners, in terms of the Act of Parliament which I have told you of. They were forty in number, of the most distinguished

of her statesmen and nobility, and were directed to proceed to the trial of Mary for her alleged accession to Babington's conspiracy.

On the 14th October, 1586, these commissioners held their court in the great hall of Fotheringay Castle. Mary, left to herself, and having counsel of no friend, advocate, or lawyer, made, nevertheless, a defence becoming her high birth and distinguished talents. She refused to plead before a court composed of persons who were of a degree inferior to her own; and when at length she agreed to hear and answer the accusation brought against her, she made her protest that she did so, not as owning the authority of the court, but purely in vindication of her own character.

The attorney and solicitor for Queen Elizabeth stated the conspiracy of Babington, as it unquestionably existed, and produced copies of letters which Mary was alleged to have written, approving the insurrection, and even the assassination of Elizabeth. The declarations of Naue and Curle, two of Mary's secretaries, went to confirm the fact of her having had correspondence with Babington, by intervention of a priest called Ballard. The confessions of Babington and his associates were then read, avowing Mary's share in their criminal undertaking.

To these charges Mary answered, by denying that she ever had any correspondence with Ballard, or that she had ever written such letters as those produced against her. She insisted that she could only be affected by such writings as bore her own hand and seal, and not by copies. She urged that the declarations of her secretaries were given in private, and probably under the influence of fear of torture, or hope of reward, of which, indeed, there is every probability.* Lastly, she pleaded that the confessions of the conspirators could not affect her, since they were infamous persons, dying for an infamous crime. If their evidence was designed to be used, they ought to have been pardoned, and brought forward in person, to bear witness against her. Mary admitted that, having for many years despaired of relief or favor from Queen Elizabeth, she had, in her distress, applied to other sovereigns, and that she had also endeavored to procure some favor for the persecuted Catholics of England; but she denied that she had endeavored to purchase liberty for herself, or advantage for the Catholics, at the expense of shedding the blood of any one; and declared, that if she had given consent in word, or even in thought, to the murder of Elizabeth, she was willing, not only to submit to the doom of men, but even to renounce the mercy of God.

The evidence which was brought to convict the Queen of Scotland was such as would not now affect the life of the meanest criminal; yet the Commission had the cruelty and meanness to declare Mary guilty of having been accessory to Babington's conspiracy, and of having contrived and endeavored the death of Queen Elizabeth, contrary to the statute made for security of the Queen's life. And the Parliament of England approved of and ratified this iniquitous sentence.

It was not perhaps to be expected that James VI. should have had much natural affection for his mother,

* "Whether these secretaries were bribed to confess this," saith Camden, "I cannot say: but it is certain," he adds, "that Walsingham had made them promises; and their credit was impeached by the Scottish Queen, as they had taken a previous oath of fidelity to her." — CHALMERS, vol. i. p. 429.

whom he had never seen since his infancy, and who had, doubtless, been represented to him as a very bad woman, and as one desirous, if she could have obtained her liberty, of dispossessing him of the crown which he wore, and resuming it herself. He had, therefore, seen Mary's captivity with little of the sympathy which a child ought to feel for a parent. But, upon learning these proceedings against her life, he must have been destitute of the most ordinary feelings of human nature, and would have made himself a reproach and scandal throughout all Europe, if he had not interfered in her behalf. He therefore sent ambassadors — first, Sir William Keith, and after him the Master of Gray — to intercede with Queen Elizabeth, and to use both persuasion and threats to preserve the life of his mother. The friendship of Scotland was at this moment of much greater importance to England than at any previous period of her history. The King of Spain was in the act of assembling a vast navy and army (boastingly called the Invincible Armada), by which he proposed to invade and conquer England; and if James VI. had been disposed to open the ports and harbors of Scotland to the Spanish fleets and armies, he might have greatly facilitated this formidable invasion, by diminishing the risk which the Armada might incur from the English fleet.

It therefore seems probable, that had James himself been very serious in his interposition, or had his ambassador been disposed to urge the interference committed to his charge with due firmness and vigor, it could scarce have failed in being successful, at least for a time. But the Master of Gray, as is now admitted, privately encouraged Elizabeth and her ministers to proceed in the cruel path they had chosen, and treacherously gave them reason to believe, that though, for the sake of decency, James found it necessary to interfere in his mother's behalf, yet, in his secret mind, he would not be very sorry that Mary, who, in the eyes of a part of his subjects, was still regarded as sovereign of Scotland, should be quietly removed out of the way. From the intrigues of this treacherous ambassador, Elizabeth was led to trust that the resentment of the King for his mother's death would neither be long nor violent; and, knowing her own influence with a great part of the Scottish nobility, and the zeal of the Scots in general for the Reformed religion, she concluded that the motives arising out of these circumstances would prevent James from making common cause against England with the King of Spain.

At any other period in the English history, it is probable that a sovereign attempting such an action as Elizabeth meditated, might have been interrupted by the generous and manly sense of justice and humanity peculiar to a free and high-minded people like those of England. But the despotic reign of Henry VIII. had too much familiarized the English with the sight of the blood of great persons, and even of Queens, poured forth by the blow of the executioner, upon the slightest pretexts; and the idea that Elizabeth's life could not be in safety while Mary existed, was, in the deep sentiment of loyalty and affection which they entertained for their Queen (and which the general tenor of her reign well deserved), strong enough to render them blind to the gross injustice exercised upon a stranger and a Catholic.

Yet, with all the prejudices of her subjects in her own favor, Elizabeth would fain have had Mary's death take place in such a way as that she herself should not appear to have any hand in it. Her ministers were employed to write letters to Mary's keepers, insinuating what a good service they would do to Elizabeth and the Protestant religion, if Mary could be privately assassinated. But these stern guardians, though strict and severe in their conduct towards the Queen, would not listen to such persuasions; and well was it for them that they did not, for Elizabeth would certainly have thrown the whole blame of the deed upon their shoulders, and left them to answer it with their lives and fortunes. She was angry with them, nevertheless, for their refusal, and called Paulet a precise fellow, loud in boasting of his fidelity, but slack in giving proof of it.

As, however, it was necessary, from the scruples of Paulet and Drury, to proceed in all form, Elizabeth signed a warrant for the execution of the sentence pronounced on Queen Mary, and gave it to Davison, her secretary of state, commanding that it should be sealed with the great seal of England. Davison laid the warrant, signed by Elizabeth, before the Privy Council, and next day the great seal was placed upon it. Elizabeth, upon hearing this, affected some displeasure that the warrant had been so speedily prepared, and told the secretary that it was the opinion of wise men that some other course might be taken with Queen Mary. Davison, in this pretended change of mind, saw some danger that his mistress might throw the fault of the execution upon him after it had taken place. He therefore informed the Keeper of the Seals what the Queen had said, protesting he would not venture further in the matter. The Privy Council, having met together, and conceiving themselves certain what were the Queen's real wishes, determined to save her the pain of expressing them more broadly, and resolving that the blame, if any might arise, should be common to them all, sent off the warrant for execution with their clerk,

Beale. The Earls of Kent and Shrewsbury, with the High Sheriff of the county, were empowered and commanded to see the fatal mandate carried into effect without delay.

Mary received the melancholy intelligence with the utmost firmness. "The soul," she said, "was undeserving of the joys of heaven, which would shrink from the blow of an executioner. She had not," she added, "expected that her kinswoman would have consented to her death, but submitted not the less willingly to her fate." She earnestly requested the assistance of a priest; but this favor, which is granted to the worst criminals, and upon which Catholics lay particular weight, was cruelly refused. The Queen then wrote her last will, and short and affectionate letters of farewell to her relations in France. She distributed among her attendants such valuables as had been left her, and desired them to keep them for her sake. This occupied the evening before the day appointed for the fatal execution.

On the 8th February, 1587, the Queen, still maintaining the same calm and undisturbed appearance which she had displayed at her pretended trial, was brought down to the great hall of the castle, where a scaffold was erected, on which were placed a block and a chair, the whole being covered with black cloth. The Master of her Household, Sir Andrew Melville, was permitted to take a last leave of the mistress whom he had served long and faithfully. He burst into loud lamentations, bewailing her fate, and deploring his own in being destined to carry such news to Scotland. "Weep not, my good Melville," said the Queen, "but rather rejoice; for thou shalt this day see Mary Stewart relieved from all her sorrows." She obtained permission, with some difficulty, that her maids should be allowed to attend her on the scaffold. It was objected to, that the extravagance of their grief might disturb the proceedings; she engaged for them that they would be silent.

When the Queen was seated in the fatal chair, she heard the death-warrant read by Beale, the clerk to the Privy Council, with an appearance of indifference; nor did she seem more attentive to the devotional exercises of the Dean of Peterborough, in which, as a Catholic, she could not conscientiously join. She implored the mercy of Heaven, after the form prescribed by her own Church. She then prepared herself for execution, taking off such parts of her dress as might interfere with the deadly blow. The executioners offered their assistance, but she modestly refused it, saying, she had neither been accustomed to undress before so many spectators, nor to be served by such grooms of the chamber. She quietly chid her maids, who were unable to withhold their cries of lamentation, and reminded them that she had engaged for their silence. Last of all, Mary laid her head on the block, which the executioner severed from her body with two strokes of his axe. The headsman held it up in his hand, and the Dean of Peterborough cried out, "So perish all Queen Elizabeth's enemies!" No voice, save that of the Earl of Kent, could answer *Amen:* the rest were choked with sobs and tears.

Thus died Queen Mary, aged a little above forty-four years. She was eminent for beauty, for talents, and accomplishments, nor is there reason to doubt her natural goodness of heart, and courageous manliness of disposition. Yet she was, in every sense, one of the most unhappy princesses that ever lived, from the moment when she came into the world, in an hour of defeat and danger, to that in which a bloody and violent death closed a weary captivity of eighteen years.

Queen Elizabeth, in the same spirit of hypocrisy which had characterized all her proceedings towards Mary, no sooner knew that the deed was done, than she hastened to deny her own share in it. She pretended that Davison had acted positively against her command in laying the warrant before the Privy Council; and that she might seem the more serious in her charge, she caused him to be fined in a large sum of money, and deprived him of his offices; and of her favor forever. She sent a special ambassador to King James, to apologize for "this unhappy accident," as she chose to term the execution of Queen Mary.

James at first testified high indignation, with which the Scottish nation was well disposed to sympathize. He refused to admit the English envoy to his presence, and uttered menaces of revenge. When a general mourning was ordered for the departed Queen, the Earl of Argyle appeared at the court in armor, as if that were the proper way of showing the national sense of the treatment which Mary had received. But James's hopes and fears were now fixed upon the succession to the English crown, which would have been forfeited by engaging in a war with Elizabeth. Most of his ancestors, indeed, would have set that objection at defiance, and have broken into the English frontier at the head of as large an army as Scotland could raise; but James was by nature timorous and unwarlike. He was conscious that the poor and divided country of Scotland was not fit, in its own strength, to encounter a kingdom so wealthy and so unanimous as England. On the other hand, if James formed an alliance with the Spanish monarch, he considered that he would probably have been deserted by the Reformed part of his subjects; and, besides, he was aware that Philip of Spain himself laid claim to the Crown of England; so that to assist that prince in his meditated invasion, would have been to rear up an important obstacle to the accomplishment of his own hopes of the English succession. James, therefore, gradually softening towards Queen Elizabeth, affected to believe the excuses which she offered; and in a short time they were upon as friendly a footing as they had been before the death of the unfortunate Mary.

James was now in full possession of the Scottish kingdom, and showed himself to as much, or greater advantage, than at any subsequent period of his life. After the removal of the vile James Stewart from his counsels, he acted chiefly by the advice of Sir John Maitland, the Chancellor, a brother of that Maitland of Lethington whom we have so often mentioned. He was a prudent and good minister; and as it was James's nature, in which there was a strange mixture of wisdom and of weakness, to act with sagacity, or otherwise, according to the counsels which he received, there now arose in Britain, and even in Europe, a more general respect for his character than was afterwards entertained when it became better known.

Besides, James's reign in Scotland was marked with so many circumstances of difficulty, and even of danger, that he was placed upon his guard, and compelled to conduct himself with the strictest attention to the rules of prudence; for he had little chance of overawing his turbulent nobility, but by maintaining the dignity of the royal character. If the King had possessed the ability of distributing largesses among his powerful subjects, his influence would have been greater; but this was so far from being the case, that his means of supporting his royal state, excepting an annuity allowed to him by Elizabeth of five thousand pounds yearly, were in the last degree precarious. This was owing in a great measure to the plundering of the revenue of the crown during the civil wars of his minority and the Regency of the Earl of Morton. The King was so dependent, that he could not even give an entertainment without begging poultry and venison from some of his more wealthy subjects; and his wardrobe was so ill furnished, that he was obliged to request the loan of a pair of silk hose from the Earl of Mar, that he might be suitably apparelled to receive the Spanish ambassador.

There were also peculiarities in James's situation which rendered it embarrassing. He had extreme difficulty in his necessary intercourse with the Scottish clergy, who possessed a strong influence over the minds of the people, and sometimes used it in interference with public affairs. Although they had not, like the bishops of England and other countries, a seat in Parliament, yet they did not the less intermeddle with politics, and often preached from the pulpit against the King and his measures. They used this freedom the more boldly, because they asserted that they were not answerable to any civil court for what they might say in their sermons, but only to the spiritual courts, as they were called; that is, the Synods and General Assemblies of the Church, composed chiefly of clergymen like themselves, and who, therefore, were not likely to put a check upon the freedom of speech used by their brethren.

Upon one occasion, which occurred 17th December, 1596, disputes of this kind between the King and the Church came to such a height that the rabble of the city, inflamed by the violence of some of the sermons which they heard, broke out into tumult, and besieged the door of the Tolbooth, where James was sitting in the administration of justice, and threatened to break it open. The King was saved by the intervention of the better disposed part of the inhabitants, who rose in arms for his protection. Nevertheless he left Edinburgh the next day in great anger, and prepared to take away the privileges of the city, as a punishment for the insolence of the rioters. He was appeased with much difficulty, and, as it seemed, was by no means entirely satisfied; for he caused the High Street to be occupied by a great number of the Border and Highland clans. The citizens, terrified by the appearance of these formidable and lawless men, concluded that the town was to be plundered, and the alarm was very great. But the King, who only desired to frighten them, made the magistrates a long harangue upon the excesses of which he complained, and admitted them to pardon, upon their submission.

Another great plague of James the Sixth's reign was the repeated insurrections of a turbulent nobleman, called Francis Stewart, Earl of Bothwell, — a different person, of course, from James Hepburn, who bore that title in the reign of Queen Mary. This second Earl of Bothwell was a relation of the King's, and made several violent attempts to get possession of his person, with the purpose of governing the state, as the Douglases did of old, by keeping the King prisoner. But although he nearly succeeded on one or two occasions, yet James was always rescued from his hands, and was finally powerful enough to banish Bothwell altogether from the country. He died in contempt end exile.*

* The Earl of Bothwell was attainted in Parliament, 12th July,

But by far the greatest pest of Scotland at that time, was the deadly feuds among the nobility and gentry, which eventually led to the most bloody consequences, and were perpetuated from father to son; while the King's good-nature, which rendered him very ready to grant pardons to those who had committed such inhuman outrages, made the evil still more frequent. The following is a remarkable instance: —

The Earl of Huntly, head of the powerful family of Gordon, and the man of greatest consequence in the North of Scotland, had chanced to have some feudal differences with the Earl of Murray, son-in-law of the Regent-earl of the same name, in the course of which, John Gordon, a brother of Gordon of Cluny, was killed by a shot from Murray's castle of Darnaway. This was enough to make the two families irreconcilable enemies, even if they had been otherwise on friendly terms. Murray was so handsome and personable a man, that he was generally known by the name of the Bonnie Earl of Murray. About 1591 – 2, an accusation was brought against Murray, for having given some countenance or assistance to Stewart, Earl of Bothwell, in a recent treasonable exploit. James, without recollecting, perhaps, the hostility between the two earls, sent Huntly with a commission to bring the Earl

1592. "He betook himself to his usual lurking-places in the north of England, but Elizabeth, in compliance with James's remonstrances, obliged him to quit his retreat. Abandoned by the Queen of England, excommunicated by the Church, and deserted in his distress by his followers, he was obliged to fly for safety to France, and thence to Spain and Italy where, after renouncing the Protestant faith, he lived many years an obscure and indigent life, remarkable only for a low and infamous debauchery." — WOOD'S *Peerage*, vol. i. pp. 232, 233. In 1594 several persons were executed for receiving and entertaining the Earl of Bothwell. — BIRRELL'S *Diary*, pp. 33, 34.

of Murray to his presence. Huntly probably rejoiced in the errand, as giving him an opportunity of avenging himself on his feudal enemy. He beset the house of Dunnibirsel, on the northern side of the Forth, and summoned Murray to surrender. In reply, a gun was fired, which mortally wounded one of the Gordons. The assailants proceeded to set fire to the house; when Dunbar, Sheriff of the county of Moray, said to the Earl, "Let us not stay to be burned in the flaming house; I will go out foremost, and the Gordons, taking me for you lordship, will kill me, while you escape in the confusion." They rushed out among their enemies accordingly, and Dunbar was slain. But his death did not save his friend, as he had generously intended. Murray indeed escaped for the moment, but as he fled towards the rocks by the sea-shore, he was traced by the silken tassels attached to his headpiece, which had taken fire as he broke out from among the flames. By this means the pursuers followed him down amongst the cliffs near the sea, and Gordon of Buckie, who is said to have been the first that overtook him, wounded him mortally. As Murray was gasping in the last agony, Huntly came up; and it is alleged by tradition, that Gordon pointed his dirk against the person of his chief, saying, "By Heaven, my lord, you shall be as deep in as I," and so compelled him to wound Murray whilst he was dying. Huntly, with a wavering hand, struck the expiring Earl on the face. Thinking of his superior beauty, even in that moment of parting life, Murray stammered out the dying words, "You have spoiled a better face than your own."

After this deed of violence, Huntly did not choose to return to Edinburgh, but departed for the North. He took refuge for the moment in the castle of Ravenscraig, belonging to the Lord Sinclair, who told him, with a mixture of Scottish caution and Scottish hospitality, that he was welcome to come in, but would have been twice as welcome to have passed by. Gordon of Buckie, when a long period had elapsed, avowed his contrition for the guilt he had. incurred.

Soon afterwards, three lords, the Earls of Huntly and Errol, who had always professed the Catholic religion, and the young Earl of Angus, who had become a convert to that faith, were accused of corresponding with the King of Spain, and of designing to introduce Spanish troops into Scotland for the restoration of the Catholic religion. The story which was told of this conspiracy does not seem very probable. However, the King ordered the Earl of Argyle to march against the Popish lords, with the northern forces of Lord Forbes and others, who were chiefly Protestants, and entered into the war with the religious emulation which divided the Reformers from the Catholics. Argyle likewise levied great bands of the Western Highlanders, who cared but little about religion, but were extremely desirous of plunder.

The army of Argyle, about ten thousand strong, encountered the forces of Huntly and Errol at Glenlivat, on the 3d of October, 1594. The shock was very smart. But the Gordons and Hays, though far inferior in numbers, were gentlemen, well mounted, and completely armed, and the followers of Argyle had only their plaids and bonnets. Besides, the two earls had two or three pieces of cannon, of which the Highlanders, unaccustomed to anything of the kind, were very apprehensive. The consequence of the encounter was, that though the cavalry had to charge up a hill, encumbered with rocks and stones, and although the Highlanders fought with great courage, the small body of Huntly and Errol, not amounting to above fifteen hundred horse, broke, and dispersed with great loss, the numerous host opposed to them. On the side of Argyle there was some treachery; the Grants, it is said, near neighbors, and some of them dependents of the Gordons, joined their old friends in the midst of the fray. The Chief of MacLean and his followers defended themselves with great courage, but were at length completely routed. This was one of the occasions on which the Highland irregular infantry were found inferior to the compact charge of the cavaliers of the Lowland counties, with their long lances, who beat them down, and scattered them in every direction.

Upon learning Argyle's defeat, the King himself advanced into the north with a small army, and restored tranquillity by punishing the insurgent earls.

We have before mentioned, that in those wild days the very children had their deadly feuds, carried weapons, and followed the bloody example of their fathers. The following instance of their early ferocity occurred in September, 1595. The scholars of the High School of Edinburgh, having a dispute with their masters about the length of their holidays, resolved to stand out for a longer vacation. Accordingly, they took possession of the school, in that sort of mutinous manner which in England is called *Barring-out*, and resisted the admission of the masters. Such foolish things have often occurred in public schools elsewhere; but what was peculiar to the High-School boys of Edinburgh was, that they defended the school with sword and pistol, and when Bailie MacMoran, one of the magistrates, gave directions to force the entrance, three of the boys fired, and killed him on the spot. There were none of them punished, because it was alleged that it could not be known which of them did the deed; but rather because two of them were gentlemen's sons. So you see the bloodthirsty spirit of the times descended even to children.

To do justice to James VI., he adopted every measure in his power to put an end to these fatal scenes of strife and bloodshed. Wise laws were made for preventing the outrages which had been so general; and in order to com-
13th May, 1586. pose the feuds amongst the nobles, James invited the principal lords who had quarrels to a great banquet, where he endeavored to make them agree together, and caused them to take each other's hands and become friends on the spot. They obeyed him; and proceeding himself at their head, he made them walk in procession to the Cross of Edinburgh,* still hand in hand, in token of perfect reconciliation, whilst the provost and magistrates danced before them for joy, to see such a prospect of peace and concord. Perhaps this reconciliation was too hasty to last long in every instance; but upon the whole, the authority of the law gradually gained strength, and the passions of men grew less fierce as it became more unsafe to indulge them.

I must now fulfil my promise, and in this place, tell you
April, 1596. of another exploit on the Borders, the last that was performed there, but certainly not the least remarkable for valor and conduct.

The English and Scottish Wardens, or their deputies, had held a day of truce for settling Border disputes, and, having parted friends, both, with their followers, were re-

* "A collation of wine and sweetmeats was prepared at the public Cross, and there they, King and nobles, drank to each other with all the signs of reciprocal forgiveness and of future friendship." — ROBERTSON, chap. vii.

turning home. At every such meeting it was the general rule on the Borders that there should be an absolute truce for twenty-four hours, and that all men who attended the Warden on either side to the field should have permission to ride home again undisturbed.

Now there had come to the meeting, with other Border men, a notorious depredator, called William Armstrong, but more commonly known by the name of Kinmont Willie. This man was riding home on the north or Scottish side of the Liddell, where that stream divides England and Scotland, when some of the English, who had enmity against him, or had suffered by his incursions, were unable to resist the temptation to attack him. They accordingly dashed across the river, pursued Kinmont Willie more than a mile within Scotland, made him prisoner, and brought him to Carlisle Castle.

As the man talked boldly and resolutely about the breach of truce in his person, and demanded peremptorily to be set at liberty, Lord Scrope told him, scoffingly, that before he left the castle he should bid him "farewell," meaning, that he should not go without his leave. The prisoner boldly answered, "that he would not go without bidding him good-night."

The Lord of Buccleuch, who was Warden, or Keeper, of Liddesdale, demanded the restoration of Kinmont Willie to liberty, and complained of his being taken and imprisoned as a breach of the Border laws, and an insult done to himself. Lord Scrope refused, or at least, evaded giving up his prisoner. Buccleuch then sent him a challenge, which Lord Scrope declined to accept, on the ground of his employment in the public service. The Scottish chief, therefore, resolved to redress by force the insult which his country, as well as himself, had sustained on the occasion. He collected about three hundred of his best men, and made a night march to Carlisle Castle. A small party of chosen men dismounted, while the rest remained on horseback to repel any attack from the town. The night being misty and rainy, the party to whom that duty was committed approached the foot of the walls, and tried to scale them by means of ladders which they had brought with them for the purpose. But the ladders were found too short. They then, with mining instruments which they had provided, burst open a postern, or wicket door, and entered the castle. Their chief had given them strict orders to do no harm save to those who opposed them, so that the few guards whom the alarm brought together were driven back without much injury. Being masters of the castle, the trumpets of the Scottish Warden were then blown, to the no small terror of the inhabitants of Carlisle, surprised out of their quiet sleep by the sounds of invasion at so early an hour. The bells of the castle rang out; those of the cathedral and Moot-hall answered; drums beat to arms; and beacons were lighted, to alarm the warlike country around.

In the mean while the Scottish party had done the errand they came for. They had freed Kinmont Willie from his dungeon. The first thing Armstrong did was to shout a good-night to Lord Scrope, asking him, at the same time, if he had any news for Scotland. The Borderers strictly obeyed the commands of their chief, in forbearing to take any booty. They returned from the castle, bringing with them their rescued countryman, and a gentleman named Spenser, an attendant on the constable of the castle. Buccleuch dismissed him, with his commendations to Salkeld the constable, whom he esteemed, he said, a better gentleman than Lord Scrope, bidding him say it was the Warden of Liddesdale who had done the exploit, and praying the constable, if he desired the name of a man of honor, to issue forth and seek a revenge. Buccleuch then ordered the retreat, which he performed with great leisure, and re-entered Scotland at sunrise in honor and safety. "There had never been a more gallant deed of vassalage done in Scotland," says an old historian, "no, not in Wallace's days."

Queen Elizabeth, as you may imagine, was dreadfully angry at this insult, and demanded that Buccleuch should be delivered up to the English, as he had committed so great an aggression upon their frontier during the time of peace. The matter was laid before the Scottish Parliament. King James himself pleaded the question on the part of Elizabeth, willing, it may be supposed, to recommend himself to that Princess by his tameness and docility. The Secretary of State replied in defence of Buccleuch; and the Scottish Parliament finally voted that they would refer the question to commissioners, to be chosen for both nations, and would abide by their decision. But concerning the proposed surrender of Buccleuch to England, the President declared, with a loud voice, that it would be time enough for Buccleuch to go to England when the King should pass there in person.

Buccleuch finally ended the discussion by going to England at the King's personal request, and on the understanding that no evil was to be done to him. Queen Elizabeth desired to see him personally, and demanded of him how he dared commit such aggression on her territory. He answered undauntedly, that he knew not that thing which a man *dared* NOT do. Elizabeth admired the answer, and treated this powerful Border chief with distinction during the time he remained in England, which was not long.

But the strangest adventure of James's reign was the event called the Gowrie conspiracy, over which there hangs a sort of mystery, which time has not even yet completely dispelled. You must recollect that there was an Earl of Gowrie condemned and executed when James was but a boy. This nobleman left two sons, bearing the family name of Ruthven, who were well educated abroad, and accounted hopeful young men. The King restored to the eldest the title and estate of Gowrie, and favored them both very much.

Now it chanced in the month of August, 1600, that Alexander Ruthven, the younger of the two brothers, came early one morning to the King, who was then hunting in the park of Falkland, and told him a story of his having seized a suspicious-looking man, a Jesuit, as he supposed, with a large pot of gold under his cloak. This man Ruthven said he had detained prisoner at his brother's house in Perth, till the King should examine him, and take possession of the treasure. With this story he decoyed James from the hunting-field, and persuaded him to ride with him to Perth, without any other company than a few noblemen and attendants, who followed the King without orders.

When they arrived at Perth, they entered Gowrie house, the mansion of the Earl, a large, massive building, having gardens which stretched down to the river Tay. The Earl a Gowrie was, or seemed surprised, to see the King arrive so unexpectedly, and caused some entertainment to be hastily prepared for his Majesty's refreshment. After the King had dined, Alexander Ruthven pressed him to come with him to see the prisoner in private; and

James, curious by nature, and sufficiently indigent to be inquisitive after money, followed him from one apartment to another, until Ruthven led him into a little turret, where there stood — not a prisoner with a pot of gold — but an armed man, prepared, as it seemed, for some violent enterprise.

The King started back, but Ruthven snatched the dagger which the man wore, and pointing it to James's breast, reminded him of his father the Earl of Gowrie's death, and commanded him, upon pain of death, to submit to his pleasure. The King replied, that he was but a boy when the Earl of Gowrie suffered, and upbraided Ruthven with ingratitude. The conspirator, moved by remorse or some other reason, assured the King that his life should be safe, and left him in the turret with the armed man, who, not very well selected to aid in a purpose so desperate, stood shaking in his armor, without assisting either his master or the King.

Let us now see what was passing below, during this strange scene betwixt the King and Ruthven. The attendants of James had begun to wonder at his absence, when they were suddenly informed by a servant of the Earl of Gowrie, that the King had mounted his horse, and had set out on his return to Falkland. The noblemen and attendants rushed into the court-yard of the mansion, and called for their horses, the Earl of Gowrie at the same time hurrying them away. Here the porter interfered, and said the King could not have left the house, since he had not passed the gate, of which he had the keys. Gowrie, on the other hand, called the man a liar, and insisted that the King had departed.

While the attendants of James knew not what to think, a half-smothered, yet terrified voice, was heard to scream from the window of a turret above their heads: "Help! Treason! Help! my Lord of Mar!" They looked upwards, and beheld James's face, in great agitation, pushed through the window, while a hand was seen grasping his throat, as if some one behind endeavored by violence to draw him back.

The explanation was as follows: "The King, when left alone with the armed man, had, it seems, prevailed upon him to open the lattice window. This was just done when Alexander Ruthven again entered the turret, and swearing that there was no remedy, but the King must needs die, he seized on him, and endeavored by main force to tie his hands with a garter. James resisted, in the extremity of despair, and dragging Ruthven to the window, now open, called out to his attendants in the manner we have described. His retinue hastened to his assistance. The greater part ran to the principal staircase, of which they found the doors shut, and immediately endeavored to force them open. Meantime a page of the King's, called Sir John Ramsay, discovered a back stair which led him to the turret, where Ruthven and the King were still struggling. Ramsay stabbed Ruthven twice with his dagger, James calling to him to strike high, as he had a doublet of proof on him. Ramsay then thrust Ruthven, now mortally wounded, towards the private staircase, where he was met by Sir Thomas Erskine and Sir Hugh Herries, two of the royal attendants, who despatched him with their swords. His last words were, "Alas! I am not to blame for this action."

This danger was scarcely over, when the Earl of Gowrie entered the outer chamber, with a drawn sword in each hand, followed by seven attendants, demanding vengeance for the death of his brother. The King's followers, only four in number, thrust James, for the safety of his person, back into the turret closet, and shut the door; and then engaged in a conflict, which was the more desperate, that they fought four to eight, and Herries was a lame and disabled man. But Sir John Ramsay having run the Earl of Gowrie through the heart, he dropped dead without speaking a word, and his servants fled. The doors of the great staircase were now opened to the nobles, who were endeavoring to force their way to the King's assistance.

In the mean time, a new peril threatened the King and his few attendants. The slain Earl of Gowrie was Provost of the town of Perth, and much beloved by the citizens. On hearing what had happened, they ran to arms, and surrounded the mansion-house where this tragedy had been acted, threatening, that if their Provost were not delivered to them safe and sound, the King's green coat should pay for it. Their violence was at last quieted by the magistrates of the town, and the mob were prevailed on to disperse.

The object of this strange conspiracy is one of the darkest in history, and what made it stranger, the armed man who was stationed in the turret could throw no light upon it. He proved to be one Henderson, steward to the Earl of Gowrie, who had been ordered to arm himself for the purpose of taking a Highland thief, and was posted in the turret by Alexander Ruthven, without any intimation what he was to do; so that the whole scene came upon him by surprise. The mystery seemed so impenetrable, and so much of the narrative rested upon James's own testimony, that many persons of that period, and even some historians of our own day, have thought that it was not a conspiracy of the brothers against the King, but of the King against the brothers; and that James, having taken a dislike to them, had contrived the bloody scene, and then thrown the blame on the Ruthvens, who suffered in it. But, besides the placability and gentleness of James's disposition, and besides the consideration that no adequate motive can be assigned, or even conjectured, for his perpetrating such an inhospitable murder, it ought to be remembered that the King was naturally timorous, and could not even look at a drawn sword without shuddering; so that it is contrary to all reason and probability to suppose that he could be the deviser of a scheme, in which his life was repeatedly exposed to the most imminent danger. However, many of the clergy refused to obey James's order to keep a day of solemn thanksgiving for the King's deliverance, intimating, without hesitation, that they greatly doubted the truth of his story. One of them being pressed by the King very hard, said: "That doubtless he must believe it, since his Majesty said he had seen it; but that, had he seen it himself, he would not have believed his own eyes." James was much vexed with this incredulity, for it was hard not to obtain credit after having been in so much danger.*

Nine years after the affair, some light was thrown upon the transaction by one Sprot, a notary-public, who, out of mere curiosity, had possessed himself of certain letters, said to have been written to the Earl of Gowrie by

* Five ministers of Edinburgh, who refused compliance, were commanded to remove from the city within forty-eight hours, and prohibited preaching within the King's dominions, under pain of death. Four of that number, acknowledging their fault, were pardoned and remitted. But Mr. Robert Bruce, taking a course by himself, and saying, "*he would reverence his Majesty's reports of that accident, but could not say he was persuaded of the truth of it*," was banished the King's dominions, and went into France. SPOTSWOOD, p. 462.

Robert Logan, of Restalrig, a scheming, turbulent, and profligate man. In these papers, allusion was repeatedly made to the death of Gowrie's father, to the revenge which was meditated, and to the execution of some great and perilous enterprise. Lastly, there was intimation that the Ruthvens were to bring a prisoner by sea to Logan's fortress of Fastcastle, a very strong and inaccessible tower, overhanging the sea, on the coast of Berwickshire. This place he recommends as suitable for keeping some important prisoner in safety and concealment, and adds, he had kept Bothwell there in his utmost distresses, let the King and his council say what they would.

All these expressions seem to point at a plot, not affecting the King's life, but his personal liberty, and make it probable, that when Alexander Ruthven had frightened the King into silence and compliance, the brothers intended to carry him through the gardens, and put him on board of a boat, and so conveying him down the Frith of Tay, might, after making a private signal, which Logan alludes to, place their royal prisoner in security at Fastcastle. The seizing upon the person of the King was a common enterprise among the Scottish nobles, and the father of the Ruthvens had lost his life for such an attempt. Adopting this as their intention, it is probable that Queen Elizabeth was privy to the attempt; and perhaps having found so much conveniency from detaining the person of Mary in captivity, she might have formed some similar plan for obtaining the custody of her son.

I must not conclude this story without observing, that Logan's bones were brought into a court of justice, for the purpose of being tried after death, and that he was declared guilty, and a sentence of forfeiture pronounced against him. But it has not been noticed that Logan, a dissolute and extravagant man, was deprived of great part of his estate before his death, and that the King, therefore, could have no lucrative object in following out this ancient and barbarous form of process. The fate of Sprot, the notary, was singular enough. He was condemned to be hanged for keeping these treasonable letters in his possession, without communicating them to the government; and he suffered death accordingly, asserting to the last that the letters were genuine, and that he had only preserved them from curiosity. This fact he testified even in the agonies of death; for, being desired to give a sign of the truth and sincerity of his confession, after he was thrown off from the ladder, he is said to have clapped his hands three times. Yet some persons continued to think that what Sprot told was untrue, and that the letters were forgeries; but it seems great incredulity to doubt the truth of a confession which brought to the gallows the man who made it; and, of late years, the letters produced by Sprot are regarded as genuine by the best judges of these matters. When so admitted, they render it evident that the purpose of the Gowrie conspiracy was to make King James a prisoner in the remote and inaccessible tower of Fastcastle, and perhaps ultimately to deliver him up to Queen Elizabeth.

We now approach the end of this collection of Tales. King James VI. of Scotland married the daughter of the King of Denmark, called Anne of Denmark. They had a family, which recommended them very much to the English people, who were tired of seeing their crown pass from one female to another, without any prospect of male succession. They began, therefore, to turn their eyes towards James, as the nearest heir of King Henry VIII., and the rightful successor, when Queen Elizabeth should fail. She was now old, her health broken, and her feelings painfully agitated by the death of Essex, her principal favorite. After his execution, she could scarcely be said ever to enjoy either health or reason. She sat on a pile of cushions, with her finger in her mouth, attending, as it seemed, to nothing, saving to the prayers which were from time to time read in her chamber.

While the Queen of England was thus struggling out the last moments of life, her subjects were making interest with her successor, James, with whom even Cecil himself, the prime minister of England, had long kept up a secret correspondence. The breath had no sooner left Elizabeth's body, than the near relation and godson of the late Queen, Sir Robert Carey, got on horseback, and, travelling with a rapidity which almost equalled that of the modern mail-coach, carried to the palace of Holyrood the news, that James was King of England, France, and Ireland, as well as of his native dominions of Scotland.

James arrived in London on the 7th of May, 1603, and took possession of his new realms without the slightest opposition; and thus the island of Great Britain, so long divided into the separate kingdoms of England and Scotland, became subject to the same prince. Here, therefore, must end the TALES of your GRANDFATHER, so far as they relate to the history of Scotland, considered as a distinct and separate kingdom.

TALES OF A GRANDFATHER.

SECOND SERIES.

DEDICATION.

TO HUGH LITTLEJOHN, ESQ.

MY DEAR CHILD:—

I NOW address to you three volumes of Scottish Stories, which bring down the History of that country from the period when England and Scotland became subject to the same King until that of the Union, when they were finally united into one kingdom. That you, and children of your age, may read these little books with pleasure and improvement, is the desire and hope of,

My dearest child,

Your very affectionate Grandfather,

WALTER SCOTT.

ABBOTSFORD, 15*th* *October*, 1828.

CHAPTER XXXIV.

Progress of Civilization in Society.

The kind reception which the former Tales, written for your amusement and edification, have met with, induces me, my dear little boy, to make an attempt to bring down my historical narrative to a period when the union of England and Scotland became as complete in the intimacy of feelings and interests, as law had declared and intended them to be, and as the mutual advantage of both countries had long, though in vain, required. The importance of events, however, and the desire to state them clearly, have induced me for the present to stop short at the period of the Union of the Kingdoms.

We left off, you may recollect, when James, the sixth of that name who reigned in Scotland, succeeded, by the death of Queen Elizabeth, to the throne of England, and thus became sovereign of the whole island of Britain. Ireland also belonged to his dominions, having been partly subdued by the arms of the English, and partly surrendered to them by the submission of the natives. There had been during Elizabeth's time many wars with the native lords and chiefs of the country; but the English finally obtained the undisturbed and undisputed possession of that rich and beautiful island. Thus the three kingdoms formed by the Britannic Islands came into the possession of one sovereign, who was thus fixed in a situation of strength and security, which was at that time the lot of few monarchs in Europe.

King James's power was the greater that the progress of human society had greatly augmented the wisdom of statesmen and counsellors, and given strength and stability to those laws which preserve the poor and helpless against the encroachments of the wealthy and the powerful.

But Master Littlejohn may ask me what I mean by the Progress of Human Society; and it is my duty to explain it as intelligibly as I can.

If you consider the lower order of animals, such as birds, dogs, cattle, or any class of the brute creation, you will find that they are, to every useful purpose, deprived of the means of communicating their ideas to each other. They have cries, indeed, by which they express pleasure or pain, fear or hope, — but they have no formed speech, by which, like men, they can converse together. God Almighty, who called all creatures into existence, in such manner as best pleased him, has imparted to those inferior animals no power of improving their situation, or of communicating with each other. There is no doubt a difference in the capacity of these inferior classes of creation. But though one bird may build her nest more neatly than one of a different class, or one dog may be more clever and more capable of learning tricks than another, yet, as it wants language to explain to its comrades the advantages which it may possess, its knowledge dies with it; thus birds and dogs continue to use the same general habits proper to the species, which they have done since the creation of the world. In other words, animals have a certain limited degree of sense, termed instinct, which teaches the present race to seek their food, and provide for their safety and comfort, in nearly the same manner as their parents did before them since the beginning of time, but does not enable them to communicate to their successors any improvement, or to derive any increase of knowledge from the practice of their predecessors. Thus you may remark that the example of the swallow, the wren, and other birds which cover their nests with a roof to protect them against the rain, is never imitated by other classes, who continue to construct theirs in the same exposed and imperfect manner since the beginning of the world.

Another circumstance which is calculated to prevent the inferior animals from rising above the rank in nature which they are destined to hold, is the short time during which they remain under the care of their parents. A few weeks gives the young nestlings of every season strength and inclination to leave the protection of the parents; the tender attachment which has subsisted while the young bird was unable to provide for itself without assistance is entirely broken off, and in a week or two more they probably do not know each other. The young of the sheep, the cow, and the horse, attend and feed by the mother's side for a certain short period, during which they are protected by her care, and supported by her milk; but they have no sooner attained the strength necessary to defend themselves, and the sense to provide for their wants, than they separate from the mother, and all intercourse between the parent and her offspring is closed forever.

Thus each separate tribe of animals retains exactly the same station in the general order of the universe which was occupied by its predecessors; and no existing generation either is, or can be, much better instructed, or more ignorant, than that which preceded or that which is to come after it.

It is widely different with mankind. God, as we are told in Scripture, was pleased to make man after his own image. By this you are not to understand that the Creator of heaven and earth has any visible form or shape, to which the human body bears a resemblance; but the meaning is, that as the God who created the world is a spirit, invisible and incomprehensible, so he joined to the human frame some portion of an essence resembling his own, which is called the human soul, and which, while the body lives, continues to animate and direct its motions, and on the dissolution of the bodily form which it has occupied, returns to the spiritual world, to be answerable for the good and evil of its works upon earth. It is therefore impossible that man, possessing this knowledge of right and wrong, proper to a spiritual essence resembling those higher orders of creation whom we call angels, and having some affinity, though at an incalculable distance, to the essence of the Deity himself, should have been placed under the same limitations in point of progressive improvement with the inferior tribes, who are neither responsible for the actions which they perform under directions of their instinct, nor capable, by any exertion of their own, of altering or improving their condition in the scale of creation. So far is this from being the case with man, that the bodily organs of the human frame bear such a correspondence with the properties of his soul as to give him the means, when they are properly used, of enlarging his powers, and becoming wiser and more skilful from hour to hour, as long as his life permits; and not only is this the case, but tribes and nations of men, assembled together for the purpose of mutual protection and defence, have the same power of alteration and improvement, and may, if circumstances are favorable, go on by gradual steps from being a wild horde of naked barbarians, till they become a powerful and civilized people.

The capacity of amending our condition by increase of knowledge, which, in fact, affords the means by which man rises to be the lord of creation, is grounded on the peculiar advantages possessed by the human race. Let us look somewhat closely into this, my dear boy, for it involves some truths equally curious and important.

If man, though possessed of the same immortal essence, or soul, which enables him to choose and refuse, to judge and condemn, to reason and conclude, were to be without the power of communicating to his fellow-men the conclusions to which his reasoning had conducted him, it is clear that the progress of each individual in knowledge, could be only in proportion to his own observation and his own powers of reasoning. But the gift of speech enables any one to communicate to others whatever idea of improvement occurs to him, and thus, instead of dying in the bosom of the individual by whom it was first thought of, it becomes a part of the stock of knowledge proper to the whole community, which is increased and rendered generally and effectually useful by the accession of further information, as opportunities occur, or men of reflecting and inventive minds arise in the state. This use of spoken language, therefore, which so gloriously distinguishes man from the beasts that perish, is the primary means of introducing and increasing knowledge in infant communities.

Another early cause of the improvement in human society is the incapacity of children to act for themselves, rendering the attention and protection of parents to their offspring necessary for so long a period. Even where the food which the earth affords without cultivation, such as fruits and herbs, is most plentifully supplied, children remain too helpless for many years to be capable of gathering it, and providing for their own support. This is still more the case where food must be procured by hunting, fishing, or cultivating the soil, occupations requiring a degree of skill and personal strength, which children cannot possess until they are twelve or fourteen years old. It follows, as a law of nature, that, instead of leaving their parents, at an early age, like the young of birds or quadrupeds, the youth of the human species necessarily remain under the protection of their father and mother for many years, during which they have time to acquire all the knowledge the parents are capable of teaching. It arises also from this wise arrangement, that the love and affection between the offspring and the parents, which among the brute creation is the produce of mere instinct, and continues for a very short time, becomes in the human race a deep and permanent feeling, founded on the attachment of the parents, the gratitude of the children, and the effect of long habit on both.

For these reasons, it usually happens that children feel no desire to desert their parents, but remain inhabitants of the same huts in which they were born, and take up the task of laboring for subsistence in their turn, when their fathers and mothers are disabled by age. One or two such families gradually unite together, and avail themselves of each other's company for mutual defence and assistance. This is the earliest stage of human society; and some savages have been found in this condition so very rude and ignorant, that they may be said to be little wiser or better than a herd of animals. The natives of New South

Wales, for example, are, even at present, in the very lowest scale of humanity, and ignorant of every art which can add comfort or decency to human life. These unfortunate savages use no clothes, construct no cabins or huts, and are ignorant even of the manner of chasing animals or catching fish, unless such of the latter as are left by the tide, or which are found on the rocks; they feed upon the most disgusting substances, snakes, worms, maggots, and whatever trash falls in their way. They know indeed how to kindle a fire, — in that respect only they have stepped beyond the deepest ignorance to which man can be subjected, — but they have not learned how to boil water; and when they see Europeans perform this ordinary operation, they have been known to run away in great terror. Voyagers tell us of other savages who are even ignorant of the use of fire, and who maintain a miserable existence by subsisting on shell-fish eaten raw.

And yet, my dear boy, out of this miserable and degraded state, which seems worse than that of the animals, man has the means and power to rise into the high place for which Providence hath destined him. In proportion as opportunities occur, these savage tribes acquire the arts of civilized life; they construct huts to shelter them against the weather; they invent arms for destroying the wild beasts by which they are annoyed, and for killing those whose flesh is adapted for food; they domesticate others, and use at pleasure their milk, flesh, and skins; and they plant fruit-trees and sow grain as soon as they discover that the productions of nature most necessary for their comfort may be increased by labor and industry. Thus, the progress of human society, unless it is interrupted by some unfortunate circumstances, continues to advance, and every new generation, without losing any of the advantages already attained, goes on to acquire others which were unknown to the preceding one.

For instance, when three or four wandering families of savages have settled in one place, and begun to cultivate the ground, and collect their huts into a hamlet or village, they usually agree in choosing some chief to be their judge, and the arbiter of their disputes in time of peace, their leader and captain when they go to war with other tribes. This is the foundation of a monarchical government. Or perhaps their public affairs are directed by a council, or senate, of the oldest and wisest of the tribe, — this is the origin of a republican state. At all events, in one way or other, they put themselves under something resembling a regular government, and obtain the protection of such laws as may prevent them from quarrelling with one another.

Other important alterations are introduced by time. At first, no doubt, the members of the community store their fruits and the produce of the chase in common. But shortly after, reason teaches them that the individual who has bestowed labor and trouble upon anything, so as to render it productive, acquires a right of property, as it is called, in the produce which his efforts have in a manner called into existence. Thus, it is soon acknowledged, that he who has planted a tree has the sole right of consuming its fruit; and that he who has sown a field of corn has the exclusive title to gather in the grain. Without the labor of the planter and husbandman, there would have been no apples or wheat, and therefore, these are justly entitled to the fruit of their labor. In like manner, the state itself is conceived to acquire a right of property in the fields cultivated by its members, and in the forests and waters where they have of old practised the rights of hunting and fishing. If men of a different tribe enter on the territory of a neighboring nation, war ensues between them, and peace is made by agreeing on both sides to reasonable conditions. Thus a young state extends its possessions; and by its communications with other tribes lays the foundation of public laws for the regulation of their behavior to each other in peace and in war.

Other arrangements arise, not less important, tending to increase the difference between mankind in their wild and original state, and that which they assume in the progress of civilization. One of the most remarkable is the separation of the citizens into different classes of society, and the introduction of the use of money. I will try to render these great changes intelligible to you.

In the earlier stages of society, every member of the community may be said to supply all his wants by his own personal labor. He acquires his food by the chase, — he sows and reaps his own grain, — he gathers his own fruit, — he cuts the skin which forms his dress so as to fit his own person, — he makes the sandals or buskins which protect his feet. He is, therefore, better or worse accommodated, exactly in proportion to the personal skill and industry which he can apply to that purpose. But it is discovered, in process of time, that one man has particular dexterity in hunting, being, we shall suppose, young, active, and enterprising; another, older and of a more staid character, has peculiar skill in tilling the ground, or in managing cattle and flocks; a third, lame perhaps, or infirm, has a happy talent for cutting out and stitching together garments, or for shaping and sewing shoes. It becomes, therefore, for the advantage of all that the first man should attend to nothing but hunting, the second confine himself to the cultivation of the land, and the third remain at home to make clothes and shoes. But then it follows, as a necessary consequence, that the huntsman must give to the man who cultivates the land a part of his venison and skins, if he desires to have grain of which to make bread, or a cow to furnish his family with milk; and that both the hunter and agriculturist must give a share of the produce of the chase, and a proportion of the grain, to the third man, to obtain from him clothes and shoes. Each is thus accommodated with what he wants a great deal better, and more easily, by every one following a separate occupation, than they could possibly have been had each of the three been hunter, farmer, and tailor, in his own person, practising two of the trades awkwardly and unwillingly, instead of confining himself to that which he perfectly understands, and pursues with success. This mode of accommodation is called barter, and is the earliest kind of traffic by which men exchange their property with each other, and satisfy their wants by parting with their superfluities.

But, in process of time, barter is found inconvenient. The husbandman, perhaps, has no use for shoes when the shoemaker is in need of corn, or the shoemaker may not want furs or venison when the hunter desires to have shoes. To remedy this, almost all nations have introduced the use of what is called *money;* that is to say, they have fixed on some particular substance capable of being divided into small portions, which, having itself little intrinsic value applicable to human use, is nevertheless, received as a representative of the value of all commodities. Particular kinds of shells are used as money in some countries; in others, leather, cloth, or iron, are employed; but gold and silver, divided into small portions, are used for this important purpose almost all over the world.

That you may understand the use of this circulating representative of the value of commodities, and comprehend the convenience which it affords, let us suppose that the hunter, as we formerly said, wanted a pair of shoes, and the shoemaker had no occasion for venison, but wanted some corn, while the husbandman, not desiring to have shoes, stood in need of some other commodity. Here are three men, each desirous of some article of necessity or convenience which he cannot obtain by barter, because the party whom he has to deal with does not want the commodity which he has to offer in exchange. But supposing the use of money introduced, and its value acknowledged, these three persons are accommodated, by means of it, in the amplest manner possible. The shoemaker does not want the venison which the hunter offers for sale, but some other man in the village is willing to purchase it for five pieces of silver; the hunter sells his commodity, and goes to the shoemaker, who, though he would not barter the shoes for the venison which he did not want, readily sells them for the money, and, going with it to the farmer, buys from him the quantity of corn he needs; while the farmer, in his turn, purchases whatever he is in want of, or, if he requires nothing at the time, lays the pieces of money aside, to use when he has occasion.

The invention of money is followed by the gradual rise of trade. There are men who make it their business to buy various articles, and sell them again for profit; that is, they sell them somewhat dearer than they bought them. This is convenient for all parties; since the original proprietors are willing to sell their commodities to those storekeepers or shopkeepers at a low rate, to be saved the trouble of hawking them about in search of a customer; while the public in general are equally willing to buy from such intermediate dealers, because they are sure to be immediately supplied with what they want.

The numerous transactions occasioned by the introduction of money, together with other circumstances, soon destroy the equality of ranks which prevails in an early stage of society. Some men hoard up quantities of gold and silver, become rich, and hire the assistance of others to do their work; some waste or spend their earnings, become poor, and sink into the capacity of servants. Some men are wise and skilful, and, distinguishing themselves by their exploits in battle and their counsels in peace, rise to the management of public affairs. Others, and much greater numbers, have no more valor than to follow where they are led, and no more talent than to act as they are commanded. These last sink, as a matter of course, into obscurity, while the others become generals and statesmen. The attainment of learning tends also to increase the difference of ranks. Those who receive a good education by the care of their parents, or possess so much strength of mind and readiness of talent as to educate themselves, become separated from the more ignorant of the community, and form a distinct class and condition of their own; holding no more communication with the others than is absolutely necessary.

In this way the whole order of society is changed, and instead of presenting the uniform appearance of one large family, each member of which has nearly the same rights, it seems to resemble a confederacy or association of different ranks, classes, and conditions of men, each rank filling up a certain department in society, and discharging a class of duties totally distinct from those of the others. The steps by which a nation advances from the natural and simple state which we have just described, into the more complicated system in which ranks are distinguished from each other, are called the progress of society, or of civilization. It is attended, like all things human, with much of evil as well as good; but it seems to be a law of our moral nature, that, faster or slower, such alterations must take place, in consequence of the inventions and improvements of succeeding generations of mankind.

Another alteration, productive of consequences not less important, arises out of the gradual progress towards civilization. In the early state of society, every man in the tribe is a warrior, and liable to serve as such when the country requires his assistance; but in progress of time the pursuit of the military art is, at least on all ordinary occasions, confined to bands of professional soldiers, whose business it is to fight the battles of the state, when required, in consideration of which they are paid by the community, the other members of which are thus left to the uninterrupted pursuit of their own peaceful occupations. This alteration is attended with more important consequences than we can at present pause to enumerate.

We have said, that those mighty changes which bring men to dwell in castles and cities, instead of huts and caves, and enable them to cultivate the sciences and subdue the elements, instead of being plunged in ignorance and superstition, are owing primarily to the reason with which God has graciously endowed the human race; and in a second degree to the power of speech, by which we enjoy the faculty of communicating to each other the result of our own reflections.

But it is evident that society, when its advance is dependent upon oral tradition alone, must be liable to many interruptions. The imagination of the speaker, and the dulness or want of comprehension of the hearer, may lead to many errors; and it is generally found that knowledge makes but very slow progress until the art of writing is discovered, by which a fixed, accurate, and substantial form can be given to the wisdom of past ages. When this noble art is attained, there is a sure foundation laid for the preservation and increase of knowledge. The record is removed from the inaccurate recollection of the aged, and placed in a safe, tangible, and imperishable form, which may be subjected to the inspection of various persons, until the sense is completely explained and comprehended, with the least possible chance of doubt or uncertainty.

By the art of writing a barrier is fixed against those violent changes so apt to take place in the early stages of society, by which all the fruits of knowledge are frequently destroyed, as those of the earth are by a hurricane. Suppose, for example, a case, which frequently happens in the early history of mankind, that some nation, which has made considerable progress in the arts, is invaded and subdued by another which is more powerful and numerous, though more ignorant than themselves. It is clear, that in this case, as the rude and ignorant victors would set no value on the knowledge of the vanquished, it would, if intrusted only to the memory of the individuals of the conquered people, be gradually lost and forgotten. But if the useful discoveries made by the ancestors of the vanquished people were recorded in writing, the manuscripts in which they were described, though they might be neglected for a season, would, if preserved at all, probably attract attention at some more fortunate period. It was thus, when the empire of Rome, having reached the utmost height of its grandeur, was broken down and conquered by numerous tribes of ignorant though brave barbarians, that those admirable works of classical learning, on which such value is justly placed in the present day, were rescued from total destruction and oblivion by manuscript copies preserved by chance in the old libraries of churches and convents. It may indeed be taken as an almost infallible maxim, that no nation can make any great progress in useful knowledge or civilization, until their improvement can be rendered stable and permanent by the invention of writing.

Another discovery, however, almost as important as that of writing, was made during the fifteenth century. I mean the invention of printing. Writing with the hand must be always a slow, difficult, and expensive operation; and when the manuscript is finished, it is perhaps laid aside among the stores of some great library, where it may be neglected by students, and must, at any rate, be accessible to very few persons, and subject to be destroyed by numerous accidents. But the admirable invention of printing enables the artist to make a thousand copies from the original manuscript, by having them stamped upon paper, in far less time and with less expense than it would cost to make half a dozen such copies with the pen. From the period of this glorious discovery, knowledge of every kind may be said to have been brought out of the darkness of cloisters and universities, where it was known only to a few scholars, into the broad light of day, where its treasures were accessible to all men.

The Bible itself, in which we find the rules of eternal life, as well as a thousand invaluable lessons for our conduct in this world, was, before the invention of printing, totally inaccessible to all save the priests of Rome, who found it their interest to discourage the perusal of the Scriptures by any except their own order, and thus screened from discovery those alterations and corruptions, which the inventions of ignorant and designing men had introduced into the beautiful simplicity of the Gospel. But when, by means of printing, the copies of the Bible became so numerous that every one above the most wretched poverty could, at a cheap price, possess himself of a copy of the blessed rule of life, there was a general appeal from the errors and encroachments of the Church of Rome, to the Divine Word on which they professed to be founded; a treasure formerly concealed from the public, but now placed within the reach of every man, whether of the clergy or laity. The consequence of these inquiries, which printing alone could have rendered practicable, was the rise of the happy Reformation of the Christian Church.

The same noble art made knowledge of a temporal kind as accessible as that which concerned religion. Whatever works of history, science, morality, or entertainment, seemed likely to instruct or amuse the reader, were printed and distributed among the people at large by printers and booksellers, who had a profit by doing so. Thus, the possibility of important discoveries being forgotten in the course of years, or of the destruction of useful arts, or elegant literature, by the loss of the records in which they are preserved, was in a great measure removed.

In a word, the printing-press is a contrivance which empowers any one individual to address his whole fellow-subjects on any topic which he thinks important, and which enables a whole nation to listen to the voice of such individual, however obscure he may be, with the same ease, and greater certainty of understanding what he says, than if a chief of Indians were haranguing the tribe at his council-fire. Nor is the important difference to be forgotten, that the orator can only speak to the persons present, while the author of a book addresses himself not only to the race now in existence, but to all succeeding generations, while his work shall be held in estimation.

I have thus endeavored to trace the steps by which a general civilization is found to take place in nations, with more or less rapidity, as laws and institutions, or external circumstances, favorable or otherwise, advance or retard the increase of knowledge, and by the course of which, man, endowed with reason, and destined for immortality, gradually improves the condition in which Providence has placed him; while the inferior animals continue to live by means of the same, or nearly the same instincts of self-preservation, which have directed their species in all its descents since the creation.

I have called your attention at some length to this matter, because you will now have to remark, that a material change had gradually and slowly taken place, both in the kingdom of England, and in that of Scotland, when their long quarrels were at length in appearance ended, by the accession of James the Sixth of Scotland to the English crown, which he held under the title of James the First of that powerful kingdom.

CHAPTER XXXV.

INFIRMITIES AND ILL-TEMPER OF ELIZABETH IN HER LATTER YEARS — ACCESSION OF JAMES VI. ACCEPTABLE ON THAT ACCOUNT TO THE ENGLISH — RESORT OF SCOTCHMEN TO THE COURT AT LONDON — QUARRELS BETWEEN THEM AND THE ENGLISH — HERBERT AND RAMSAY — DUELLING — DUEL OF STEWART AND WHARTON — ATTEMPT BY SIR JOHN AYRES TO ASSASSINATE LORD HERBERT — MURDER OF TURNER, A FENCING-MASTER, BY TWO FOLLOWERS OF LORD SANQUHAR, AND EXECUTION OF THE THREE MURDERERS — STATUTE AGAINST STABBING.

[1603 — 1612.]

THE whole island of Great Britain was now united under one king, though it remained in effect two separate kingdoms, governed by their own separate constitutions, and their own distinct codes of laws, and liable again to be separated, in case, by the death of King James without issue, the kingdoms might have been claimed by different heirs. For although James had two sons, yet there was a possibility that they might have both died before their father, in which case the sceptres of England and Scotland must have passed once more into different hands. The Hamilton family would, in that case, have succeeded to the kingdom of Scotland, and the next heir of Elizabeth to that of England. Who that heir was it might have been found difficult to determine.

It was, in these circumstances, to be apprehended that James, the sovereign of a poor and barren kingdom, which had for so many ages maintained an almost perpetual war with England, would have met with a prejudiced and unpleasant reception from a nation long accustomed to despise the Scotch for their poverty, and to regard them with enmity on account of their constant hostility to the English blood and name. It might have been supposed also, that a people so proud as the English, and having so many justifiable reasons for their pride, would have regarded with an evil eye the transferrence of the sceptre from the hand of the Tudors, who had swayed it during five successive reigns, to those of a Stewart, descended from the ancient and determined enemies of the English nation. But it was the wise and gracious pleasure of Providence, that while so many reasons existed to render the accession of James, and, in consequence, the union of the two crowns, obnoxious to the English people, others should occur, which not only balanced, but for a time completely overpowered those objections, as well in the minds of men of sense and education, as in the judgment of the populace, who are usually averse to foreign rulers, for no other reason than that they are such.*

* "It is seldom that the accession of a foreigner is tranquil, and James was peculiarly obnoxious, from his birthplace, to the antipathy of a people among whom his mother had suffered an ignominious death. But his accession was promoted by the expectations of every religious, and the interests of almost every political party in England. The Puritans, who had experienced his friendly intercession with Elizabeth, anticipated a reformation in the Church, if not the downfall and destruction of the hierarchy, from a prince whose professed religion was congenial to their own. The established clergy had examined his character with more anxious attention; and discovered, both in his conduct and in his controversial discourses, a strong predilection for the episcopal order. The Catholics, then a numerous and powerful party, expected greater indulgence in their religion; and entertained a persuasion that its doctrines and its votaries were secretly not indifferent to a monarch, the pretensions of whose family they had

Queen Elizabeth, after a long and glorious reign, had, in her latter days, become much more cross and uncertain in her temper than had been the case in her youth, more wilful also, and more inclined to exert her arbitrary power on slight occasions. One peculiar cause of offence given to her people was her obstinate refusal to gratify their anxiety, by making, as the nation earnestly desired, some arrangement for the succession to the throne after her own death. On this subject,* indeed, she nursed so much suspicion and jealousy, as gave rise to more than one extraordinary scene. The following is a whimsical instance, among others, of her unwillingness to hear of anything respecting old age and its consequences.

The Bishop of St. David's, preaching in her Majesty's presence, took occasion from his text, which was Psalm xc. v. 12, "So teach us to number our days, that we may apply our hearts unto wisdom," to allude to the Queen's advanced period of life, she being then sixty-three, and to the consequent infirmities attending upon old age; as, for example, when the grinders shall be few in number, and they wax dark who look out at windows,—when the

first supported, and whose mother they regarded as a martyr to their cause. But his peaceful and undisturbed accession must be ascribed to the absence of every competitor by whom his title could be contested, or the affections of the people pre-occupied or divided."—*History of Scotland from the Union of the Crowns to the Union of the Kingdoms.* By MALCOLM LAING, Esq., 1800. Vol. i. pp. 2, 3.

* "A short time before her death," says Robertson, "she broke the silence which she had so long preserved on that subject, and told Cecil and the Lord Admiral 'that her throne was the throne of kings; that she would have no mean person to ascend it, and that her cousin the King of Scots should be her successor.' This she confirmed on her death-bed."—B. viii. The continuator of Sir James M'Intosh's history adds, "She was then speechless, Cecil asked her to answer by a sign, and she joined both her hands above her head."—Vol. iv. p. 145.

daughters of singing shall be abased, and more to the like purpose. With the tone of these admonitions the Queen was so ill-satisfied, that she flung open the window of the closet in which she sat, and told the preacher to keep his admonitions to himself, since she plainly saw the greatest clerks (meaning scholars) were not the wisest men. Nor did her displeasure end here. The bishop was commanded to confine himself to his house for a time, and the Queen, referring to the circumstance some time afterwards, told her courtiers how much the prelate was mistaken in supposing her to be as much decayed as perhaps he might feel himself to be. As for her, she thanked God, neither her stomach nor her strength, — her voice for singing, nor her art of fingering instruments, were any whit decayed. And to prove the goodness of her eyes, she produced a little jewel, with an inscription in very small letters, which she offered to Lord Worcester and Sir James Crofts to read. They had too much tact to be sharp-sighted on the occasion; she, therefore, read it herself with apparent ease, and laughed at the error of the good bishop.*

* "One Sunday," says Sir John Harrington, "the Bishop of London preached to the Queen's Majesty; and seemed to touch on the vanity of decking the body too finely. Her Majesty told the ladies, that if the Bishop held more discourse on such matters, she would fit him for heaven; but he should walk thither without a staff, and leave his mantle behind him." — *Nugæ Antiquæ.* "Throughout the whole of her reign," says Sir Walter Scott elsewhere, "Queen Elizabeth, pre-eminent as a sovereign, had never been able to forbear the exertion of her claims as a wit and a beauty. When verging to the extremity of life, her mirror presented her with hair too gray and features too withered to reflect, even in her own opinion, the features of that fairy queen, of immortal youth and beauty, in which she had been painted by one of the most beautiful poets of that poetic age. She avenged herself by discontinuing the consultation of her looking-glass, which no longer flattered her principal failing of personal vanity, and exchanged that monitor of the toilet, which cannot flatter, for the more false, favorable, and pleasing, though less accurate reports of the

The faults of Elizabeth, though arising chiefly from age and ill-temper, were noticed and resented by her subjects, who began openly to show themselves weary of a female reign, forgetting how glorious it had been, and manifested a general desire to have a king to rule over them. With this almost univeral feeling, all eyes, even those of Elizabeth's most confidential statesman and counsellor, Sir Robert Cecil, afterwards Earl of Salisbury, were turned to the King of Scotland as next heir to the crown. He was a Protestant prince, which assured him the favor of the Church of England, and of the numerous and strong adherents to the Protestant religion. As such, Cecil entered into a secret correspondence with him, in which he pointed out the line of conduct proper on James's part to secure his interest in England. On the other hand, the English Catholics, on whom Queen Elizabeth's government had imposed many severe penal laws, were equally friendly to the succession of King James, since from that Prince, whose mother had been a strict Catholic, they might hope for favor, to the extent at least of some release from the various hardships which the laws of England imposed on them. The Earl of Northumberland conducted a correspondence with James on the part of the Catholics, in which he held high language, and offered to assert the Scottish King's right of succession by force of arms.*

ladies who attended her. This indulgence of vanity brought as usual its own punishment. The young females who waited upon the Queen turned her pretensions into ridicule; and if the report of the times is true, ventured even to personal ridicule, by misplacing the cosmetics which she used for the repair of her faded charms,—sometimes venturing to lay upon the royal nose the carmine which ought to have embellished the cheeks."—LARDNER, vol. ii. pp. 411, 412.

* "Nor did the King himself believe he should have come in with a sheathed sword, which appeared by that letter he produced of the

These intrigues were kept by James as secret as was in his power. If Elizabeth had discovered either the one or the other, neither the services of Cecil, nor the high birth and power of the great Earl of Northumberland could have saved them from experiencing the extremity of her indignation. Cecil, in particular, was at one time on the point of ruin. A post from Scotland delivered into his hands a private packet from the Scottish King, when the secretary was in attendance on Elizabeth. "Open your despatches," said Elizabeth, "and let us hear the news from Scotland." A man of less presence of mind would have been ruined; for if the Queen had seen the least hesitation in her minister's manner, her suspicions would have been instantly awakened, and detection must have followed. But Cecil recollected the Queen's sensitive aversion to any disagreeable smell, which was strengthened by the belief of the time, that infectious diseases and subtile poisons could be communicated by means of scent alone. The artful secretary availed himself of this, and while he seemed to be cutting the strings which held the packet, he observed it had a singular and unpleasant odor; on which Elizabeth desired it might be taken from her presence, and opened elsewhere with due precaution. Thus Cecil got an opportunity to withdraw from the packet whatever could have betrayed his correspondence with King James.* Cecil's policy and inclina-

Earl of Northumberland, that if he made any doubt hereof, he would bring him forty thousand Catholics, who should conduct him into England."—SIR ANTHONY WELDON, apud *Secret History*, vol. ii. p. 70. Edinburgh, 1811. *Edited by Sir W. Scott.*

* The correspondence alluded to was conducted on the part of Cecil by Lord Henry Howard, afterwards Earl of Northampton: The confidants employed by King James were the Earl of Mar, and Mr. Edward Bruce of Kinloss. Notwithstanding the anxious and repeated injunc-

tions were very generally followed in the English Court; indeed there appeared no heir to the crown, male or female, whose right could be placed in competition with that of James.

It may be added to this general inclination in James's favor, that the defects of his character were of a kind which did not attract much attention while he occupied the throne of Scotland. The delicacy of his situation was then so great, and he was exposed to so many dangers from the dislike of the clergy, the feuds of the nobles, and the tumultuous disposition of the common people, that he dared not indulge in any of those childish freaks of which he was found capable when his motions were more completely at his own disposal. On the contrary, he was compelled to seek out the sagest counsellors, to listen to the wisest advice, and to put a restraint on his own natural disposition for encouraging idle favorites, parasites, and flatterers, as well as to suppress his inward desire to extend the limits of his authority further than the constitution of the country permitted.

At this period James governed by the advice of such ministers as the Chancellor Maitland, and afterwards of Home, Earl of Dunbar, men of thought and action, of whose steady measures and prudent laws the King naturally obtained the credit. Neither was James himself deficient in a certain degree of sagacity. He possessed all that could be derived from learning alloyed by pedantry, and from a natural shrewdness of wit, which enabled him to play the part of a man of sense, when either acting under the influence of constraint and fear,

tions of Cecil "to destroy every letter," great part of this correspondence has been preserved, and was for the first time published by Lord Hailes, Edinburgh, 1766.

or where no temptation occurred to induce him to be guilty of some folly. It was by these specious accomplishments that he acquired in his youth the character of an able and wise monarch, although when he was afterwards brought on a more conspicuous stage, and his character better understood, he was found entitled to no better epithet than that conferred on him by an able French politician, who called him the "wisest fool in Christendom."

Such, however, as King James was, England now received him with more universal acclamation than had attended any of her princes on their ascent to the throne. Multitudes, of every description, hastened to accompany him on his journey through England to the capital city. The wealthy placed their gold at his disposal, the powerful opened their halls for the most magnificent entertainments, the clergy hailed him as the head of the Church, and the poor, who had nothing to offer but their lives, seemed ready to devote them to his service. Some of the Scottish retinue, who were acquainted with James's character, saw and feared the unfavorable effect which such a change of circumstances was likely to work on him. "A plague of these people!" said one of his old domestics; "they will spoil a good king."

Another Scot made an equally shrewd answer to an Englishman, who desired to know from him the King's real character. "Did you ever see a jackanapes?" said the Scotchman, meaning a tame monkey; "if you have, you must be aware that if you hold the creature in your hands you can make him bite me, and if I hold him in my hands, I can make him bite you."

Both these sayings were shown to be true in course of time. King James, brought from poverty to wealth, became thoughtless and prodigal, indolent, and addicted to idle pleasures. From hearing the smooth flatteries of the clergy of England, who recognized him as head of the Church, instead of the rude attacks of the Presbyterian ministers of Scotland, who had hardly admitted his claim to be one of its inferior members, he entertained new and more lofty pretensions to divine right. Finally, brought from a country where his personal liberty and the freedom of his government were frequently placed under restraint, and his life sometimes in danger, he was overjoyed to find himself in a condition where his own will was not only unfettered, as far as he himself was concerned, but appeared to be the model by which all loyal subjects were desirous to accommodate theirs; and he seemed readily enough disposed to stretch to its utmost limits the power thus presented to him. Thus, from being a just and equitable monarch, he was inspired with a love of arbitrary power; and from attending, as had been his custom, to state business, he now minded little save hunting and festivals.

In this manner James, though possessing a large stock of pedantic wisdom, came to place himself under the management of a succession of unworthy favorites, and although particularly good-natured, and naturally a lover of justice, was often hurried into actions and measures, which, if they could not be termed absolutely tyrannical, were nevertheless illegal and unjust. It is, however, of his Scottish government that we are now to treat, and therefore I am to explain to you, as well as I can, the consequences of the union with England to the people and country of Scotland.

If the English nation were at first delighted to receive King James as their sovereign, the Scottish people were no less enchanted by the prospect of their monarch's ascent to this wealthy and pre-eminent situation. They considered the promotion of their countryman and Prince as an omen of good fortune to their nation; each individual Scotchman expected to secure some part of the good things with which England was supposed to abound, and multitudes hurried to court, to put themselves in the way of obtaining their share.

James was shocked at the greediness and importunity of his hungry countrymen, and scandalized besides at the poor and miserable appearance which many of them made among the rich Englishmen, which brought discredit on the country to which he himself, as well as they, belonged. He sent instructions to the Scottish Privy Council to prevent such intruders from leaving their country, complaining of their manners and appearance, as calculated to bring disgrace upon all the natives of Scotland. A proclamation was accordingly issued at Edinburgh, setting forth that great numbers of men and women of base sort and condition, and without any certain trade, calling, or dependence, repaired from Scotland to court, which was almost filled with them, to the great annoyance of his Majesty, and to the heavy disgrace of the Scottish nation; for these suitors being, in the judgment of all who saw them, but "idle rascals, and poor miserable bodies," their importunity and numbers raised an opinion that there were no persons of good rank, comeliness, or credit in the country which sent forth such a flight of locusts. Further, it was complained that these unseemly supplicants usually alleged that the cause of their repairing to court was to desire payment of old debts due by the King, "which, of all kinds of importunity," says the proclamation, with great simplicity, "is the most unpleasing to his

Majesty." Therefore, general proclamation was directed to be made at all the market-crosses in Scotland, that no Scottish person should be permitted to travel to England without leave of the Privy Council; and that vessels transporting individuals, who had not obtained due license, should be liable to confiscation.

But although the King did all that was in his power to prevent these uncouth suitors from repairing to his court, yet there were many other natives of Scotland of a higher description, the sons of men of rank and quality, who, by birth and condition, had the right of attending his court, and approaching his presence, whom he could not prohibit from doing so, without positively disowning all former affections, national feeling, and sympathy or gratitude for past services. The benefits which he conferred on these were ill construed by the English, who seem to have accounted everything as taken from themselves which was bestowed on a Scotchman. The King, though it does not appear that he acted with any unjust purpose, was hardly judged, both by his own countrymen and the English. The Scots, who had been his friends in his inferior situation, and, as it might be called, his adversity, naturally expected a share of his bounty when he was advanced to such high prosperity; while the English, with a jealousy for which much allowance is also to be made, regarded these northern suitors with an evil eye. In short, the Scottish courtiers thought that their claims of ancient services, of allegiance tried under difficult circumstances, of favor due to countrymen, and perhaps even to kindred, which no people carry so far, entitled them to all the advantages which the King might have to bestow; while the English, on the other hand, considered everything given to the Scots as conferred at their expense, and used many rhymes and satirical expressions to that purpose, such as occur in the old song: —

> "Bonny Scot, all witness can
> England has made thee a gentleman."
>
> "Thy blue bonnet, when thou came hither,
> Would scarcely keep out the wind or weather;
> But now it is turned to a hat and a feather —
> The bonnet is blown the devil knows whither.
> The sword at thy haunch was a huge black blade,
> With a great basket-hilt of iron made;
> But now a long rapier doth hang by his side,
> And huffingly doth this bonny Scot ride."

Another rhyme, to the same purpose, described a Scottish courtier thus: —

> "In Scotland he was born and bred,
> And, though a beggar, must be fed." *

It is said, that when the Scots complained to the King of this last aspersion, James replied, "Hold your peace, for I will soon make the English as poor as yourselves, and so end that controversy." † But as it was not in the power of wit to appease the feud betwixt the nobility and gentry of two proud nations, so lately enemies, all the efforts of the King were unequal to prevent bloody and desperate quarrels between his countrymen and his new subjects, to the great disquiet of the court, and the

* Ritson's North Country Chorister. — In reference to the quatrain which follows, Osborne remarks, "In the mean time this nation was rooted up by those Caledonian bores, as these homely verses do attest, which were everywhere posted, and do contain as many stories as lines.

> They beg our lands, our goods, our lives,
> They switch our nobles, . . .
> They pinch our gentry, and send for our benchers,
> They stab our sergeants, and pistoll our fencers."
>
> — *Secret History*, vol. i. p. 217.

† Ibid., vol. i. p. 371.

distress of the good-natured monarch, who, averse to war in all its shapes, and even to the sight of a drawn sword, suffered greviously on such occasions.

There was one of those incidents which assumed a character so formidable, that it threatened the destruction of all the Scots at the court and in the capital, and, in consequence, a breach between the kingdoms so lately and happily brought into alliance. At a public horse-race at Croydon, Philip Herbert, an Englishman of high birth, though, as it fortunately chanced, of no degree of corresponding spirit, received, in a quârrel, a blow in the face by a switch or horsewhip, from one Ramsay, a Scottish gentleman in attendance on the court. The rashness and violence of Ramsay was construed into a national point of quarrel by the English present, who proposed revenging themselves on the spot by a general attack upon all the Scots on the race-ground. One gentleman, named Pinchbeck, although ill-fitted for such a strife, for he had but the use of two fingers on his right hand, rode furiously through the multitude, with his dagger ready drawn, exhorting all the English to imitate him in an immediate attack on the Scots, exclaiming, "Let us breakfast with those that are here, and dine with the rest in London." But as Herbert did not return the blow, no scuffle or assault actually took place; otherwise, it is probable, a dreadful scene must have ensued. James, with whom Herbert was a particular favorite, rewarded his moderation or timidity by raising him to the rank of Knight, Baron, Viscount, and Earl of Montgomery, all in one day. Ramsay was banished the court for a season; and thus the immediate affront was in some degree alleviated. But the new Earl of Montgomery remained, in the opinion of his countrymen, a dishonored man; and it is said his mother, the sister of Sir Philip Sidney, wept and tore her hair when she heard of his having endured with patience the insult offered by Ramsay. This is the lady whom, in a beautiful epitaph, Ben Jonson has described as

"Sidney's sister, Pembroke's mother;
Death, ere thou hast slain another
Wise, and good, and learn'd as she,
Time shall throw a dart at thee." *

Yet the patience of Herbert under the insult was the fortunate prevention of a great national misfortune, for which, if his after conduct had not given tokens of an abject spirit, he might have been praised as a patriot, who had preferred the good of his country to the gratification of his own immediate resentment. †

Another offence given by the haughty and irascible temper of a Scotchman, was also likely to have produced disastrous consequences. The Inns of Court are the places of resort and study appointed for those young men who are destined to the profession of the law in England,

* Osborne, *apud* Secret History, vol. i. pp. 218-225. Sir Walter Scott, editor of this work, adds, "Philip, Earl of Pembroke and Montgomery, had no qualities to recommend him as a royal favorite saving two; any one of which, however, would have rendered him acceptable to James I. These were comeliness of person, and indefatigable zeal in hunting. His character was that of Squire Western, choleric, boisterous, illiterate, selfish, absurd, and cowardly. He was, besides, a profligate, a gambler, and, above all, an ungrateful rebel to the son of the Prince who raised him, as he adhered with great vehemence to the cause of the Parliament, and afterwards to that of Cromwell." — *Note, Ibid.* p. 218.

† "One thing was then remarkable at Croydon Field," says Osborne, "that none but Sir Edward Sackville, of the English, went on the Scots side (and he, out of love to the Lord Bruce, whom after he killed in a duel), which was so ill taken by his countrymen, as divers protested, that if the fray had succeeded, he was the first likely to have fallen." — *Secret History*, vol. i. p. 227.

and they are filled with students, men often of high family and accomplishments, and who, living together in the sort of colleges set apart for their residence, have always kept up the ideas of privilege and distinction to which their destination to a highly honorable profession, as well as their own birth and condition, entitles them. One of these gentlemen, by name Edward Hawley, appeared at court on a public occasion, and probably intruded further than his rank authorized; so that Maxwell, a Scotchman, much favored by James, and an usher of his chamber, not only thrust him back, but actually pulled him out of the presence chamber by a black ribbon, which, like other gallants of the time, Hawley wore at his ear. Hawley, who was a man of spirit, instantly challenged Maxwell to fight; and his second, who carried the challenge, informed him, that if he declined such meeting, Hawley would assault him wherever they should meet, and either kill him or be killed on the spot. James, by his royal interference, was able to solder up this quarrel also. He compelled Maxwell to make an apology to Hawley; and for the more full accommodation of the dispute, accepted of a splendid masque and entertainment offered on the occasion by the students of Gray's Inn Lane, the society to which the injured gentleman belonged.

We may here remark a great change in the manners of the gallants of the time, which had taken place in the progress of civilization, to which I formerly alluded. The ancient practice of trial by combat, which made a principal part of the feudal law, and which was resorted to in so many cases, had now fallen into disuse. The progress of reason, and the principles of justice, concurred to prove that a combat in the lists might indeed show which of two knights was the best rider and the stoutest swordsman, but that such an encounter could afford no evidence which of the two was innocent or guilty; since it can only be believed in a very ignorant age that Providence is to work a miracle in case of every chance combat, and award success to the party whose virtue best deserves it. The trial by combat, therefore, though it was not actually removed from the statute-book, was in fact only once appealed to after the accession of James, and even then the combat, as a mode of trial unsuited to enlightened times, did not take place.

For the same reason the other sovereigns of Europe discountenanced these challenges and combats, undertaken for pure honor or in revenge of some injury, which it used to be their custom to encourage, and to sanction with their own presence. Such rencounters were now generally accounted by all sensible persons an inexcusable waste of gallant men's lives for matters of mere punctilio; and were strictly forbidden, under the highest penalties, by the Kings both of England and France, and, generally speaking, throughout the civilized world. But the royal command could not change the hearts of those to whom it was addressed, nor could the penalties annexed to the breach of the law intimidate men, whom a sense of honor, though a false one, had already induced to hold life cheap. Men fought as many, perhaps even more, single combats than formerly; and although such meetings took place without the publicity and formal show of lists, armor, horses, and the attendance of heralds and judges of the field, yet they were not less bloody than those which had been formerly fought with the observance of every point of chivalry.*

* "Lady Mary Wortley Montague has said, with equal truth and taste, that the most romantic region of every country is that where the mountains unite themselves with the plains or lowlands. For similar

According to the more modern practice, combatants met in some solitary place, alone, or each accompanied by a single friend called a second, who were supposed to see fair play. The combat was generally fought with the rapier or small sword, a peculiarly deadly weapon, and the combatants, to show they wore no defensive armor under their clothes, threw off their coats and waistcoats, and fought in their shirts. The duty of the seconds, properly interpreted, was only to see fair play; but as these hot-spirited young men felt it difficult to remain cool and inactive when they saw their friends engaged, it was very common for them, though without even the shadow of a quarrel, to fight also; and, in that case, whoever first despatched his anatagonist, or rendered him incapable of further resistance, came without hesitation to the assistance of his comrade, and thus the decisive superiority was brought on by odds of numbers, which contradicts all our modern ideas of honor or of gallantry.

Such were the rules of the duel, as these single combats were called. The fashion came from France to England, and was adopted by the Scots and English as the readiest way of settling their national quarrels, which became very numerous.

reasons, it may be in like manner said, that the most picturesque period of history is that when the ancient, rough, and wild manners of a barbarous age are just becoming innovated upon, and contrasted by, the illumination of increased or revived learning, and the instructions of renewed or reformed religion. The reign of James I. of England possessed this advantage in a peculiar degree. Some beams of chivalry, although its planet had been for some time set, continued to animate and gild the horizon: and although probably no one acted precisely on its Quixotic dictates, men and women still talked the chivalrous language of Sir Philip Sidney's Arcadia; and the ceremonial of the tilt-yard was yet exhibited, though it now only flourished as a *Place de Carrousel.*" — *Introduction to the Fortunes of Nigel.*

One of the most noted of these was the bloody and fatal conflict between Sir James Stewart, eldest son of the first Lord Blantyre, a Scottish Knight of the Bath, and Sir George Wharton, an Englishman, eldest son of Lord Wharton, a Knight of the same order. These gentlemen were friends; and, if family report speaks truth, Sir James Stewart was one of the most accomplished young men of his time. A trifling dispute at play led to uncivil expressions on the part of Wharton, to which Stewart answered by a blow. A defiance was exchanged on the spot, and they resolved to fight next day at an appointed place, near Waltham. This fatal appointment made, they carried their resentment with a show of friendship, and drank some wine together; after finishing which, Wharton observed to his opponent, "Our next meeting will not part so easily." The fatal rencounter took place; both gentlemen fought with the most determined courage, and both fell with many wounds, and died on the field of battle.*

Sometimes the rage and passion of the gallants of the day did not take the fairest, but the shortest road to revenge; and the courtiers of James I., men of honorable birth and title, were, in some instances, known to attack an enemy by surprise, without regard to the previous

* "The letters that passed betwixt Sir James Stewart and Sir George Wharton previous to the duel are printed in the Gentleman's Magazine, November, 1800. The challenge was sent by Sir George and accepted by Sir James, who wrote, 'To that end I have sent you the length of my rapyer, which I will use with a dagger, and so meet you at the further end of Islington, at three of the clocke in the afternoon.'—They fought the duel at Islington, 8th November, 1609, were both killed on the spot, and were interred in one grave in the churchyard there, 10th November."—Wood's *Peerage*, vol. i. p. 214. The old ballad on the duel states it to have been fought at Waltham.—See it in *The Border Minstrelsy*, New Edit., vol. iii. p. 77.

appointment of a place of meeting, or any regulation as to the number of the combatants. Nay, it seems as if, on occasions of special provocation, the English did not disdain to use the swords of hired assassins in aid of their revenge, and all punctilios of equality of arms or numbers were set aside as idle ceremonies.

Sir John Ayres, a man of rank and fortune, entertained jealousy of Lord Herbert of Cherbury, celebrated as a soldier and philosopher, from having discovered that his wife, Lady Ayres, wore around her neck the picture of that high-spirited and accomplished nobleman. Incensed by the suspicions thus excited, Sir John watched Lord Herbert, and, meeting him on his return from court, attended by only two servants, he attacked him furiously, backed by four of his followers with drawn weapons, and accompanied by many others, who, though they did not directly unsheath their swords, yet served to lend countenance to the assault. Lord Herbert was thrown down under his horse; his sword, with which he endeavored to defend himself, was broken in his hand; and the weight of the horse prevented him from rising. One of his lackeys ran away on seeing his master attacked by such odds; the other stood by him, and released his foot, which was entangled in the stirrup. At this moment Sir John Ayres was standing over him, and in the act of attempting to plunge his sword into his body; but Lord Herbert, catching him by the legs, brought him also to the ground; and, although the young lord had but a fragment of his sword remaining, he struck his unmanly antagonist on the stomach with such force as deprived him of the power to prosecute his bloody purpose; and some of Lord Herbert's friends coming up, the assassin thought it prudent to withdraw, vomiting blood in consequence of the blow he had received.

This scuffle lasted for some time in the streets of London, without any person feeling himself called upon to interfere in behalf of the weaker party; and Sir John Ayres seems to have entertained no shame for the enterprise, but only regret that it had not succeeded. Lord Herbert sent him a challenge as soon as his wounds were in the way of being cured; and the gentleman who bore it, placed the letter on the point of his sword, and in that manner delivered it publicly to the person whom he addressed. Sir John Ayres replied, that the injury he had received from Lord Herbert was of such a nature, that he would not consent to any terms of fair play, but would shoot him from a window with a musket, if he could find an opportunity. Lord Herbert protests, in his Memoirs, that there was no cause given on his part for the jealousy which drove Sir John Ayres to such desperate measures of revenge.

A still more noted case of cruel vengeance, and which served to imbitter the general hatred against the Scots, was a crime committed by Lord Sanquhar, a nobleman of that country, the representative of the ancient family of Creichton. This young lord, in fencing with a man called Turner, a teacher of the science of defence, had the misfortune to be deprived of an eye by the accidental thrust of a foil. The mishap was, doubtless, both distressing and provoking; but there was no room to blame Turner, by whom no injury had been intended, and who greatly regretted the accident. One or two years after this, Lord Sanquhar being at the court of France, Henry IV., then King, asked him how he had lost his eye. Lord Sanquhar, not wishing to dwell on the subject, answered in general terms, that it was by the thrust of a sword. "Does the man who did the injury still live?" asked the

King; and the unhappy question impressed it indelibly upon the heart of the infatuated Lord Sanquhar that his honor required the death of the poor fencing-master. Accordingly, he despatched his page and another of his followers, who pistolled Turner in his own school. The murderers were taken, and acknowledged they had been employed to do the deed by their lord, whose commands, they said, they had been bred up to hold as indisputable warrants for the execution of whatever he might enjoin. All the culprits being brought to trial and condemned, much interest was made for Lord Sanquhar, who was a young man, it is said, of eminent parts. But to have pardoned him would have argued too gross a partiality in James towards his countrymen and original subjects. He was hanged, therefore, along with his two associates; which Lord Bacon termed the most exemplary piece of justice in any king's reign.*

To sum up the account of these acts of violence, they gave occasion to a severe law, called the statute of stabbing. Hitherto, in the mild spirit of English jurisprudence, the crime of a person slaying another without premeditation only amounted to the lesser denomination of murder which the law calls manslaughter, and which had been only punishable by fine and imprisonment. But, to check the use of short-swords and poniards, weapons easily concealed, and capable of being suddenly produced, it was provided, that if any one, though without forethought

* See the State Trials, vol. vii. p. 86. Osborne says, "By the death of Lord Sanquhar the King satisfied in part the people, and wholly himself; it being thought he hated him for his love to the King of France, and not making any reply when he [the French King] said in his presence, to one that called our James a second Solomon, that he hoped he was not the son of David the fiddler" (i. e. Rizzio). — *Secret History*, vol. i. p. 231.

or premeditation, with sword or dagger, attacked and wounded another whose weapon was not drawn, of which wound the party should die within six months after receiving it, the crime should not be accounted homicide, but rise into the higher class of murder, and be as such punished with death accordingly.

CHAPTER XXXVI.

ATTEMPT OF JAMES TO REDUCE THE INSTITUTIONS OF SCOTLAND TO A STATE OF UNIFORMITY WITH THOSE OF ENGLAND — COMMISSIONERS APPOINTED TO EFFECT THIS — THE PROJECT FAILS — DISTINCTIONS BETWEEN THE FORMS OF CHURCH GOVERNMENT IN THE TWO COUNTRIES — INTRODUCTION OF EPISCOPACY INTO THE SCOTTISH CHURCH — FIVE ARTICLES OF PERTH — DISSATISFACTION OF THE PEOPLE WITH THESE INNOVATIONS.

[1612 — 1618.]

WHILE the quarrels of the English and Scottish nobility disturbed the comfort of James the First's reign, it must be admitted that the monarch applied himself with some diligence to cement as much as possible the union of the two kingdoms, and to impart to each such advantages as they might be found capable of borrowing from the other. The love of power, natural to him as a sovereign, combined with a sincere wish for what would be most advantageous to both countries, — for James, when not carried off by his love of idle pleasures, and the influence of unworthy favorites, possessed the power of seeing, and the disposition to advance, the interests of his subjects, — alike induced him to accelerate, by every means, the uniting the two separate portions of Britain into one solid and inseparable state, for which nature designed the inhabitants of the same island. He was not negligent in adopting measures to attain so desirable an object, though circumstances deferred the accomplishment of his wishes till the lapse of a century. To explain the nature of his attempt, and the causes of its failure, we must consider the respective condition of England and Scotland as regarded their political institutions.

The long and bloody wars between the houses of York and Lancaster, who for more than thirty years contended for the throne of England, had, by slaughter in numerous battles, by repeated proscriptions, public executions, and forfeitures, reduced to a comparatively inconsiderable number, and to a much greater state of disability and weakness, the nobility and great gentry of the kingdom, by whom the crown had been alternately bestowed on one or other of the contending parties. Henry the Seventh, a wise and subtle prince, had by his success in the decisive battle of Bosworth, attained a secure seat upon the English throne. He availed himself of the weak state of the peers and barons, and the rising power of the cities and boroughs, to undermine and destroy the influence which the feudal system had formerly given to the aristocracy over their vassals; and they submitted to this diminution of their authority, as men who felt that the stormy independence possessed by their ancestors had cost them very dear, and that it was better to live at ease under the King, as a common head of the state, than to possess, each on his own domains, the ruinous power of petty sovereigns, making war upon, and ruining others, and incurring destruction themselves. They therefore relinquished, without much open discontent, most of their oppressive rights of sovereignty over their vassals, and were satisfied to be honored and respected masters of their own lands, without retaining the power of princes over those who cultivated them. They exacted rents from their tenants instead of service in battle, and attendance in peace, and became peaceful and wealthy, instead of being great and turbulent.

As the nobles sunk in political consideration, the citizens of the towns and seaports, and the smaller gentry and cultivators of the soil, increased in importance as well as in prosperity and happiness. These commoners felt, indeed, and sometimes murmured against the ascendence acquired by the King, but were conscious, at the same time, that it was the power of the crown which had relieved them from the far more vexatious and frequent exactions of their late feudal lords; and as the burden fell equally on all, they were better contented to live under the sway of one king, who imposed the national burdens on the people at large, than under that of a number of proud lords. Henry VII. availed himself of these favorable dispositions to raise large taxes, which he partly hoarded up for occasions of emergency, and partly expended on levying bands of soldiers, both foreign and domestic, by whom he carried on such wars as he engaged in, without finding any necessity to call out the feudal array of the kingdom. In this manner he avoided rendering himself dependent on his nobles.

Henry VIII. was a prince of a very different temper, and yet his reign contributed greatly to extend and confirm the power of the English Crown. He expended, indeed, lavishly, the treasures of his father; but he replenished them, in a great measure, by the spoils of the Roman Catholic Church, and he confirmed the usurpation of arbitrary authority, by the vigor with which he wielded it. The tyranny which he exercised in his family and court, was unfelt by the citizens and common people, with whom he continued to be rather popular from his splendor than dreaded for his violence. His power wrested from them, in the shape of compulsory loans and benevolences, large sums of money which he was not entitled to by the grant of Parliament; but though he could not directly compel them to pay such exactions, yet he could exert, as in the case of Alderman Read,* the power of sending the refusing party to undergo the dangers and hardships of foreign service, which most wealthy citizens thought still harder than the alternative of paying a sum of money.

The reign of the English Queen Mary was short and inglorious, but she pursued the arbitrary steps of her father, and in no degree relaxed the power which the Crown had acquired since the accession of Henry VII. That of Elizabeth tended considerably to increase it. The success of the wise measures which she adopted for maintaining the Protestant religion, and making the power of England respected by foreign states, flattered the vanity, and conciliated the affection, of her subjects. The wisdom and economy with which she distributed the treasures of the state added to the general disposition of her subjects to place them at her command; and the arbitrary authority which her grandfather acquired by subtlety, which her father maintained by violence, and which her sister preserved by bigotry, was readily conceded to Elizabeth by the love and esteem of her people. It was, moreover, to be considered that, like the rest of the Tudor family, the Queen nourished high ideas of royal prerogative; and, when thwarted in her wishes by any opposition, not unfrequently called to lively recollection, both by expression and action, whose daughter she was.

In a word, the almost absolute authority of the House of Tudor may be understood from the single circumstance,

* See *ante*, p. 84.

that although religion is the point on which men do, and ought to think their individual feelings and sentiments particularly at liberty; yet, at the arbitrary will of the sovereign, the Church of England was disjoined from that of Rome by Henry the Eighth, was restored to the Roman Catholic faith by Queen Mary, and again declared Protestant by Elizabeth; and on each occasion the change was effected without any commotion or resistance, beyond such temporary tumults as were soon put down by the power of the Crown.

Thus, on succeeding to the English throne, James found himself at the head of a nobility who had lost both the habit and power of contesting the pleasure of the sovereign, and of a wealthy body of commons, who, satisfied with being liberated from the power of the aristocracy, were little disposed to resist the exactions of the Crown.

His ancient kingdom of Scotland was in a directly different situation. The feudal nobility had retained their territorial jurisdictions, and their signorial privileges, in as full extent as their ancestors had possessed them, and therefore had at once the power and the inclination to resist the arbitrary will of the sovereign, as James himself had felt on more occasions than one. Thus, though the body of the Scottish people had not the same protection from just and equal laws, as was the happy lot of the inhabitants of England, and were much less wealthy and independent, yet the spirit of the constitution possessed all the freedom which was inherent in the ancient feudal institutions, and it was impossible for the monarch of Scotland so to influence the Parliament of the country, as to accomplish any considerable encroachment on the privileges of the nation.

It was therefore obvious, that besides the numerous reasons of a public nature for uniting South and North Britain under a similar system of government, James saw a strong, personal interest for reducing the turbulent nobles and people of Scotland to the same submissive and quiet state in which he found England, but in which it was not his good fortune to leave it. With this view he proposed that the Legislature of each nation should appoint commissioners, to consider of the terms on which it might be possible to unite both under the same constitution. With some difficulty on both sides, the Parliament of England was prevailed on to name forty-four commissioners, while the Scottish Parliament appointed thirty-six, to consider this important subject.

The very first conferences showed how impossible it was to accomplish the desired object until time should have removed or softened those prejudices which had existed during the long state of separation and hostility betwixt the two nations. The English commissioners demanded, as a preliminary stipulation, that the whole system of English law should be at once extended to Scotland. The Scots rejected the proposal with disdain, justly alleging, that nothing less than absolute conquest by force of arms could authorize the subjection of an independent nation to the customs and laws of a foreign country. The treaty, therefore, was in a great degree shipwrecked at the very commencement, — the proposal for the union was suffered to fall asleep, and the King only reaped from his attempt the disadvantage of having excited the suspicions and fears of the Scottish lawyers, who had been threatened with the total destruction of their national system of jurisprudence. This impression was the deeper, as the profession of the law, which must be influential in every government, was particularly so in Scotland, it being chiefly practised in that kingdom by the sons of the higher class of gentry.

Though in a great measure disappointed in his efforts for effecting a general union and correspondence of laws between the two nations, James remained extremely desirous to obtain at least an ecclesiastical conformity of opinion, by bringing the form and constitution of the Scottish Church as near as possible to that of England. What he attempted and accomplished in this respect constitutes an important part of the history of his reign, and gave occasion to some of the most remarkable and calamitous events in that of his successor.

I must remind you, my dear child, that the Reformation was effected by very different agency in England, from the causes which produced a similar change in Scotland. The new plans of church government adopted in the two nations did not in the least resemble each other, although the doctrines which they teach are so nearly alike that little distinction can be traced, save what is of a very subtle and metaphysical character. But the outward forms of the two churches are totally different.

You must remember that the Reformation of the Church of England was originally brought about by Henry VIII., whose principal object was to destroy the dependence of the clergy upon the Pope, and transfer to himself, whom he declared head of the Church in his own regal right, all the authority and influence which had formerly been enjoyed by the Papal See. When, therefore, Henry had destroyed the monastic establishments, and confiscated their possessions, and had reformed such doctrines of the Church as he judged to require amendment, it became his object to preserve the general constitution and hierarchy, that is, the gradation of superior and inferior clergy, by whom her functions were administered. The chief difference therefore was, that the patronage exercised by the Pope was, in a great measure, transferred to the Crown, and distributed by the hands of the King himself, to whom, therefore, the inferior clergy must naturally be attached by hope of preferment, and the superior orders by gratitude for past favors, and the expectation of further advancement. The order of bishops, in particular, raised to that rank by the Crown, and enjoying seats in the House of Lords, must be supposed, on most occasions, willing to espouse the cause, and forward the views of the King, in such debates as might occur in that assembly.

The Reformation in Scotland had taken place by a sudden popular impulse, and the form of church government adopted by Knox, and the other preachers under whose influence it had been accomplished, was studiously rendered as different as possible from the Roman hierarchy. The Presbyterian system, as I said in a former chapter, was upon the model of the purest republican simplicity; the brethren who served the altar claimed and allowed of no superiority of ranks, and of no influence but what individuals might attach to themselves by superior worth or superior talent. The representatives who formed their church courts, were selected by plurality of votes, and no other Head of the Church, visible or invisible, was acknowledged, save the blessed Founder of the Christian Religion, in whose name the church courts of Scotland were and still are convoked and dismissed.

Over a body so constituted, the King could have little influence or power; nor did James acquire any by his personal conduct. It was, indeed, partly by the influence of the clergy that he had been in infancy placed upon the throne; but, as their conduct in this was regarded by James, in his secret soul, as an act of rebellion against his mother's authority, he gave the Kirk of Scotland little thanks for what they had done. It must be owned the preachers made no attempt to conciliate his favor; for, although they had no legal call to speak their sentiments upon public and political affairs, they yet entered into them without ceremony, whenever they could show that the interest of the Church gave a specious apology for interference. The Scottish pulpits rang with invectives against the King's ministers, and sometimes against the King himself; and the more hot-headed among the clergy were disposed not only to thwart James's inclinations, and put the worst construction upon his intentions, but even publicly to insult him in their sermons, and favor the insurrections attempted by Stewart, Earl of Bothwell, and others, against his authority. They often entertained him with violent invectives against his mother's memory; and, it is said, that on one occasion, when the King, losing patience, commanded one of these zealots either to speak sense or come down from the pulpit, the preacher replied to this request, which one would have thought a very reasonable one, "I tell thee, man, I will neither speak sense nor come down."

James did not see that these acts of petulance and contumacy arose, in a great measure, from the suspicions which the Scottish clergy justly entertained of his desiring to innovate upon the Presbyterian model;* and

* "K. James having gone to Edinburgh, attended worship in the High Church. Balcanquhall, in the course of his sermon, advanced something which was derogatory to the authority of bishops; upon which James rose from his seat and interrupting the preacher, asked him what Scripture he had for that assertion. Balcanquhall said, he

hastily concluded, that their refractory conduct, which was the result of mutual jealousies, was essential to the character of the peculiar form of church government, and that the spirit of Presbytery was in itself inimical to a monarchical establishment.

As soon, therefore, as the King obtained the high increase of power which arose from his accession to the English throne, he set himself gradually to new-model the Scottish Church, so as to bring it nearer to that of England, and to obtain for the Crown some preponderating influence in its councils. But the suspicions of the Presbyterian clergy were constantly alive to their sovereign's intentions. It was in vain he endeavored to avail himself of the institution of an order of men called Superintendents, to whom the Book of Discipline, drawn up by Knox himself, had assigned a sort of presidency in certain cases, with power of inspecting the merits of the clergy. By re-establishing superior offices among the clergy, James endeavored to introduce a sort of permanent presidents into the several presbyteries. But the ministers clearly saw his ultimate object. "Busk (dress), busk him as bonnily as you can," cried Mr. John Davidson, "bring him in as fairly as you will, we see the horns of his mitre weel enough;" and the horns of the mitre were, to their

could bring sufficient proof from Scripture for all that he had asserted. The King denied this, and pledged his kingdom that he would prove the contrary; adding, that it was the practice of the preachers to busy themselves about such causes in the pulpit, but he was aware of their intentions, and would look after them. This interlude continued upwards of a quarter of an hour, to the great edification of the audience; after which James resumed his seat, and heard the sermon to the end. But he was not satisfied with this skirmish. The preacher was sent for to the palace, where his Majesty had the satisfaction of engaging him in close combat for more than an hour." — *Henry Widdrington to Secretary Walsingham*, ap. M'Crie's *Life of Melville*, vol. i. p. 344.

apprehension, as odious as the horns of the Pope's tiara, or those of Satan himself. At last the King ventured on a decisive stroke. He named thirteen bishops, and obtained the consent of Parliament for restoring them to the small remains of their dilapidated bishoprics. The other bishoprics, seventeen in number, were converted into temporal lordships.

It cannot be denied that the leaders of the Presbyterian clergy showed the utmost skill and courage in the defence of the immunities of their Church. They were endeared to the people by the purity of their lives, by the depth of learning possessed by some, and the powerful talents exhibited by others; above all, perhaps, by the willingness with which they submitted to deprivation of office, accompanied by poverty, penalties, and banishment, rather than betray the cause which they considered as sacred. The King had, in 1605, openly asserted his right to call and to dissolve the General Assemblies of the Church. Several of the clergy, however, in contempt of the monarch, summoned and attended a General Assembly at Aberdeen independent of his authority. This opportunity was taken to chastise the refractory clergymen. Five of their number were punished with banishment. In 1606, the two celebrated preachers named Melville were summoned before the Council, and upbraided by the King with their resistance to his will. They defended themselves with courage, and claimed the right of being tried by the laws of Scotland, a free kingdom, having laws and privileges of its own. But the elder Melville furnished a handle against them by his own imprudence.

In a debate before the Privy Council, concerning a Latin copy of verses, which Andrew Melville had written in derision of the ceremonies of the Church of England,* the old man gave way to indecent violence, seized the Archbishop of Canterbury by the lawn sleeves, which he shook, calling them Romish rags, and charged the prelate as a breaker of the Sabbath, the maintainer of an antichristian hierarchy, the persecutor of true preachers, the enemy of reformed churches, and proclaimed himself his mortal enemy to the last drop of his blood. This indiscretion and violence afforded a pretext for committing the hot old Presbyterian divine to the Tower; and he was afterwards exiled, and died at Sedan. The younger Melville was confined to Berwick, several other clergymen were banished from their parishes to remote parts, and the Kirk of Scotland was for the time reduced to reluctant submission to the King's will. Thus the order of bishops was once more introduced into the Scottish Church.

James's projects of innovation were not entirely accomplished by the introduction of prelacy. The Church of

* On the 29th September, 1600, Melville and his nephew, by command of the King, attended the festival of St. Michael in the Royal Chapel; where, on the altar, were placed two shut books, two empty chalices, and two candlesticks with unlighted candles. On returning to his lodgings, Melville composed the following epigram on the ceremonials he had just witnessed:—

> "Cur stant clausi Anglis libri duo regia in ara,
> Lumina cæca duo, pallubra sicca duo?
> Num sensum cultumque Dei tenet Anglia clausum,
> Lumine cæca suo, sorde sepulta sua?
> Romano an ritu dum regalem instruit aram,
> Purpuream pingit religiosa lupam?"

In those days rendered,—

> "Why stand there on the royal altar hie
> Two closed books, blind lights, two basins drie?
> Doth England hold God's mind and worship closs,
> Blind of her sight, and buried in her dross?
> Doth she, with chapel put in Romish dress,
> The purple whore religiously express?"

England, at the Reformation, had retained some particular rites in observance, which had decency at least to recommend them, but which the headlong opposition of the Presbyterians to everything approaching to the Popish ritual induced them to reject with horror. Five of these were introduced into Scotland, by an enactment passed by a parliament held at Perth [1618,] and thence distinguished as the Five Articles of Perth. In modern times, when the mere ceremonial part of divine worship is supposed to be of little consequence, compared with the temper and spirit in which we approach the Deity, the Five Articles of Perth seem to involve matters which might be dispensed or complied with, without being considered as essential to salvation. They were as follows: I. It was ordained that the communion should be received in a kneeling posture, and not sitting, as hitherto practised in the Scottish churches. II. That, in extreme cases, the communion might be administered in private. III. That baptism also might, when necessary, be administered in private. IV. That youth, as they grew up, should be confirmed, as it is termed, by the bishop; being a kind of personal avowal of the engagements entered into by godfathers and godmothers at the time of baptism. V. That four days, distinguished by events of the utmost importance to the Christian religion, should be observed as holidays. These were, — Christmas, on which day our Saviour was born; Good Friday, when he suffered death; Easter, when he arose from the dead; and Pentecost, when the Holy Spirit descended on the Apostles.

But, notwithstanding the moderate character of these innovations, the utmost difficulty was found in persuading even those of the Scottish clergy who were most favorable to the King to receive them into the Church, and they only did so on the assurance that they should not be required to adopt any additional changes. The main body of the churchmen, though terrified into sullen acquiescence, were unanimous in opinion that the new regulations indicated a manifest return towards Popery. The common people held the same opinion; and a thunder-storm of unusual violence, which took place at the time the Parliament was sitting in debate upon the adoption of these obnoxious articles, was considered as a declaration of the wrath of Heaven against those who were again introducing the rites and festivals of the Roman Church into the pure and reformed Kirk of Scotland. In short, this attempt to infuse into the Presbyterian model something of the principles of a moderate prelacy, and to bring it, in a few particulars, into conformity with that of the sister kingdom, was generally unacceptable to the Church and to the nation; and it will be hereafter shown, that an endeavor to extend and heighten the edifice which his father had commenced, led the way to those acts of violence which cost Charles I. his throne and life.*

* When Cowper was made Bishop of Galloway, an old woman, who had been one of his parishioners at Perth, and a favorite, could not be persuaded that her minister had deserted the Presbyterian cause, and resolved to satisfy herself. She paid him a visit in the Canongate, where he had his residence as Dean of the Chapel Royal. The retinue of servants through which she passed staggered the good woman's confidence; and, on being ushered into the room where the Bishop sat in state, she exclaimed, "Oh, sir! what's this? And ye hae really left the guid cause, and turned prelate!" — "Janet," said the Bishop, "I have got new light upon these things." — "So I see, sir," replied Janet; "for when ye was at Perth, ye had but ae candle, and now ye've got twa before ye, — that's a' your *new light.*" — M'Crie's *Life of Melville*, vol. ii. p. 379.

CHAPTER XXXVII.

Disorderly State of the Borders — Characteristic Example of Border Match-making — Deadly Feud between the Maxwells and Johnstones — Battle of Dryfe Sands — James's Power of Enforcing the Laws increased after his Accession to the English Throne — Measures for Restraining the Border Marauders — The Clan Graham Removed from the Debatable Land to Ulster in Ireland — Levies of Soldiers to serve in Foreign Parts — Mutual Bonds among the Chiefs for the Preservation of Good Order — Severe Prosecution of Offenders — The Town of Berwick-upon-Tweed an Independent Jurisdiction.

We are next to examine the effect which James's accession to the throne of England had upon those lawless parts of his kingdom, the Borders and the Highlands, as well as on the more civilized provinces of Scotland, — of which I shall take notice in their order.

The consequences of the union of the crowns were more immediately felt on the Borders, which, from being the extremity of both countries, were now converted into the centre of the kingdom. But it was not easy to see how the restless and violent inhabitants, who had been for so many centuries accustomed to a lawless and military life, were to conduct themselves, when the general peace around left them no enemies either to fight with or plunder.

These Borderers were, as I have elsewhere told you, divided into families, or clans, who followed a leader supposed to be descended from the original father of the tribe. They lived in a great measure by the rapine which they exercised indiscriminately on the English or their own countrymen, the inhabitants of the more inland districts, or by the protection-money which they exacted for leaving them undisturbed. This kind of plundering was esteemed by them in the highest degree honorable and praiseworthy; and the following, as well as many other curious stories, is an example of this: —

A young gentleman,* of a distinguished family belonging to one of these Border tribes, or clans, made, either from the desire of plunder, or from revenge, a raid, or incursion, upon the lands of Sir Gideon Murray of Elibank, afterwards Deputy Treasurer of Scotland, and a great favorite of James VI. The Laird of Elibank having got his people under arms, engaged the invaders, and, encountering them when they were encumbered with spoil, defeated them, and made the leader of the band prisoner. He was brought to the castle of his conqueror, when the lady inquired of her victorious husband, "What he intended to do with his captive?" — "I design," said the fierce baron, "to hang him instantly, dame, as a man taken red-hand in the act of robbery and violence." — "That is not like your wisdom, Sir Gideon," answered his more considerate lady. "If you put to death this young gentleman, you will enter into deadly feud with his numerous and powerful clan. You must therefore do

* "William (afterwards Sir William) Scott, eldest son of Walter Scott of Harden, and of his lady, the celebrated Mary Scott, 'the Flower of Yarrow,' of whose way of living it is mentioned that when the last bullock was killed and devoured, it was the lady's custom to place on the table a dish, which, on being uncovered, was found to contain a pair of clean spurs; a hint to the riders that they must shift for their next meal." — Note, *Border Minstrelsy*, new ed., vol. i. p. 211.

a wiser thing, and, instead of hanging him, we will cause him to marry our youngest daughter, Meg with the meikle mouth, without any tocher" (that is, without any portion). The laird joyfully consented; for this Meg with the large mouth was so ugly, that there was very little chance of her getting a husband in any other circumstances; and, in fact, when the alternative of such a marriage, or death by the gallows, was proposed to the poor prisoner, he was for some time disposed to choose the latter; nor was it without difficulty that he could be persuaded to save his life at the expense of marrying Meg Murray. He did so at last, however; and it is said that Meg, thus forced upon him, made an excellent and affectionate wife; but the unusual size of mouth was supposed to remain discernible in their descendants for several generations.* I mention this anecdote because it occurred during James the Sixth's reign, and shows in a striking manner how

* See in James Hogg's *Mountain Bard* (3d ed., pp. 67-86) a metrical version of this narrative, entitled "The Fray of Elibank, with notes." — The verses conclude: —

> "So Willie took Meg to the forest sae fair,
> An' they lived a most happy an' social life;
> The langer he ken'd her, he lo'ed her the mair,
> For a prudent, a virtuous, and honourable wife.
> An' muckle gude blude frae that union has flow'd,
> An' mony a brave fellow, an' mony a brave feat,
> *I darena just say they are a' muckle-mou'd,*
> *But they rather have still a gude luck for their meat.*" — p. 81.

The union contracted under such singular circumstances give birth to, — 1. Sir William Scott the second, who carried on the line of the family of Harden. 2. Sir Gideon Scott of High Chester, whose son was created Earl of Tarras on his marriage with Agnes, Countess of Buccleuch; but having no issue, the honors and estates of Buccleuch devolved upon her younger sister Anne, married to the unfortunate Duke of Monmouth. 3. Walter Scott of Raeburn, progenitor of our author. 4. John, of whom are descended the Scotts of Wool.

little the Borderers had improved in their sense of morality, or distinctions between right and wrong.

A more important, but not more characteristic event, which happened not long afterwards, shows, in its progress, the utter lawlessness and contempt of legal authority which prevailed on the Borders in the commencement of this reign, and, in its conclusion, the increased power of the monarch after the Union of the Crowns.

There had been long and deadly feud, on the West Borders, betwixt the two great families of Maxwell and Johnstone. The former house was the most wealthy and powerful family in Dumfries-shire and its vicinity, and had great influence among the families inhabiting the more level part of that county. Their chieftain had the title of Lord Maxwell, and claimed that of Earl of Morton. The Johnstones, on the other hand, were neither equal to the Maxwells in numbers nor in power; but they were a race of uncommon hardihood, much attached to each other and their chieftain, and who, residing in the strong and mountainous district of Annandale, used to sally from thence as from a fortress, and return to its fastnesses, after having accomplished their inroads. They were, therefore, able to maintain their ground against the Maxwells, though more numerous than themselves.

So well was this known to be the case, that when, in 1585, the Lord Maxwell was declared to be a rebel, a commission was given to the Laird of Johnstone to pursue and apprehend him. In this, however, Johnstone was unsuccessful. Two bands of hired soldiers, whom the Government had sent to his assistance, were destroyed by the Maxwells; and Lochwood, the chief house of the Laird, was taken and wantonly burnt, in order, as the Maxwells expressed it, that Lady Johnstone might have light to put on her hood. Johnstone himself was subsequently defeated and made prisoner. Being a man of a proud and haughty temper, he is said to have died of grief at the disgrace which he incurred; and thus there commenced a long series of mutual injuries between the hostile clans.

Shortly after this catastrophe, Maxwell, being restored to the King's favor, was once more placed in the situation of Warden of the West Borders, and an alliance was made betwixt him and Sir James Johnstone, in which they and their two clans agreed to stand by each other against all the world. This agreement being entered into, the clan of Johnstone concluded they had little to apprehend from the justice of the new Lord Warden, so long as they did not plunder any of the name of Maxwell. They accordingly descended into the valley of the Nith, and committed great spoil on the lands belonging to Douglas of Drumlanrig, Creichton Lord Sanquhar, Grierson of Lagg, and Kirkpatrick of Closeburn, all of them independent barons of high birth and great power. The injured parties pursued the depredators with forces hastily assembled, but were defeated with slaughter in their attempt to recover the prey. The despoiled and injured barons next carried their complaints to Maxwell, the Warden, who alleged his late alliance with Johnstone as a reason why he could not yield them the redress which his office entitled them to expect at his hands. But when, to make up for such risk as he might incur by renewing his enmity with the Johnstones, the barons of Nithsdale offered to bind themselves by a bond of manrent, as it was called, to become the favorers and followers of Lord Maxwell in all his quarrels, excepting against the King, the temptation became too strong to be overcome, and the ambitious Warden resolved to sacrifice his newly formed friendship with Johnstone to the desire of extending his authority over so powerful a confederacy.

The secret of this association did not long remain concealed from Johnstone, who saw that his own destruction and the ruin of his clan were the objects aimed at, and hastened to apply to his neighbors in the east and south for assistance. Buccleuch, the relative of Johnstone, and by far his most powerful ally, was then in foreign parts. But the Laird of Elibank, mentioned in the last story, bore the banner of Buccleuch in person, and assembled five hundred men of the clan of Scott, whom our historians term the greatest robbers and fiercest fighters among the Border clans. The Elliots of Liddesdale also assisted Johnstone; and his neighbors on the southern parts, the Grahams of the Debatable Land, from hopes of plunder and ancient enmity to the Maxwells, sent also a considerable number of spears.

Thus prepared for war, Johnstone took the field with activity, while Maxwell, on the other part, hastily assembling his own forces, and those of his new followers, the Nithsdale barons, Drumlanrig, Lagg, Closeburn, the Creichtons, and others, invaded Annandale with the royal banner displayed, and a force of upwards of two thousand men. Johnstone, unequal in numbers, stood on the defensive, and kept possession of the woods and strong ground, waiting an opportunity of fighting to advantage; while Maxwell, in contempt of him, formed the siege of the castle or tower of Lockerby, the fortress of a Johnstone, who was then in arms with his chief. His wife, a woman of a masculine disposition, the sister or daughter of the laird who had died in Maxwell's prison, defended his place of residence. While Maxwell endeavored to storm the castle, and while it was bravely defended by its female captain, the chief received information that the Laird of Johnstone was advancing to its relief. He drew off from the siege, marched towards his feudal enemy, and caused it to be published through his little army that he would give a "ten-pound land," that is, land rated in the cess-books at that yearly amount, "to any one who would bring him the head or hand of the Laird of Johnstone." When this was reported to Johnstone, he said he had no ten-pound lands to offer, but that he would bestow a five-merk land upon the man who should bring him the head or hand of Lord Maxwell.

The conflict took place close by the river Dryfe,* near Lochmaben, and is called the Battle of Dryfe Sands. It was managed by Johnstone with considerable military skill. He showed at first only a handful of horsemen, who made a hasty attack upon Maxwell's army, and then retired in a manner which induced the enemy to consider them as defeated, and led them to pursue in disorder with

* The Dryfe rises in the northern end of Hutton parish, and runs a course directly south about eleven miles, passing through the parish of Dryfesdale for about three miles on the N. W. part, it empties itself into the Annan in a direct line between the market town of Lockerby and the royal burgh of Lochmaben. It is said that in the year 1670, Dryfe swept away the original church and burying-ground then in the middle of the holm, now called the *Sand Bed*. In 1671, the late church and burial-ground was established at a small distance, upon the skirt of the present glebe, thought to be perfectly secure from the swellings of Dryfe; but the water in process of time approached the new burying-ground, carrying a good deal of it away; and threatening the church itself, as if to verify the old saying or prophecy of Thomas the Rhymer, —

"Let spades and shools do what they may,
Dryfe will have Dry'sdale kirk away."

The parish church now stands upon an eminence at the north end of the town of Lockerby. *Statistical Account.*

loud acclamations of victory. The Maxwells and their confederates were thus exposed to a sudden and desperate charge from the main body of the Johnstones and their allies who fell upon them while their ranks were broken, and compelled them to take to flight. The Maxwells and the confederated barons suffered grievously in the retreat, — many were overtaken in the streets of Lockerby, and cut down or slashed in the face by the pursuers; a kind of blow, which to this day is called in that country a "Lockerby lick."

Maxwell himself, an elderly man and heavily armed, was borne down from his horse in the beginning of the conflict; and, as he named his name and offered to surrender, his right hand, which he stretched out for mercy, was cut from his body. Thus far history; but family tradition adds the following circumstance: The Lady of Lockerby, who was besieged in her tower as already mentioned, had witnessed from the battlements the approach of the Laird of Johnstone, and as soon as the enemy withdrew from the blockade of the fortress, had sent to the assistance of her chief the few servants who had assisted in the defence. After this she heard the tumult of battle, but as she could not from the tower see the place where it was fought, she remained in an agony of suspense, until, as the noise seemed to pass away in a westerly direction, she could endure the uncertainty no longer, but sallied out from the tower, with only one female attendant, to see how the day had gone. As a measure of precaution, she locked the strong oaken door and the iron grate with which a Border fortress was commonly secured, and knitting the large keys on a thong, took them with her, hanging on her arm.

When the Lady of Lockerby entered on the field of

battle, she found all the relics of a bloody fight; the little valley was covered with slain men and horses, and broken armor, besides many wounded, who were incapable of further effort for saving themselves. Amongst others, she saw lying beneath a thorn-tree a tall, gray-haired, noble-looking man, arrayed in bright armor, but bareheaded, and bleeding to death from the loss of his right hand. He asked her for mercy and help with a faltering voice; but the idea of deadly feud in that time and country closed all access to compassion even in the female bosom. She saw before her only the enemy of her clan, and the cause of her father's captivity and death; and raising the ponderous keys which she bore along with her, the Lady of Lockerby is commonly reported to have dashed out the brains of the vanquished Lord Maxwell.

The battle of Dryfe Sands was remarkable as the last great clan battle fought on the Borders, and it led to the renewal of the strife betwixt the Maxwells and Johnstones, with every circumstance of ferocity which could add horror to civil war. The last distinguished act of the tragedy took place thus:—

The son of the slain Lord Maxwell invited Sir James Johnstone to a friendly conference, to which each chieftain engaged to bring one friend only. They met at a place called Auchman-hill, on the 6th August, 1608, when the attendant of Lord Maxwell, after falling into bitter and reproachful language with Johnstone of Gunmanlie, who was in attendance on his chief, at length fired his pistol. Sir James Johnstone turning round to see what had happened, Lord Maxwell treacherously shot him through the back with a pistol charged with a brace of poisoned bullets. While the gallant old knight lay dying on the ground, Maxwell rode round him with the view of completing his crime, but Johnstone defended himself with his sword till strength and life failed him.

This final catastrophe of such a succession of bloody acts of revenge took place several years after the union of the crowns, and the consequences, so different from those which ensued on former occasions, show how effectually the King's authority, and the power of enforcing the course of equal justice, had increased in consequence of that desirable event. You may observe, from the incidents mentioned, that, in 1585, when Lord Maxwell assaulted and made prisoner the Laird of Johnstone, then the King's warden, and acting in his name, and committed him to the captivity in which he died, James was totally unequal to the task of vindicating his royal authority, and saw himself compelled to receive Maxwell into favor and trust, as if he had done nothing contrary to the laws. Nor was the royal authority more effectual in 1593, when Maxwell, acting as royal warden, and having the King's banner displayed, was in his turn defeated and slain, in so melancholy and cruel a manner, at Dryfe Sands. On the contrary, Sir James Johnstone was not only pardoned, but restored to favor and trust by the King. But there was a conspicuous difference in the consequences of the murder which took place at Auchmanhill in 1608. Lord Maxwell, finding no refuge in the Border country, was obliged to escape to France, where he resided for two or three years; but afterwards venturing to return to Scotland, he was apprehended in the wilds of Caithness, and brought to trial at Edinburgh. James, desirous on this occasion to strike terror, by a salutary warning, into the factious nobility and disorderly Borderers, caused the criminal to be publicly beheaded on 21st May, 1613.*

* "Thus," says Sir Walter Scott, "was finally ended, by a salutary

Many instances might be added to show that the course of justice on the Border began, after the accession of James to the English throne, to flow with a less interrupted stream, even where men of rank and power were concerned.

The inferior class of freebooters was treated with much less ceremony. Proclamations were made, that none of the inhabitants of either side of the Border (except noblemen and gentlemen of unsuspected character) should retain in their possession armor or weapons, offensive or defensive, or keep any horse above the value of fifty shillings. Particular clans, described as broken men, were especially forbid the use of weapons. The celebrated clan of Armstrong had, on the very night in which Queen Elizabeth's death became public, concluding that a time of such misrule as that in which they had hitherto made their harvest was again approaching, and desirous of losing no time, made a fierce incursion into England, extending their ravages as far as Penrith, and done much mischief. But such a consequence had been foreseen and provided against. A strong body of soldiers, both English and Scots, swept along the Border, and severely punished the marauders, blowing up their fortresses with gunpowder, destroying their lands, and driving away their cattle and flocks. Several of the principal leaders were taken and executed at Carlisle. The Armstrongs appear never to have recovered their consequence after this severe chastisement; nor are there many of this celebrated

example of severity, the 'foul debate' betwixt the Maxwells and Johnstones, in the course of which each family lost two chieftains; one dying of a broken heart, one in the field of battle, one by assassination, and one by the sword of the executioner." — *See Notes to the Ballads of "Lord Maxwell's Good Night," and "The Lads of Wamphray," Border Minstrelsy*, new edit., vol. ii. pp. 133-153.

clan now to be found among the landholders of Liddesdale, where they once possessed the whole district.*

The Grahams, long the inhabitants of the Debatable Land, which was claimed both by England and Scotland, were still more severely dealt with. They were very brave and active Borderers, attached to England, for which country, and particularly in Edward VI.'s time, they had often done good service. But they were also very lawless plunderers, and their incursions were as much dreaded by the inhabitants of Cumberland as by those of the Scottish frontier. Thus their conduct was equally the subject of complaint on both sides of the Border; and the poor Grahams, seeing no alternative, were compelled to sign a petition to the King, confessing themselves to be unfit persons to dwell in the country which they now inhabited, and praying that he would provide the means of transporting them elsewhere, where his paternal goodness should assign them the means of subsistence. The whole clan, a very few individuals excepted, were thus deprived of their lands and residences, and transported to the county of Ulster, in Ireland, where they were settled on lands which had been acquired from the conquered Irish. There is a list in existence, which shows the rate at which the county of Cumberland was taxed for the exportation of these poor Borderers, as if they had been so many bullocks.†

* For an account of the Armstrongs, see the *Border Minstrelsy*, new edit., vol. i. pp. 392-406.

† See Essay on Border Antiquities, Sir Walter Scott's Prose Works, vol. vii. pp. 86-134. "The space betwixt the (waters of) *Esk* and the *Sark*," says Pennant, "bounded on the third side by the *march* dike, which crosses from one river to the other, seems properly to belong to Scotland; but having been disputed by both crowns, was styled *the Debatable Land*. In the reign of K. James VI., Sir Richard Graham, obtaining from the Earl of Cumberland (to whom it was granted

Another efficient mode of getting rid of a warlike and disorderly population, who, though an admirable defence of a country in time of war, must have been great scourges in time of the profound peace to which the Border districts were consigned after the close of the English wars, was the levying a large body of soldiers to serve in foreign countries. The love of military adventure had already carried one legion of Scots to serve the Dutch in their defence against the Spaniards, and they had done great service in the Low Countries, and particularly at the battle of Mechline, in 1578; where, impatient of the heat of the weather, to the astonishment of both friends and enemies, the Scottish auxiliaries flung off their upper garments, and fought like furies in their shirts. The circumstance is pointed out in the plan of the battle, which is to be found in Strada's history,* with the explanation, "Here the Scots fought naked."

Buccleuch levied a large additional force from the Border, whose occupation in their native country was gone forever. These also distinguished themselves in the wars of the Low Countries. It may be supposed that very many of them perished in the field, and the descendants of others still survive in the Netherlands and in Germany.

In addition to the relief afforded by such an outlet for a superfluous military population, whose numbers greatly exceeded what the land could have supplied with food, and who, in fact, had only lived upon plunder, bonds

by Queen Elizabeth) a lease of this tract, bought it from the needy monarch, and had interest enough to get it united to the county of Cumberland, it being indifferent to James, then in possession of both kingdoms, to which of them it was annexed." — *Tour in Scotland*, vol. ii. p. 82.

* De Bello Belgico. Of the Belgic War; translated into English by Sir Robert Stapleton. Folio. Lond. 1650.

were entered into by the men of substance and family on the Borders, not only obliging themselves to abstain from depredations, but to stand by each other in putting down and preventing such evil doings at the hand of others, and in making common cause against any clan, branch, or surname, who might take offence at any individual for acting in prosecution of this engagement. They engaged also to the King and to each other, not only to seize and deliver to justice such thieves as should take refuge in their grounds, but to discharge from their families or estates, all persons, domestics, tenants, or others, who could be suspected of such offences, and to supply their place with honest and peaceable subjects. I am possessed of such a bond, dated in the year 1612, and subscribed by about twenty landholders, chiefly of the name of Scott.

Finally, an unusually severe and keen prosecution of all who were convicted, accused, or even suspected, of offence against the peace of the Border, was set on foot by George Home, Earl of Dunbar, James's able but not very scrupulous minister; * and these judicial measures were conducted so severely as to give rise to the proverb of Jeddart (or Jedburgh) justice, by which it is said a criminal was hanged first and tried afterwards: the truth of which is affirmed by historians as a well-known fact, occurring in numerous instances.

Cruel as these measures were, they tended to remedy a disease which seemed almost desperate. Rent, the very name of which had till that period scarcely been heard on the Border, began to be paid for property, and the propri-

* "A man of deep wit," says Spotswoode, "of few words, and in his Majestie's service no less faithful than fortunate. The most difficile affairs he compassed without any noise, and never returned when he was employed without the work performed that he was sent to do." — p. 516.

etors of land turned their thoughts to rural industry, instead of the arts of predatory warfare. But is was more than a century ere the country, so long a harassed and disputed frontier, gained the undisturbed appearance of a civilized land.

Before leaving the subject of the Borders, I ought to explain to you, that as the possession of the strong and important town of Berwick had been long and fiercely disputed between England and Scotland, and as the latter country had never surrendered or abandoned her claim to the place, though it had so long remained an English possession, James, to avoid giving offence to either nation, left the question undecided; and since the union of the Crowns, the city is never spoken of as part of England or Scotland, but as the King's Good Town of Berwick-upon-Tweed; and when a law is made for North and South Britain, without special and distinct mention of this ancient town, that law is of no force or avail within its precincts.

CHAPTER XXXVIII.

Wild State of the Western Islands — Suffocation by Smoke of the Inhabitants of Eigg in a Cave — Story of Allan-a-Sop — Dreadful Death by Thirst — Massacre of Lowlanders in Lewis and Harris — The Western Isles, excepting Skye and Lewis, offered for £800 to the Marquis of Huntly.

The Highlands and Western Islands were in no respect so much affected by the union of the Crowns as the inhabitants of the Borders. The accession of James to the English throne was of little consequence to them, unless in so far as it rendered the King more powerful, and gave him the means of occasionally sending bodies of troops into their fortresses to compel them to order; and this was a measure of unusual rigor, which was but seldom resorted to.

The Highland tribes, therefore, remained in the same state as before, using the same dress, wielding the same arms, divided into the same clans, each governed by its own patriarch, and living in all respects as their ancestors had lived for many centuries before them. Or if there were some marks of softened manners among those Gaelic tribes who resided on the mainland, the inhabitants of the Hebrides or Western Isles, adjacent to the coast of Scotland, are described to us as utterly barbarous. A historian of the period says, "that the Highlanders who dwell on the mainland, though sufficiently wild, show some shade of civilization; but those in the islands are without laws or morals, and totally destitute of religion and humanity." * Some stories of their feuds are indeed preserved, which go far to support this general accusation. I will tell you one or two of them.

The principal possessors of the Hebrides were originally of the name of MacDonald, the whole being under the government of a succession of chiefs, who bore the name of Donald of the Isles, as we have already mentioned, and were possessed of authority almost independent of the Kings of Scotland. But this great family becoming divided into two or three branches, other chiefs settled in some of the islands, and disputed the property of the original proprietors. Thus, the MacLeods, a powerful and numerous clan, who had extensive estates on the mainland, made themselves masters, at a very early period, of a great part of the large island of Skye, seized upon much of the Long Island, as the Isles of Lewis and Harris are called, and fought fiercely with the MacDonalds, and other tribes of the islands. The following is an example of the mode in which these feuds were conducted.

About the end of the sixteenth century, a boat, manned by one or two of the MacLeods, landed in Eigg, a small island, peopled by the MacDonalds. They were at first hospitably received; but having been guilty of some incivility to the young women on the island, it was so much resented by the inhabitants, that they tied the MacLeods hand and foot, and putting them on board of their own

* "Insulani occidentales, immanitate barbari, feritate, ignavia, luxuria, superbia, deterrimi — Kornines agrestes, sine legibus, sine moribus, sine urbium cultu, ac prope omnia humanitatis et religionis expertes." — *Johnstoni Historia*, apud LAING, v. i. p. 48.

boat, towed it to sea, and set it adrift, leaving the wretched men, bound as they were, to perish by famine, or by the winds and waves, as chance should determine. But fate so ordered it, that a boat belonging to the Laird of MacLeod fell in with that which had the captives on board, and brought them in safety to the Laird's castle of Dunvegan in Skye, where they complained of the injury which they had sustained from the MacDonalds of Eigg. MacLeod, in a great rage, put to sea with his galleys, manned by a large body of his people, which the men of Eigg could not entertain any rational hope of resisting. Learning that their incensed enemy was approaching with superior forces, and deep vows of revenge, the inhabitants, who knew they had no mercy to expect at MacLeod's hands, resolved, as the best chance of safety in their power, to conceal themselves in a large cavern on the sea-shore.

This place was particularly well calculated for that purpose. The entrance resembles that of a fox-earth, being an opening so small that a man cannot enter save by creeping on hands and knees. A rill of water falls from the top of the rock, and serves, or rather served at the period we speak of, wholly to conceal the aperture. A stranger, even when apprised of the existence of such a cave, would find the greatest difficulty in discovering the entrance. Within, the cavern rises to a great height,* and the floor is covered with white dry sand. It is extensive enough to contain a great number of people. The

* "*Uamba Fhraine* (the cave of Francis), remarkable not only for its form, but also for the murder of the inhabitants of this island by Alistiar Creloch, Laird of M'Leod. The entrance of this cave is so small that a person must creep on four for about 12 feet; it then becomes pretty capacious, its length being 213 feet, breadth 22, and height 17 feet." — *Statistical Account*, vol. xvii. p. 288.

whole inhabitants of Eigg,* who, with their wives and families, amounted to nearly two hundred souls, took refuge within its precincts.

MacLeod arrived with his armament, and landed on the island, but could discover no one on whom to wreak his vengeance — all was desert. The MacLeods destroyed the huts of the islanders, and plundered what property they could discover; but the vengeance of the chieftain could not be satisfied with such petty injuries. He knew that the inhabitants must either have fled in their boats to one of the islands possessed by the MacDonalds, or that they must be concealed somewhere in Eigg. After making a strict but unsuccessful search for two days, MacLeod had appointed the third to leave his anchorage, when, in the gray of the morning, one of the seamen beheld from the deck of his galley the figure of a man on the island. This was a spy whom the MacDonalds, impatient of their confinement in the cavern, had imprudently sent out to see whether MacLeod had retired or no. The poor fellow, when he saw himself discovered, endeavored, by doubling, after the manner of a hare or fox, to obliterate the track of his footsteps on the snow, and prevent its being discovered where he had re-entered the cavern. But all the arts he could use were fruitless, the invaders again landed, and tracked him to the entrance of the den.

MacLeod then summoned those who were within it, and called upon them to deliver up the individuals who had maltreated his men, to be disposed of at his pleasure. The MacDonalds, still confident in the strength of their

* The Rev. D. M'Lean, minister of Eigg, says, "excepting three, who took other places of refuge, and a boat's crew then in Glasgow." — *Statistical Account*, vol. xvii. p. 288.

fastness, which no assailant could enter but on hands and knees, refused to surrender their clansmen.

MacLeod next commenced a dreadful work of indiscriminate vengeance. He caused his people, by means of a ditch cut above the top of the rock, to turn away the stream of water which fell over the entrance of the cavern. This being done, the MacLeods collected all the combustibles which could be found on the island, particularly turf and quantities of dry heather, piled them up against the aperture, and maintained an immense fire for many hours, until the smoke, penetrating into the inmost recesses of the cavern, stifled to death every creature within. There is no doubt of the truth of this story, dreadful as it is. The cavern is often visited by strangers; and I have myself seen the place where the bones of the murdered MacDonalds still remain, lying as thick on the floor of the cave as in the charnel-house of a church.*

The MacLeans, in like manner, a bold and hardy race, who, originally followers of the Lords of the Isles, had assumed independence, seized upon great part both of the Isle of Mull and the still more valuable island of Ilay, and made war on the MacDonalds with various success. There is a story belonging to this clan, which I may tell you, as giving another striking picture of the manners of the Hebrideans.

* In the confined air of this cave the bones are still pretty fresh (1796), some of the skulls entire, and the teeth in their sockets. Above 40 skulls have been lately numbered here. It is probable a greater number was destroyed, and that their neighboring friends carried them off for burial in consecrated ground." — *Statistical Account*, vol. xvii. p. 289. — In the journal of his voyage to the Hebrides, August, 1814, Sir Walter Scott says, "I brought off, in spite of the prejudices of our sailors, a skull from among the numerous specimens of mortality which the cavern afforded." — *See Note*, "*Lord of the Isles*," *Poetical Works*, vol. x. p. 322 - 4.

The chief of the clan, MacLean of Duart, in the Isle of Mull, had an intrigue with a beautiful young woman of his own clan, who bore a son to him. In consequence of the child's being, by some accident, born on a heap of straw, he received the name of Allan-a-Sop, or Allan of the Straw, by which he was distinguished from others of his clan. As his father and mother were not married, Allan was of course a bastard, or natural son, and had no inheritance to look for, save that which he might win for himself.

But the beauty of the boy's mother having captivated a man of rank in the clan, called MacLean of Torloisk, he married her, and took her to reside with him at his castle of Torloisk, situated on the shores of the Sound, or small strait of the sea, which divides the smaller Island of Ulva from that of Mull. Allan-a-Sop paid his mother frequent visits at her new residence, and she was naturally glad to see the poor boy, both from affection, and on account of his personal strength and beauty, which distinguished him above other youths of his age. But she was obliged to confer marks of her attachment on him as privately as she could, for Allan's visits were by no means so acceptable to her husband as to herself. Indeed, Torloisk liked so little to see the lad, that he determined to put some affront on him, which should prevent his returning to the castle for some time. An opportunity for executing his purpose soon occurred.

The lady one morning looking from the window, saw her son coming wandering down the hill, and hastened to put a girdle-cake upon the fire, that he might have hot bread for breakfast. Something called her out of the apartment after making this preparation, and her husband, entering at the same time, saw at once what she had been about, and determined to give the boy such a reception as should disgust him for the future. He snatched the cake from the girdle, thrust it into his step-son's hands, which he forcibly closed on the scalding bread, saying, "Here Allan — here is a cake which your mother has got ready for your breakfast." Allan's hands were severely burnt; and, being a sharp-witted and proud boy, he resented this mark of his step-father's ill-will, and came not again to Torloisk.

At this time the western seas were covered with the vessels of pirates, who, not unlike the Sea-Kings of Denmark at an early period, sometimes settled and made conquests on the islands. Allan-a-Sop was young, strong, and brave to desperation. He entered as a mariner on board of one of these ships, and in process of time obtained the command, first of one galley, then of a small flotilla, with which he sailed round the seas, and collected considerable plunder, until his name became both feared and famous. At length he proposed to himself to pay a visit to his mother, whom he had not seen for many years; and setting sail for this purpose, he anchored one morning in the Sound of Ulva, and in front of the house of Torloisk. His mother was dead, but his step-father, to whom he was now as much an object of fear as he had been formerly of aversion, hastened to the shore to receive his formidable step-son, with great affectation of kindness and interest in his prosperity; while Allan-a-Sop, who, though very rough and hasty, does not appear to have been sullen or vindictive, seemed to take his kind reception in good part.

The crafty old man succeeded so well, as he thought, in securing Allan's friendship, and obliterating all recollections of the former affront put on him, that he began to think it possible to employ his step-son in executing his own private revenge upon MacQuarrie of Ulva,* with whom, as was usual between such neighbors, he had some feud. With this purpose, he offered what he called the following good advice to his son-in-law: "My dear Allan, you have now wandered over the seas long enough; it is time you should have some footing upon land, a castle to protect yourself in winter, a village and cattle for your men, and a harbor to lay up your galleys. Now, here is the Island of Ulva, near at hand, which lies ready for your occupation, and it will cost you no trouble, save that of putting to death the present proprietor, the Laird of MacQuarrie, a useless old carle, who has cumbered the world long enough."

Allan-a-Sop thanked his step-father for so happy a suggestion, which he declared he would put in execution forthwith. Accordingly, setting sail the next morning, he appeared before MacQuarrie's house an hour before noon. The old chief of Ulva was much alarmed at the menacing apparition of so many galleys, and his anxiety was not lessened by the news that they were commanded by the redoubted Allan-a-Sop. Having no effectual means of resistance, MacQuarrie, who was a man of shrewd sense, saw no alternative save that of receiving the invaders, whatever might be their purpose, with all outward demonstrations of joy and satisfaction; the more especially as he recollected having taken some occasional notice of Allan during his early youth, which he now resolved to make the most of. Accordingly, MacQuarrie caused immediate preparations to be made for a banquet as splen-

* By an error, unpardonable in one who had read Boswell's tour to the Hebrides, and seen the late venerable Laird of MacQuarrie, the name of MacKinnon was inserted in the former editions. 1830.

did as circumstances admitted, hastened down to the shore to meet the rover, and welcomed him to Ulva with such an appearance of sincerity, that the pirate found it impossible to pick any quarrel, which might afford a pretence for executing the violent purpose which he had been led to meditate.

They feasted together the whole day; and in the evening, as Allan-a-Sop was about to retire to his ships, he thanked the Laird for his hospitality, but remarked, with a sigh, that it had cost him very dear. "How can that be," said MacQuarrie, "when I bestowed this entertainment upon you in free good-will?"—"It is true, my friend," replied the pirate; "but then it has quite disconcerted the purpose for which I came hither, which was to put you to death, my good friend, and seize upon your house and island, and so settle myself in the world. It would have been very convenient for me this Island of Ulva; but your friendly reception has rendered it impossible for me to execute my purpose: so that I must be a wanderer on the seas for some time longer." Whatever MacQuarrie felt at learning he had been so near to destruction, he took care to show no emotion save surprise, and replied to his visitor, "My dear Allan, who was it that put into your mind so unkind a purpose towards your old friend; for I am sure it never arose from your own generous nature? It must have been old Torloisk, who made such an indifferent husband to your mother, and such an unfriendly step-father to you when you were a helpless boy; but now, when he sees you a bold and powerful leader, he desires to make a quarrel betwixt you and those who were the friends of your youth. If you consider this matter rightly, Allan, you will see that the estate and harbor of Torloisk lie to the full as conveniently for you as those of Ulva, and that, if you are disposed (as is very natural) to make a settlement by force, it is much better it should be at the expense of the old churl, who never showed you kindness or countenance, than at that of a friend like me, who always loved and honored you."

Allan-a-Sop was struck with the justice of this reasoning; and the old offence of his scalded fingers was suddenly recalled to his mind. "It is very true what you say, MacQuarrie," he replied; "and, besides, I have not forgotten what a hot breakfast my step-father treated me to one morning. Farewell for the present; you shall soon hear news of me from the other side of the Sound." Having said thus much, the pirate got on board, and, commanding his men to unmoor the galleys, sailed back to Torloisk, and prepared to land in arms. MacLean hastened to meet him, in expectation to hear of the death of his enemy, MacQuarrie. But Allan greeted him in a very different manner from what he expected. "You hoary old traitor," he said, "you instigated my simple good-nature to murder a better man than yourself! But have you forgotten how you scorched my fingers twenty years ago, with a burning cake? The day is come that that breakfast must be paid for." So saying, he dashed out the old man's brains with a battle-axe, took possession of his castle and property, and established there a distinguished branch of the clan of MacLean.

It is told of another of these western chiefs, who is said, upon the whole, to have been a kind and good-natured man, that he was subjected to repeated risk and injury by the treachery of an ungrateful nephew, who attempted to surprise his castle, in order to put his uncle to death, and obtain for himself the command of the tribe. Being detected on the first occasion, and brought before his uncle as a prisoner, the chief dismissed him unharmed; with a warning, however, not to repeat the offence, since, if he did so, he would cause him to be put to a death so fearful that all Scotland should ring with it. The wicked young man persevered, and renewed his attempts against his uncle's castle and life. Falling a second time into the hands of the offended chieftain, the prisoner had reason to term him as good as his word. He was confined in the pit, or dungeon of the castle, a deep, dark vault, to which there was no access save through a hole in the roof. He was left without food till his appetite grew voracious; the more so, as he had reason to apprehend that it was intended to starve him to death. But the vengeance of his uncle was of a more refined character. The stone which covered the aperture in the roof was lifted, and a quantity of salt beef let down to the prisoner, who devoured it eagerly. When he had glutted himself with this food, and expected to be supplied with liquor, to quench the raging thirst which the diet had excited, a cup was slowly lowered down, which, when he eagerly grasped it, he found to be empty! Then they rolled the stone on the opening in the vault, and left the captive to perish by thirst, the most dreadful of all deaths.

Many similar stories could be told you of the wild wars of the islanders; but these may suffice at present to give you some idea of the fierceness of their manners, the low value at which they held human life, the cruel manner in which wrongs were revenged, and the unscrupulous violence by which property was acquired.

The Hebrideans seem to have been accounted by King James a race whom it was impossible to subdue, conciliate, or improve by civilization; and the only remedy which occurred to him was to settle Lowlanders in the islands, and drive away or extirpate the people by whom they were inhabited. For this purpose the King authorized an association of many gentlemen in the county of Fife, then the wealthiest and most civilized part of Scotland, who undertook to make a settlement in the isles of Lewis and Harris. These undertakers, as they were called, levied money, assembled soldiers, and manned a fleet, with which they landed on the Lewis, and effected a settlement at Stornoway in that country, as they would have done in establishing a colony on the desert shores of a distant continent.

At this time the property of the Lewis was disputed between the sons of Rory MacLeod, the last lord, who had two families by separate wives. The undertakers, finding the natives thus quarreling among themselves, had little difficulty in building a small town and fortifying it; and their enterprise in the beginning assumed a promising appearance. But the Lord of Kintail, chief of the numerous and powerful clan of MacKenzie, was little disposed to let this fair island fall into the possession of a company of Lowland adventurers. He had himself some views of obtaining it in the name of Torquil Connaldagh MacLeod, one of the Hebridean claimants, who was closely connected with the family of MacKenzie, and disposed to act as his powerful ally desired. Thus privately encouraged, the islanders united themselves against the undertakers; and, after a war of various fortune, attacked their camp of Stornoway, took it by storm, burnt the fort, slew many of them, and made the rest prisoners. They were not expelled, you may be sure, without bloodshed and massacre. Some of the old persons still alive in the Lewis, talk of a very old woman, living in their youth, who used to say, that she had held the light while her countrymen were cutting the throats of the Fife adventurers.

A lady, the wife of one of the principal gentlemen in the expedition, fled from the scene of violence into a wild and pathless desert of rock and morass, called the forest of Fannig. In this wilderness she became the mother of a child. A Hebridean, who chanced to pass on one of the ponies of the country, saw the mother and infant in the act of perishing with cold, and being struck with the misery of their condition, contrived a strange manner of preserving them. He killed his pony, and opening its belly, and removing the entrails, he put the new-born infant and the helpless mother into the inside of the carcass, to have the advantage of the warmth which this strange and shocking receptacle for some time afforded. In this manner, with or without assistance, he contrived to bear them to some place of security, where the lady remained till she could get back in safety to her own country.

The lady who experienced this remarkable deliverance, became afterwards, by a second marriage, the wife of a person of consequence and influence in Edinburgh, a judge, I believe, of the Court of Session. One evening, while she looked out of the window of her house in the Canongate, just as a heavy storm was coming on, she heard a man in the Highland dress say in the Gaelic language, to another with whom he was walking, "This would be a rough night for the forest of Fannig." The lady's attention was immediately attracted by the name of a place which she had such awful reasons for remembering, and, on looking attentively at the man who spoke, she recognized her preserver. She called him into the house, received him in the most cordial manner, and finding that he was come from the Western Islands on some law business of great importance to his family, she interested her husband in his favor, by whose influence it was speedily and successfully settled, and the Hebridean, loaded with kindness and presents, returned to his native island, with reason to congratulate himself on the humanity which he had shown in so singular a manner.

After the surprise of their fort, and the massacre of the defenders, the Fife gentlemen tired of their undertaking; and the Lord of Kintail had the whole advantage of the dispute, for he contrived to get possession of the Lewis for himself, and transmitted it to his family, with whom it still remains.

It appears, however, that King James did not utterly despair of improving the Hebrides by means of colonization. It was supposed that the powerful Marquis of Huntly might have been able to acquire the property, and had wealth enough to pay the Crown something for the grant. The whole archipelago was offered to him, with the exception of Skye and Lewis, at the cheap price of ten thousand pounds Scots, or about £800; but the Marquis would not give more than half the sum demanded, for what he justly considered as merely a permission to conquer a sterile region, inhabited by a warlike race.*

* To these conditions, the Marquis answers, "1st, His lordship offers to tak in hand the service and settlings of the haill north yles under his Majestie's obedience, except the Skye and Lewis, without a lieutenand, and that he shall put an end to that service, *be extirpation of the barbarous people thairof, within the space of ane year. Item*, His lordship offers yearly to his Majestie for the said yles, £400 Scots, viz. iiic lb. for the Ust, and ic lb. for the rest of the yles, *nomine fudiefirme;* and craves only ane suspension fra the payment for the space of ane year." —*Account of the Clan Macdonald*, Edin., 1819, 8vo, pp. 111, 112.

Such was the ineffectual result of the efforts to introduce some civilization into these islands. In the next chapter we shall show that the improvement of the Highlanders on the mainland was not much more satisfactory.

END OF VOLUME II.